THE FIFTH KIND

ASCENSION

JAMES D. PRESCOTT

Books by James D. Prescott

The Genesis Conspiracy

Augmented

Extinction Code

Extinction Countdown

Extinction Crisis

The Fifth Kind: Arrival

The Fifth Kind: Awakening

The Fifth Kind: Ascension

Dedication

To my editor RJ, my incredible beta team, and my dedicated readers.

Character List:

Dr. Katherine Shepard: Civilian expert in languages and exobiology.

Colonel Devon Peters: Administrative head of the UFO crash retrieval program (CRP).

Commander Bradshaw: Director of the CRP.

Dr. Debra Mercer: Medical research director at Joint Base Andrews.

Special Agent Dwight Douglas: FBI agent. Runs the Washington, D.C., field office.

Desiree Douglas: Dwight's elder daughter. Drax agent.

Monique Douglas: Dwight's younger daughter.

Special Agent Sue Keller: FBI agent. Washington, D.C., field office.

Anastasia Petrova: Computer prodigy.

Miguel Alvarez: Delta operator. Marksman.

Jake Thompson: Delta operator. Communications specialist.

Nash: Delta operator. Heavy weapons.

Dr. Rajan Singh: Lead scientist for the CRP.

U.S. Senator Donovan Ravencroft: Drax replacement.

Isadora: Thalasian assassin and operative.

Dr. Mateo Vargas: Physicist who discovered the fifth force.

Recap of Books One and Two

Book 1

In an ancient Egyptian tomb, archaeologists make a startling discovery—the mummified body of a man in a space suit.

Meanwhile, exobiologist Dr. Katherine Shepard is summoned to a mysterious crash site in the Pacific. Here, she encounters Colonel Devon Peters along with the wreckage of a UFO. Inside is a lone survivor along with the glowing orb he was transporting.

En route back to the US, an advanced team of intruders ambushes the site, attempting to seize the orb and eliminate the extraterrestrial survivor. The attack raises alarms about a betrayal from within. They soon learn that the answers they seek may be related to three ancient monoliths that may not have originated on Earth.

In Washington, D.C., FBI Agent Dwight Douglas is investigating the peculiar murder of Senator Michael Miller. His findings lead him to a sinister revelation that synthetic beings may be walking among the human population.

Shepard and Peters, joined by Dr. Rajan Singh, grapple with the mysteries of the alien orb. Their continued quest to secure the monoliths takes them from the Sahara Desert to ancient crypts in Southern France, each discovery unearthing more questions than answers.

Meanwhile, Douglas' world turns surreal when the Thalasian agent Isadora reveals the impending threat of the Drax, an alien race bent on Earth's destruction. He wrestles with his duty as an agent against the staggering revelations of extraterrestrial machinations.

The path to the third and final monolith leads them to Norway, where Shepard's team discovers an ancient city, believed to be Atlantis, buried beneath the ice. Here, they unearth technological marvels hinting at the city's true nature—a possible spacecraft.

For his part, Douglas uncovers a chilling facility where the Drax have been orchestrating an elaborate ruse by creating human duplicates.

A final showdown takes place in Atlantis between the humans and the Drax. After a narrow victory, the team powers up the city and meets its owners, the Council.

After stepping through a portal to a Council base on the moon, they are confronted with the grim reality of the Drax's exploitation of humans and their sinister plans for Earth. For eons they have used humans as cattle, harvesting a rare substance called Drahk'noth. Processed into glowing orbs, this powerful dark matter energy powers all of the Drax technology.

The only force standing with Earth is the Council, a ragtag group of humans previously seeded on other planets by the Drax. But will it be enough to avert disaster and save humanity?

Book 2

As global tensions rise, Shepard and her team learn of a new Drax offensive aimed at eliminating the Council and tightening their control over humanity. An anomaly discovered in the Chilean Atacama Desert is initially believed to be part of this plan. Seeking answers, the crash retrieval team is sent to investigate, where they find a strange world populated by unusual creatures.

Meanwhile, Agents Douglas and Keller are drawn into the investigation of a Pentagon UFO whistleblower's assassination. Their trail leads to a Japanese corporation harboring a two-hundred-year-old secret.

In Atacama, the team's search for answers yields two significant leads. The first is Dr. Mateo's discovery of a fifth fundamental force, which governs the emergence of matter in the universe. Manipulating this force produces potent radiation that mutates living and dead matter, explaining the anomaly. Further investigation reveals that a meteor from Mars, laced with this radiation, landed on Earth, creating the anomaly.

It becomes clear that both the Drax and the Council aim to control this powerful force. The team then heads to Mars, where they discover the ruins of an ancient alien race called the Endarians. The Endarians were masters of using the fifth force, but its dangerous radioactive byproduct—in the form of lethal crystals—led to their civilization's downfall. While at the facility, Shepard and her team inadvertently tamper with a piece of ancient technology, creating a half-human, half-Endarian child.

Following a battle with the Drax and their Council allies, the humans emerge victorious and return home, hopeful that the Endarian child will hold the key to defeating the Drax once and for all.

"There are multiple accounts from credible witnesses, including senior military officials, of UFOs disabling nuclear weapons. This should be a matter of urgent national security interest."

—Christopher Mellon
Former Deputy Assistant Secretary of Defense for Intelligence

Act 1

Ezekiel's Wheel

Chapter 1

Aurora, Texas, 1897

The townspeople stood in the dusty road, decked out in their finest. Although this wasn't so much a meeting as it was an inauguration, perhaps even a celebration.

With a population just shy of 400 souls, Aurora wasn't big enough to justify a full-time mayor. These were simple farmers and ranchers, after all, struggling to eke out a living in an unforgiving environment. As a result, there were no signs of ostentatious wealth here, only decent God-fearing folks who fought every day to stave off famine, locusts, disease, and a host of other threats, natural and unnatural.

All of which made the brand-new water tower, the town's first, all the more impressive. In the end, it had cost $300 and taken six weeks to build, an endeavor spearheaded by Henry McCulloch. Originally from the Isle of Skye, Scotland, he had emigrated to America with less than a dollar in his pocket. Over the next fifteen years, he had worked every menial job imaginable, eventually earning enough to head west. Today, he was a rancher with 100 head of Hereford cows. He was also the de facto leader of Aurora.

While he had had a remarkable beginning, the water tower itself was no less impressive. Built from wrought iron, it rose sixty feet into the air, by far the tallest structure within 500 miles. Its presence served as a symbol of the bright future that lay ahead for the humble town of Aurora.

Henry rose and gripped the edges of the podium, blinking away the oppressive heat from the midafternoon sun bearing down on him. His heart filled with pride as he began his speech.

He had gotten no further than a dozen words into his prepared remarks when he caught sight of a glimmer in the distance. Focused on the task at hand, Henry drew his attention back to the festivities until that glimmer became a flash.

A handful of onlookers seemed to notice the brief pause in Henry's speech, along with the crease forming on his brow. They turned, curious about what had caught his attention, and gasped at what they saw. A deafening roar accompanied the terrifying sight, shattering the peaceful tranquility and replacing it with panic.

The world was ending, Henry was certain of it.

The object, a ball of flame the size of the general store, streaked overhead, no higher than twenty yards. The townspeople recoiled, fearful they were about to be incinerated by the very hand of God. Instead, the object veered to the left and collided with the newly minted tower. The resulting explosion of water, steam, and steel was tremendous.

Henry and the other dignitaries dived for cover. A half second later, the object struck the ground, shaking them violently. If the Lord wasn't punishing them for their sins, it surely felt that way.

The moment the fire and brimstone was over, Henry scrambled to his feet, aware that the world had, in fact, not ended. And apart from having been nearly scared to death, everyone present appeared to be unharmed. Rushing to the edge of the clearing, he surveyed the damage.

The water tower was no more. That much was clear. But the once-empty field behind Aurora's main thoroughfare now bore a long, ragged scar where the object had impacted the ground. Curls of smoke rose from the gash where the earth had been torn up, as though churned by a giant's plow.

Hunks of metal littered the debris field, a mixture of the water tower and whatever had hit it. In the distance, Henry could only just make out the contours of the object. It was no longer on fire—the water tower had seen to that. Instead, it was blinking through a series of colors that bore no resemblance to anything he had ever seen before.

Just then, a sandy-haired boy named Timothy ran up to him, his clothes wet from the watery explosion. The child began frantically waving in the object's direction. Henry's gaze bounced between the boy and the object, still blinking and smoking.

"Do you know what that thing is, son?" Henry asked, his mind reeling.

The boy nodded. "Pa read it to us last night in the Good Book."

A look of surprise flashed across Henry's weathered features. "Did he now?"

"Yessir. Sure as shine, there ain't no doubt. That thing we just seen was Ezekiel's Wheel."

Chapter 2

The black Chevy Suburban kicked up a trail of dust as it sped along the backcountry road.

"Slow down, will you?" Dr. Lena Lang snapped, annoyed. Her co-host of the TV program *Paranormal Places*, Dr. John Avery, had a foot she swore was much further down on the periodic table than anything resembling lead.

It was early evening, and the sun was already beginning its retreat, spreading ribbons of gold and orange across the sky. In the back was their director, Marcus Lee. Talented and calculating, he had once been a highly sought-after Hollywood director before reality TV had come along in the early 2000s and cut his career short. Next to him was their producer, Alex Rivera. His background in journalism made him an asset, but his addiction to risky behavior often got them into trouble.

Alex laughed. "You're lucky I'm not driving."

Grinning, Lena peered back at him. "I had them put it in my contract. 'If Alex gets behind the wheel again, I walk.'"

A light shone in John's eyes. As the host, he was ruggedly handsome—that much wasn't a shock—but

4

also well-educated, with a degree in religious studies from Yale University. Behind his back, he was often referred to as John "did I mention I went to Yale?" Avery.

That didn't impress Lena one bit. She'd studied physics at Princeton and spent the following ten years at CERN cracking the secrets of the universe. Then, two years ago, an unexpected offer had fallen into her lap: a guest appearance in a talking head documentary on the History Channel. Cheesy, yes, but it had demonstrated she had both the looks and the brains for show business. Not long after, the network had pitched her on a new program they were putting together called *Paranormal Places*. The premise was simple: in each episode, she and her co-host, John Avery, would visit remote locations around the world in search of strange and unexplained phenomena.

She was a devout skeptic, while John, on the other hand, believed just about anything put in front of him. Lena suspected their pairing hadn't been as accidental as it might seem. The tension between the two was evident on and off air. The truth was, she found John arrogant and perhaps even a little gullible. Of course, she would never say any of that to his face. His ego was far too delicate for the full truth.

And yet Lena was also aware she could also be somewhat difficult and inflexible. They were opposites. For the purposes of the show, at least, the odd pairing worked well. The ratings were strong, and the History Channel had already ordered a third season.

That was why they'd come to the Apache Hollow cave in Texas, a vast subterranean system that was said to be haunted. Over the years, a laundry list of bizarre supernatural occurrences had been attributed to the caves: werewolves, chupacabra, and even vengeful spirits.

As far as she was concerned, all of it amounted to a giant sack of BS. A remote Texas mining town in the middle of nowhere suddenly becoming a hotbed of paranormal activity just as the municipality had been on the verge of bankruptcy? The coincidence was too hard to ignore. None of this had made a difference to John, of course. Growing up in the region, he'd heard the stories for years. So when he'd pitched this location for the first episode of season three, no one had been one bit surprised.

"How's the equipment holding up?" Marcus asked Alex.

"So far, so good," Alex replied. "We got it tucked away in Faraday cages."

In the last few weeks, the sun had grown even more unstable, bombarding the Earth with plasma storms multiple times a day. In most cases, the only logical response had been to protect anything electronic, lest it should get zapped and turned into a rather expensive brick.

Marcus nodded, apparently working out a few final points of the script. They would arrive at the entrance just after nightfall, find it sealed shut, and then retreat to town. There they would wait for morning and question the locals on what they knew. In the end, they would find no sign of anything, leaving Lena to secretly wonder whether the inflated History Channel paycheck was worth selling her soul.

Knowing Alex, perhaps she should have guessed that wasn't how things would turn out.

They pulled up to the cave entrance a dozen miles outside of town. Lena got out and stretched her legs.

John did the same, checking his reflection in the side mirror and warming up his voice. In the distance came the faint echo of a freight train. The light was fading fast.

Marcus opened the back hatch and removed a Canon EOS C300 camera and attached an Aputure LS C300d light. He buzzed around Lena and John as they recounted the unsettling history of Apache Hollow. Every now and then, mostly for effect, John would pause and look around, speaking into a walkie-talkie.

"Was that you, Alex?" he asked, with mock concern.

Of course, Alex was barely twenty feet away, digging through the back of the truck.

"Nope, wasn't me," Alex replied, acting oblivious.

When Alex did finally join them, he was carrying a plastic container about the size of a breadbox.

"What's that for?" Lena asked, distinctly aware this was not something they'd discussed beforehand.

Marcus' gaze turned to John. "You got a lighter?"

John nodded, producing a silver Zippo from the pocket of his shirt. The sun was nearly gone now.

"I'm not sure I like where this is going," Lena said, trying desperately to avoid always sounding like someone's mother. But with this gang of yahoos, that was becoming harder every day.

They made their way to the entrance of Apache Hollow, which looked large enough to drive a truck through. Unfortunately for them, it had been bricked up seventy-five years ago after a group of kids in the 1940s had gone inside on a dare and failed to come out again. According to legend, around midnight on a full moon, you could hear the sound of claws scratching to get out. While the cave's reputation for spookiness had already been established by that point, this had definitely cemented it.

Alex removed a small stick of what looked like dynamite, searching for a chink in the masonry where he could insert it.

"Have you lost your mind?" Lena shouted.

He half-turned. "You and John look for ghosts. As the producer, it's my job to keep the ratings high."

"Yeah, the difference is ghosts aren't real, Alex," she shot back. "But blowing shit up with dynamite, especially when we don't even have permission to film, is insane."

"Guerrilla filmmaking at its best," Alex said, a grin on his face he couldn't quite peel away. "Besides, it isn't dynamite. It's a lot less powerful, but gives off a lot of smoke." He gave her jazz hands—"That's showbiz, folks!"—before pressing the explosive into a crack and flicking the Zippo lid open. "You might wanna get back behind the SUV."

She glared at him, arms crossed. Lena could easily quit over such a flagrant disregard for safety. And yet, twisted as it was, a part of her wanted to know what was in there.

Lena, John, and Marcus hurried behind the Suburban, peering over the hood. A second later, Alex came running. He had just reached the front of the vehicle when the explosion went off, the blast wave knocking him off his feet. Lena ducked behind the wheel well, watching a layer of dust rise up off the ground as the air was sucked from her lungs.

Alex was now ten feet behind them, laughing hysterically.

"Less powerful than dynamite, my ass," John said, fixing his disheveled hair. Marcus swung the camera around as the smoke began to clear. While the blast had been powerful, it had only opened a single five-foot hole in the barrier, just enough to press in one by one.

"All right," John said as he shrugged on a backpack. "This cave's not gonna explore itself."

Chapter 3

One by one, they stepped over chunks of broken brick and squeezed through the entrance. The acrid odor of nitroglycerin gave way to something earthy, almost tropical. The sound of flowing water echoed in the distance. Lena flashed her light around, noting the wet stone walls. While the chamber looked large enough to drive a truck through, the sounds up ahead suggested this was little more than a foyer.

John pushed past her, as he tended to do once the cameras were rolling. No sooner had he done it than he put a hand over his mouth.

"Oh, my God," John cried. "Do you smell that?"

She nodded, her eyes watering. Marcus swung around to catch their disgusted expressions.

Peering down, Lena speared something on the ground with the beam from her flashlight. Her right eyebrow rose. She pulled the six-inch blade from her belt and flicked what looked like a pile of droppings.

John moved in for a closer look. "Coyote?"

She shook her head. "Can't be. Coyote scat isn't deposited in mounds. The only cave-dwelling creature I know that does that is a bat."

John straightened his back, a crack suddenly appearing in his confidence. "I've seen bat droppings before, and they're not this big."

Lena put her hands on her hips. "I'm not getting such a good feeling about this place." She turned and looked at Alex.

"Okay, cut," he called out, exasperated.

Marcus let the camera settle against his belly.

"Are you for real?" Alex snapped. "I didn't break the law getting us into this cave only to have us turn tail and run the minute things got interesting. Besides, we do this right and we could win an Emmy. I'm not kidding."

That got John's attention. He turned to Lena, hands clasped together. "Stop being silly. How about we go just a little further?" He took her by the shoulders when he saw her expression shift. "I'm sorry, I didn't mean you were silly. But an Emmy, Lena! Think about it."

Awards were the last thing on her mind, but she could see she was outnumbered and relented.

On they went, deeper into the cave. Before long, the ground at their feet began to slope downward. At one point, they spotted a faint bluish glow up ahead. As they approached, the cave opened into a truly enormous chamber. And it soon became clear what they'd been seeing. Bioluminescent moss hung from the cave walls, filling this giant space with shimmering azure light, but that wasn't all. Dotting this alien-looking landscape were cypress trees, ribbons of blue moss dripping from each branch. It looked like something out of a fairy tale.

"Oh, my, this just might be the most beautiful thing I've ever seen," Lena said, drinking in the wondrous sight before her.

"I knew it," Alex shouted, unable to control himself. "We hit the jackpot."

John ventured to a nearby tree and touched a patch of moss hanging at eye level. "Shouldn't this be green? I mean, I've never heard of glowing blue moss before."

He had a point. Lena was no expert, but it didn't look like any species she was familiar with.

"First unusual droppings and now this," Alex said, unable to keep from grinning. "Marcus, get as many shots of this as you can."

"Way ahead of you, Captain," Marcus shot back.

The others were still marveling over the bioluminescent moss when Lena pushed ahead. She kept her light on, but with the ambient glow around them, she didn't really need it. Something else had caught her eye— a different kind of light against the far wall, blinking red, green, and yellow. She took a series of cautious steps toward it when something caught the toe of her boot. She fell forward, scraping her bare hands on the cave floor.

"Dang it," she said, rolling into a seated position as she surveyed the damage. Not surprisingly, the others were far too preoccupied to even notice she'd taken a spill. Perhaps that was best, or else Alex would surely be tempted to include it on the gag reel.

A distant and rather distracted voice called out to her. "You okay, Lena?"

Dusting her hands, she got to her feet. "Fine. Just tripped on a tree root." She glanced down to confirm the obvious and froze in confusion. The thing sticking up from the ground wasn't a root. It looked more like a dirty piece of fabric. She tugged at it until it finally gave up its secrets. With a final yank, a white bone came loose and tumbled onto the ground. It looked like a femur, and a short one at that.

"Um, Alex?"

No response.

"John… Marcus… Alex… anyone? Hello?"

She could hear them talking excitedly among themselves.

Feeling numb with shock, Lena decided to float the question anyway. "Didn't you say a group of children came in here and never left?"

"Yeah," Alex replied without much interest. "Four kids, I believe. Back in the forties."

The obvious follow-up to that statement was, "Get over here and take a look at this then." Except she never got a chance to utter those words because she was immediately overwhelmed with the eerie feeling that something or someone was behind her. The most disturbing part was that she could see the other three fifty feet away, shooting B-roll and collecting samples.

A cold hand closed around her heart when the clicking sound came. Whatever this was, it didn't sound natural.

But you're a ghost hunter. Isn't that why you're here?

She told that voice to shut the hell up as she slowly turned to find a giant pair of almond-shaped eyes staring back at her through the dim blue haze.

Chapter 4

A shriek of terror would certainly have been appropriate, but Lena's entire body had frozen stiff. Everything slowed as her brain attempted to make sense of this strange face staring back at her. Its head was about the same size as hers, except it was long, narrow, and scaly. Those eyes, the first things she'd seen, were situated on either side of its head. Between them sat a long pair of antennae. A thin appendage rose out of nowhere and pulled one of the antennae down to its mouth, a barely visible section at the bottom of its face.

Click, click, click. It watched her intently as it repeated the act with the other antenna. Click, click, click.

"Lena?" a voice called from a distant place.

She blinked and all at once realized this wasn't an alien at all. It was a grasshopper the size of a Rottweiler. Lena began shuffling away from it right as the others arrived.

"Holy shit, what is that?" John shouted. Gone was the bravado that normally kicked in the moment someone screamed 'action.'

Alex ripped the camera from Marcus' hands and started filming.

"Hey, what the hell, man?" the director fired back. "Not cool."

"I'm sorry, Marcus, but you weren't rolling, and this is without a doubt the opportunity of a lifetime. Lena, go try and pet it."

She half-turned. "Pet it?" She pointed at the ground. "I just found a child's bones, Alex. For all we know one of these things ate it."

"Grasshoppers are herbivores," he replied, freeing up a hand to wave her on.

Lena wasn't going to take that particular bit of stage direction. If Alex wanted to see someone's hand get chewed off, he better offer his own. No, her real attention had returned to the blinking lights she'd seen in the distance. Giving their new friend a wide berth, Lena headed toward them.

"Hey, where you going?" Alex asked incredulously. He turned to John and saw that the co-host's face had blanched with fear.

"Don't look at me. I'm not touching that thing."

A second later, Lena called out. "Hey, come check this out."

She spun to see Alex feeding the grasshopper a handful of moss. When they finally gathered by her side, each of them glanced down with a look of confusion.

The object before them was smooth, black and about the size of a VW Beetle. At least half of it appeared to be encased in a stalagmite, a rock-like formation created when calcium carbonate dripped from cave ceilings. But that process took thousands of years. Was there something about this device that was distorting the space-time around it?

"How long do you think this thing's been down here?" Marcus asked, mesmerized.

15

John steadied himself. "Rumors of paranormal activity in Aurora, Texas, are really just the tip of the iceberg. But even I didn't believe them."

Lena glanced over, surprised. "Tip of the iceberg?"

"In 1897 a newspaper story came out of Aurora about a crashed UFO," Alex explained. "No one ever found anything and so it was chalked up to a town's desperate attempt to bring in some tourists. In fact, it was so far-fetched, we weren't even going to cover it on this episode."

"And yet here we are," Lena said, reaching out.

John caught her hand. "What do you think you're doing?"

"Don't you wanna open it up?" she asked, incredulous.

"Uh, are you insane? I say we get the heck out of here and call the police, the National Guard, and maybe even the president."

She took him by the shoulders. "John, stop being silly. You talked me into this and now you want to leave?"

"I'm not going anywhere," Alex said, handing the camera back to Marcus.

"Yeah, I'm not so sure," John said, rubbing his hands together. "Especially if you're going to start punching buttons on that thing."

Alex spoke to Marcus. "Okay, let's start with a wide shot. Lena, stand next to that thing."

John stayed behind them, slowly backing away.

"If you want that Emmy," Alex said, as though speaking to a disobedient child, "I suggest you join your co-host."

John merely shook his head. So long as ghosts stayed invisible, he was just fine. The moment they actually materialized into something tangible, he was no longer interested.

"Suit yourself," Alex said, turning his attention back to Lena, who was now standing next to the object.

"It appears to have burn marks," Lena observed, running her hand over its surface. She leaned forward, her fingers hovering over the three glowing buttons. "Red, green, and yellow." She turned back to Alex. "Which one should I press?"

Alex thought for a moment before that old gambler's light shone in his eye. "All of them."

Still backing away, John let out a whimper.

Lena laid her fingers on the red button, feeling the warmth coming off it. She took a deep breath and applied pressure. The button went down and turned off. A moment later, she repeated the process two more times. Soon, all three lights were off.

Thirty full seconds passed and nothing happened. She turned back to first Alex and then John. The latter looked mighty relieved.

Then the object shuddered, startling each of them. A moment later came the sound of the stalagmites cracking and falling away. Then a seam appeared, and out came a thick cloud of white mist. Lena took several steps back.

"Holy crap, it's opening up," Alex said, his voice a mixture of elation and terror.

What exactly would they find inside? Was there some kind of alien lifeform?

Just then, a flat horizontal beam of blue laser light flashed, running up and down each of their bodies.

"What's it doing?" Marcus asked, the camera drooping.

Alex pulled the camera back into place. "If you miss this, I swear to God…"

17

Seconds passed before the mist dissipated, revealing the object's interior. Inside was one big control panel. They'd hoped for an alien who had traveled trillions of miles to make contact. And yet this thing didn't even have a seat.

"Maybe it's some sort of probe," Lena said, her breath only now beginning to settle in her chest.

Suddenly, the blue laser light was back, hovering in empty space before them. Only this time, rather than scanning their bodies, it began to resolve into a shape. At first a pair of arms and legs. Then a torso and a head. Whatever this was, it looked like a human.

"Greetings," he said in a kind voice. Lena couldn't shake the feeling that voice sounded strangely familiar, as though someone had recorded each of them on a separate track and had then merged them together. Even the hologram's physique looked amorphic. "Does this form please you?"

"What form?" Alex asked the flickering image.

The hologram turned to him. "The one you have chosen for what's to come."

"Wait a minute," Lena blurted out, a tinge of fear in her voice. "W-who are you exactly?"

"We have been known by many names. Mungu, Theos, Ishwar."

"We don't speak any of those languages," Alex told him. "What about in English?"

The hologram smiled patiently, regarding them as a father might look upon a child. "In your language, you might call us God."

Lena felt the skin on her cheeks grow warm, and at the same time a chill ran up her spine, such was the depth of her shock.

"You said before something was about to happen," Lena said. "What did you mean by that?"

"Let me show you."

Suddenly, Lena felt a bolt of electrical energy course through her. It was as though every cell in her body was destroyed and remade in the same instant. She collapsed to the floor. Alex and Marcus rushed to help her.

"Now do you see?" the hologram asked, watching her expectantly.

Lena's head was swimming. Her arms and legs felt like gelatin. She searched her mind and to her dismay found no new information. "I don't."

A knowing grin eased onto the hologram's lips. "Fear not. In time you will."

With each of them struggling to understand what had just happened, they missed the flap of leathery wings whooshing through the air, followed by the thud from the impact of something large slamming onto the ground.

A terrified scream echoed from John. Each of them spun to see something that resembled a giant, mutated bat had just landed next to him. In one deft motion, it snatched the grasshopper into its powerful jaws and crunched it.

Lena turned back to the hologram, but it was gone. And while the capsule remained, the hatch was sealed shut and the three lights were blinking as they had before.

"Where did God go?" Marcus stammered.

The bat continued to munch as a green, viscous liquid ran down its maw. John was frozen solid in fear. If they didn't do something quick, they might all be next.

Lena ran over to him, her boots clomping on the moist ground. "Snap out of it, will ya? We're leaving."

He didn't start moving until she grabbed his arm and shook him. She could see now it wasn't the creature before them he was staring at. His head was craned upward as he stared in horror at the ceiling, a living tableau of movement.

"There must be thousands of them up there," he whispered.

Just then, Alex and Marcus charged past them, the latter struggling with the weight of the camera. John and Lena followed closely behind, gnawed by fear that any second, the entire cave system would be swarming with giant, hungry bats.

"How the hell did they get so big?" was all John kept asking. "Never seen anything like it in all my life."

Up ahead, nearly out of breath, Alex couldn't help himself. "Marcus, tell me you got a shot of that creature."

Behind them came the sound of hundreds, maybe thousands, of wings pushing against the air. The beam from their flashlights speared the entrance up ahead.

"Don't you dare stop," Alex yelled. "And for goodness' sake, don't look back."

That terrible sound was growing louder. These things, whatever they were, could surely fly faster than they could run.

They were twenty feet away from freedom when something heavy landed in front of them, blocking the entrance. Its eyes were like two blood-red jewels.

Lena's heart dropped. This was it. How ironic that she was about to meet God for the second time in one day.

The creature hissed just as three shots rang out. Then three more. The creature's chest exploded outward before it slumped to the ground. As it fell, a new figure came into view. He looked like a sheriff. He waved at them frantically.

"Hurry up, before the rest show up."

None of them needed to be told twice. They charged past the now-dead bat thing and pushed through the narrow entrance. Two more deputies were there with a sheet of plywood, which they set in place and reinforced with bracers set into the ground.

The four of them leaned on the nearest cruiser, its lights bathing the area in an eerie display.

"Thank you, Sheriff Dixon," Alex said, reading his nametag. He put out his hand.

Dixon took it and cinched a cuff around his wrist. "You're all under arrest." One of the deputies took Marcus' camera.

"Wait a minute," Alex protested to no avail.

They were put into two cruisers. Lena sat next to John. Glancing in the rearview mirror, she could see her face was covered in dirt. Her hands were also chewed up, likely from the fall.

"Better to be arrested than eaten alive, right?" she said, trying to lighten the mood. She thought at once of her husband and kids. Who would let them know she was all right? She glanced over at John and saw sweat pouring down his face.

"Hey, you okay?" she asked.

He threw her a sideways glance. "You feel weird at all?"

She grew quiet for a moment. "Yeah, but I can think of at least a dozen reasons why." Her gaze dropped from his face to movement underneath his collar. Her pulse quickened. Had some creature hitched a ride out with them?

21

"Your neck," she said, trying with everything she had to stay calm.

"I know, it hurts like hell."

With her hands cuffed, there wasn't much she could do. "Hey, lean this way, let me have a look."

John shuffled over to the right and then leaned left as far as he could go. Slowly, the area beneath John's left ear came into view and Lena gasped.

"Oh, crap, is it that bad? Am I cut or something?"

Lena stared in abject horror, trying to make some sense of what she was seeing. Her co-host, John, hadn't been cut. That was the good news. The bad news was he had a finger growing out of the side of his neck.

Chapter 5

Dr. Katherine Shepard stepped out of the SUV and surveyed the scene. The brick wall sealing the entrance to the cave had been widened enough by the military to allow a four-wheeler to pass.

The area was awash with military vehicles and soldiers busy securing the location. Her convoy had gone through at least three checkpoints on the way here from the local landing strip. Even the town of Aurora was under quarantine. Not surprisingly, the Pentagon had already cooked up a cover story to explain away the heavy military presence in the area—something about a leak of hazardous material from the local train yard.

Dr. Mateo Vargas stepped out next, rubbing at the back of his neck. He checked his watch. "Oh, man, it's nearly three a.m. Who else needs a double espresso?"

Shepard laughed. "Around here? You'll be lucky if the coffee doesn't taste like motor oil."

"Right about now, I can't say I'd mind."

Commander Bradshaw caught sight of them and headed over. Next to him was Colonel Devon Peters. Protocol she'd once helped to develop stipulated soldiers with guns were always the first on scene, followed by the scientists.

"What do we have here, Commander?" she asked.

One of his eyebrows rose. "Seems the crew of a cable television show entered the cave and located what appears to be a crashed UAP."

She glanced over his shoulder. A series of military spotlights had been set up near the entrance.

A young officer pulled up at Bradshaw's left elbow. "Sir, the removal team is ready for the extraction."

"Any issue with the lifeforms inside the cave?" he asked.

She shook her head. "They've been careful not to disturb them."

Shepard noticed what looked like a large hairy body near the cave's entrance.

Peters followed her gaze. "That was the local sheriff's handiwork. Not that it'll make much difference. Once we lug that thing out of there it won't last long."

She caught his meaning at once. "You mean fifth force radiation?"

She was referring to the waste byproduct that resulted from the manipulation of the fifth force itself. For decades, scientists had believed the universe was governed by only four fundamental forces (gravity, electromagnetism, the strong nuclear force and the weak nuclear force). In a sense, these forces were believed to lay out the basic rules of how the universe worked. After their recent discoveries on Mars, Mateo and the other government scientists had soon realized that a fifth and even more powerful force existed, one that regulated the emergence of matter in the universe. And as with nuclear power, there was a flipside. When manipulated, the fifth force was known to create a waste byproduct in the form of crystals that emanated fifth force radiation. While the fifth force was the engine that created new matter, the resulting radiation mutated existing matter. Creatures altered by the fifth force perished soon after being removed from its powerful energy.

Dr. Rajan Singh appeared wearing a hazmat suit. "Precisely. But there's no need to worry. The levels out here are low, although I wouldn't recommend going inside that cave without adequate protection."

Shepard thought at once of the TV crew, but before she could ask…

"They're also in quarantine," Bradshaw said, reading her concern. "They left an hour ago for Joint Base Andrews to undergo further testing."

Shepard's gaze fell on Singh. "Speaking of testing, I heard the lab made a breakthrough on the crystal Captain Miller brought back from Mars."

Singh's eyes lit up. "When we subjected the crystal to low levels of electromagnetic energy, the outputs went off the chart…"

Intrigued, Mateo cut in. "Which points to an amplification effect, suggesting there might be a way to boost the output."

"It certainly looks that way," Singh replied. "Although we will need to perform additional tests before we can be certain."

A blank wall inside Shepard's mind filled with warning signs, but there would be a time and a place to voice those concerns. For now, her thoughts turned back to the UAP they'd just retrieved from the cave. Rubbing her hands to ward off the chill in the early morning air, she said, "If this thing's bleeding fifth force radiation, then it must be Endarian."

She was referring to the ancient race that had once spanned the galaxy before their desire to tap into the most powerful force in the universe proved their undoing.

25

Peters nodded. "That was our assessment as well."

"Any idea how long it's been in there?" Mateo asked, struggling with the tablet in his hands.

"Right now, all we have are legends and ghost stories," Peters told them.

Intrigued, Shepard asked, "What kind of legends?"

"That in 1897, something made a crash landing in Aurora and took out the town's water tower. The wreckage was apparently buried, which just as well could have meant sealed into a cave."

Just then a four-wheeler with a flatbed rolled out from the cave entrance carrying out the UAP, a black object about the size of a small car.

"Any idea where it came from?" Shepard asked, knowing the question was a long shot, but throwing it out anyway.

"We might," Singh replied eagerly. "Aerial surveillance was able to identify a disturbance in the ground where we suspect the object crashed. Working backwards from there, and judging from the object's speed, we suspect it was stationed in Earth's orbit."

"A satellite? But for what purpose?"

"That's where the science team comes in," Mateo replied.

"I expect I might also be able to lend a hand," a soft female voice said.

It was RUTH, the team's powerful AI system, which seemed to become increasingly intelligent with every passing day.

Singh laughed. "You already have." He turned to the others. "Who do you think calculated the object's likely orbit?"

RUTH laughed too.

Peters leaned closer to the head scientist. "One day that old girl may rule us all."

A chuckle this time. "I promise to govern with wisdom and mercy."

"How sweet," Peters said, his eyes wide with feigned alarm.

They watched as the retrieval team loaded the UAP into the back of an eighteen-wheeler.

From inside the cave came the sound of a screech, followed by a wet plop. Shepard felt a pain in her heart. She knew what that sound meant. Whatever irradiated ecosystem had sprung up over the past hundred years, drip-fed by the slow leakage of fifth force radiation, was now coming undone. She needed to keep reminding herself those things were nothing more than mutations. That the crash retrieval team wasn't wiping out lifeforms that might otherwise have thrived. And yet each time her reassurances seemed to ring ever more hollow.

Chapter 6

The team didn't arrive back to Andrews until late evening on the following day. After touchdown and a quick debriefing, Shepard collapsed into bed, sleeping all the way until morning.

She rose feeling groggy and only half-rested, as though she'd spent the night fighting demons in her dreams. Normally, she might have rushed home to see her son Ryan—it didn't matter how late she might have landed. But not anymore.

She kept a picture on her bedside table of what had once been her family: Phil, Ryan and her at a cottage in the Azores. They were smiling. Phil and Ryan had just got done catching fish and prepping them for dinner. Their eyes were bright, their cheeks sun-kissed from hours on the lake. The fingers of some powerful fist closed around her heart and began to squeeze. Slowly, she reached over and set the picture face down.

The pain of loss was so strong she could only bear it in short spurts. Anything more and she feared she might collapse and never get up again. There was a job to do, an entire civilization to keep from enslavement and destruction. Seconds passed before the pain began to subside into the background. And yet it was always there, like tinnitus, although sometimes if she could force herself to think of something else, she could almost forget the agonizing heartache.

Exercise helped. It kept her from becoming stationary and wallowing. And so she went for her daily five-mile run. When she was done and showered, Shepard made her way across the base to the medical wing to see Dr. Mercer.

The two women were standing before a glass partition. On the other side was a young man in his early twenties sitting in a chair as two doctors ran a series of tests on him. If Shepard hadn't known Sam was aging more rapidly than a normal human, she might not have recognized him. The fact Sam had been born in an alien container on Mars was still hard to fathom.

"I heard a rumor you found another UAP last night," Mercer said, flicking a clump of her gray hair out of her face. She was talking about their trip to Aurora.

Shepard nodded at Mercer's question. "We did indeed, but this one isn't like the others."

This piqued the doctor's interest. "Really? How so?"

"For starters, it looks like it might be Endarian."

Both of the women's gazes settled on Sam.

"I understand he looks human," Mercer began.

"Trust me, you don't need to explain it to me. He's an alien."

A troubled look flashed across Mercer's face. "It's just you've been to see him every day."

"Why shouldn't I? Don't forget, he's got some of my DNA in there." The Endarian box on Mars Shepard and Peters had both touched to produce Sam was still crystalized in her mind.

Mercer crossed her arms. "And Colonel Peters' DNA as well. But he belongs—" Her voice cut off.

Shepard threw her a look. "To the US government? Is that what you were about to say?"

The doctor's eyes swept back to Sam. "I'm just saying we need to follow protocol. We don't want him getting too attached. It may not be safe."

"For him or for us?"

The corner of Mercer's mouth twitched. "Good question. I wasn't going to mention this, but when you were gone, there was an incident."

Both of Shepard's eyebrows rose in surprise. "Another one?"

"A nurse sent in to take blood couldn't find a vein. She must have hurt him, because the objects in the room started to vibrate. Thankfully, she had enough sense to get out of there."

"You think he's a ticking time bomb, don't you?" Shepard asked point blank.

Mercer's eyes fell. "I worry that if he isn't managed properly, innocent people could get hurt."

"Let me have a chat with him."

The tension on Mercer's face was readily apparent.

"I promise you, I'll be all right. Just give me five minutes."

"Fine, but don't do anything to agitate him."

Moments later, Shepard passed through the decontamination corridor, a section about ten feet long where ultraviolet germicidal irradiation ensured she wasn't dragging any viruses or bacteria into Sam's living space.

"How's my guy doing?" she said casually.

Sam looked up and grinned widely. His dark brown hair was short. He also looked a few years older than the

30

first time she'd seen him in this particular viewing chamber. "Hi, Dr. Shepard."

She was amazed at how much he looked like Peters. They had the same nose and facial structure. It was uncanny. "I see you got a haircut."

He ran a hand along the back and sides of his head. "What do you think?"

She smiled. "It suits you. Was getting a little long for my taste, if I'm going to be honest." Given the accelerated rate at which he was growing, if he went more than three days without cutting his hair, he'd be little more than a mess of wild curls.

"I missed you," he said, fixing her with his deep brown eyes. "I wish you'd come more often."

Shepard glanced over at the two-way mirror, distinctly aware that Mercer would scrutinize her every word. "Yeah, well, I've been busy lately, Ryan... I mean Sam. I just wanted to make sure you had everything else you needed."

"Let's see," he said, counting on his fingers. "Blood tests in the morning. Usually after that a bunch of guys in lab coats strip me naked and measure every part of my body. For lunch, they send in something they call food, but it looks more like slop to me."

She could see the frustration mounting. Reaching out, she cupped the side of his face. "That doesn't sound nice at all. Maybe I could smuggle you in a candy bar. Would you like that?"

He nodded vigorously.

"Dr. Mercer mentioned that you got annoyed the other day and things in the room started to shake. Do you remember that?"

"A little."

"Any idea how that happened?"

Sam grew quiet as he mulled over her words. "She hurt me. I got angry."

"I understand." Shepard decided to change tack. "I guess what I'm asking is, how do you think you were able to affect the objects in the room? You know, to make them move without touching them?"

"I'm not sure." His eyes locked onto hers. They were filled with curiosity. "Can't you do the same?"

She shook her head. "No, we can't."

"We?"

"The human race, I mean."

Sam grew quiet and Shepard wondered whether she had said something wrong. She rose to leave.

"So soon?" Sam said, a pleading quality to his voice. "Can't you stay a little longer?"

Her soul ached for what this poor child must be going through. But he wasn't a child, was he? Every physiological reading suggested he was somewhere between twenty and twenty-three. But with so little proper human contact, he had the emotional depth of someone half his age. Such a situation wasn't simply sad. As Mercer would point out, when you were dealing with someone who could access the very fundamental laws of the universe, it was also incredibly dangerous.

"Sure, I can stay a few more minutes. Have I ever told you how much my son liked baseball?"

Sam leaned in, grinning with the pleasure of a child allowed to stay up way past their bedtime.

Chapter 7

Shepard was heading through the base's main complex on her way to the computer science lab when the lights flickered and then went out. Moments later the hallway came back to life. Then a female voice came over the loudspeaker.

"Be aware of the increased frequency of solar storms expected throughout the week. The Air Force is working to ensure all critical infrastructure is properly shielded."

The handful of military personnel nearby exchanged an uneasy look.

"It's getting worse," Peters said, sliding in beside her, dressed in his blue camo battle uniform. Towering over her by a full foot, he cut quite the dashing figure. The two continued walking together.

She didn't need him telling her the sun was growing more unstable to see how serious the situation was becoming.

"You know," he went on, "one day the lights might just go out for good. Heard an astronomer on the news say the sun could go at any minute."

She threw him a look. "Go?"

Peters balled up his hands and then extended them. "Kaboom. Supernova. Adios, amigos. Au revoir. Sayonara."

"Yeah, I got the point," she said, grinning despite her annoyance. "Like many of us, I'd hoped we had years to stop the Drax from destroying our solar system, but that doesn't appear to be the case."

Peters fished out a graph from a folder he was carrying and showed it to her.

"What's this?"

"It's a stellar evolution chart," he explained. "You can see key points highlighting the sun's deterioration."

The first was in 1945, just after the explosion of the atomic bomb. That made sense since the Council had explained during their initial meeting on the moon that setting off the bomb had put a bullseye on the Earth. Once humans developed the technology to fight back, the Drax knew it was time to move to the next star system. They had probably done this hundreds if not thousands of times. But there was another uptick on the graph and it coincided perfectly with their realization that the human race had been living in bondage.

Shepard tensed her lips. "So you're saying the Drax have probably stepped up their exit plan, in part because of us."

Peters nodded. "Yes, although it would have been next to impossible to hide that we'd discovered their presence. I mean, how could we have known the enemy was living among us?"

"Hindsight is…" She stopped herself. "Well, you know."

He smiled, revealing a pair of dimples. "My grandma used to always say, 'If I had my druthers, I'd have done it differently.'"

"That pretty much sums it up. Not that we needed any more pressure, but I suppose some invisible clock really is ticking in a way it wasn't before."

34

They passed by the operations center, where a series of senior staff were shuffling about running damage reports and trying to ensure the base's systems were all back up and running.

Peters drew in a deep breath. "I heard you went in to see Sam again."

"Mercer?"

A guilty look flashed over his face. "She's worried. And so am I. Look, I know why you might feel a bond with the kid. Especially after what happened to Ryan."

Hearing his name spoken out loud felt like an ice pick being jammed into her belly. He must have noticed her visceral reaction. "Trust me, this isn't a conversation I was eager to have."

She stopped and set her hands on her hips. "Is that why we just so happened to bump into each other? So you could tell me to lay off of Sam?"

His eyes fell. "Mercer's right on this one. I know he looks and sounds human and that he was created from our DNA…"

"Which in a way makes us his parents, doesn't it?"

Peters' eyes flicked around, as though processing her statement.

"Wait a second," she continued. "I seem to remember you were the guy who was desperate to have a family."

"Yeah, but—"

She could see a strange expression settle over his rugged features. The realization hit her at once. "You've been going to see him too, haven't you?"

"Not as often as you have."

She laughed sardonically. "Maybe not, but clearly you feel some kind of way or you wouldn't waste your time."

Peters shifted the folder into his other hand. "I think what I'm trying to say is both of us need to detach and back off. We don't know what he's really capable of. Genetically speaking, he may be our…"

"Child? Go ahead and say it."

"Yes, you're right. But that doesn't change the fact that he may be our only ticket to saving the entire human race. If that means poking and prodding him and doing whatever we can to figure out how he ticks, then so be it."

Deep down she knew Peters was right. But that didn't change the fact that she found his automatic deferral to logic and reason a little cold and somewhat disheartening.

Moments later, they reached the IT lab, where an argument was already underway.

The loudest voice belonged to Anastasia Petrova, the computer prodigy who had been RUTH's co-creator. Facing her were the three Delta operators: the marksman, Miguel Alvarez; the comms specialist, Jake Thompson; and Nash, the heavy weapons operator. Their voices only rose as Shepard and Peters entered the room.

"What's going on here?" Peters bellowed, his voice drawing them all to attention.

"These idiots are asking me to break the law," Petrova said, her thin and normally pale face now flushed with anger.

"Who are you calling an idiot?" Jake shot back. Motioning to Nash and Alvarez, he said, "You better be talking about them."

Peters turned to Alvarez, who also looked annoyed. "What's this all about?"

The table next to the marksman was cluttered with electronic bits and pieces. "We were simply asking Anastasia if she could give RUTH a firing proficiency. That way we could rig up a drone with a rifle and have her cover us from above."

Petrova raised her hands. "Now do you see? They want RUTH to become a cold-blooded assassin. Murder was not the reason we made her." Peters didn't look nearly as outraged as Petrova had hoped. "Oh, please tell me you're not about to agree with them."

The colonel cocked his head to one side, letting the notion percolate. "I gotta say, the idea isn't half bad."

The three Delta operators whooped and hollered.

Petrova crossed her arms and stormed to the other side of the lab. Shepard went after her. "I couldn't agree more with everything you said. Don't worry, I'll talk them out of it."

"You better, or I'll walk," Petrova warned. "I'll not have my life's work turned into a mass murderer."

"*Our* lives' work," Shepard reminded her old partner.

Some of the rage cleared from Petrova's eyes. "Yes, of course. My apologies."

"I'm here because I received your message. You said you had something for me."

"Ah, yes." Petrova reached into the pocket of her lab coat and produced an earbud. It very much resembled the kind you could get at any big-box electronic store.

"What's this?"

"Put it on and tap the side," Petrova encouraged her. Shepard did so and at once heard a familiar voice.

"Hello, Dr. Shepard."

"RUTH, don't tell me they got you squeezed down into this tiny little earpiece."

A gentle laugh. "That's right. With my help, we found an efficient way of shrinking the superconducting quantum chips by nearly eighty-five percent."

"Humble and wickedly smart," Shepard said. "But will there be any loss in functionality?"

"Quite the opposite," RUTH informed her. "My capabilities have improved fivefold."

"Wow," Shepard said, truly amazed. "Won't be long before you don't need us anymore." She'd only been partly joking, but the finer edges of humor still eluded even the most adroit AIs.

"I can only speak for myself, but I have grown quite fond of you and the other members of the crash retrieval team. I could not imagine trading all of you for some stuffy large language model."

Shepard couldn't help laughing out loud. Confident with a touch of snobbery. Had she been told only a handful of years ago what AI could achieve, she wouldn't have believed it.

"Dr. Shepard, I also wanted to inform you that my analysis of the Endarian facility markings is now complete. I've categorized all twenty-five thousand of them according to form, content and meaning."

"Yes, I recall," Shepard reminded her. "The Endarian facility on Mars was really little more than a waste disposal plant for fifth force radiation crystals."

"That is correct. However, upon conducting a more thorough analysis, I discovered something new. Something that might help us to further our mission."

A dozen yards away, Peters and the other three Delta operators were discussing the optimal use of AI control firing platforms.

The creases in Shepard's brow smoothed as she homed in on what RUTH was telling her. "Okay, you've got my attention. Spill it."

"I'm sorry, I am not detecting a spilled liquid."

Petrova frowned, listening in on their conversation through an earpiece of her own. "She's still learning slang."

"No kidding." To RUTH—"It's an expression. 'Spill the beans,' as in 'get to the point.'"

"Ah, I see. I'll make a note of that. Yes, as I was saying, of the twenty-five thousand pictographs I was able to record and translate, a single mention occurred more often than any other."

"You're killing me, RUTH."

"More irony," Petrova cut in.

RUTH chuckled. "Duly noted, Anastasia. As I was saying, the pictographs make repeated mention of a device best translated as a 'galactic forge.'"

Shepard's eyebrows knit together. "Galactic forge? Any idea what that is?"

"I have an idea," the AI replied, "although my level of confidence can only be placed at eighty-three point seven percent."

"So then give me your best guess," Shepard said, crossing her arms and leaning her back against a nearby worktable.

"It appears to be describing a device of immense power, capable of harnessing and directing the fifth force."

"A weapon," Shepard said almost as a statement of fact.

"A tool," RUTH amended. "Capable of incredible acts of creation as well as destruction."

"This forge, do you think it might be capable of stabilizing the sun?"

"Most definitely, Dr. Shepard. And perhaps much more."

Shepard's head tilted slightly. "A device that powerful could help free us from the Drax."

"Although not without its risks, it could turn whoever wields it into a veritable god."

The implications were swirling about her. The prospect was certainly a hopeful one, but not without an equal or greater level of concern. What if this galactic forge got into the wrong hands? And if it was as powerful as RUTH suspected, surely the Drax were already busy trying to find it.

"By the way, RUTH, how can we be sure the Drax don't already have one?"

"There are a few reasons, Dr. Shepard. First, the forge utilizes the fifth force, while the basis of the Drax technology is refined dark matter. This is the reason they have enslaved humanity, as well as the reason they will move on to the next habitable planet once they have extracted everything they are able to. The other reason we can be confident the Drax do not already possess this device comes down to detection. Now that our scientists can detect fifth force energy, or FFE, as they're calling it, if the Drax had a forge of their own, such readings would be off the chart."

"I see. Thank you, RUTH. I suppose that leaves one final question. If this thing is real, where can we find it?"

"An excellent inquiry, Dr. Shepard. At the moment, the truth is, we do not know."

Chapter 8

The Drax cybernetics facility was located an hour outside of D.C., ten stories beneath the abandoned Potomac Steelworks. Here, US Senator Donovan Ravencroft grinned as he reviewed the latest batch of elite Drax units. Pairs of blood-red eyes stared back at him. Shielded by plates of white ballistic armor, these menacing machines stood taller than the average Drax soldier and outweighed them by a hundred pounds. The extra bulk wasn't simply to make them appear more imposing. In hand-to-hand combat, it would make them nearly unstoppable.

Like the regular Drax units, these new soldiers did not wear human skins. The reason for that was very simple. Their purpose was not to blend in, but rather to accomplish whatever mission Ravencroft gave them. Orders they were expected to carry out with extreme prejudice.

"They're magnificent, don't you think?" he asked, his deep voice echoing through the immense space. "I call them the Praetorian Guard."

Desiree looked on with a mix of awe and concern. "A guard fit for an emperor," she said, tickling his ego.

Ravencroft paused and drank in the possibilities. In spite of the Praetorians' height, Ravencroft was still notably taller, with graying hair and the sharp eyes of a pit viper. "Yes, I like that."

"What was it that took you so long?" she asked.

"Necessity is the mother of invention, as they say. Prior to the humans waking up to our activities, there wasn't really a need to alter the way things had been done for eons. Why change what isn't broken, right?" A sudden light shone in his eyes. "Yet another tidbit of human wisdom."

"'Human wisdom' strikes me as an oxymoron."

Ravencroft laughed. "Touché." He turned to her and, as he did, two of the Praetorian Guards broke formation and positioned themselves behind her.

Desiree glanced back, wondering what Ravencroft was up to.

He stood before her and raised his arms to either side of him. "The suit is also new. Stuart Hughes Diamond Edition. Just shy of a million dollars."

"It sure looks it," she said, that feeling of dread growing. "You've always had such refined tastes."

Ravencroft smiled again, but this time his eyes were dead. "You were given the task of inserting an operative into the Pentagon's crash retrieval program."

"Yes," Desiree replied quickly. The moisture in her mouth was gone. "The Council beat us to it. And once Dr. Yamada's deceit was uncovered, the humans immediately stepped up their security measures."

"I see."

The Praetorian on her right laid a hand on her shoulder and began squeezing. It took everything Desiree had not to cry out in pain. Soon she heard a crunching sound and her legs gave out. The other Praetorian reached out and held her aloft.

"Quite strong, aren't they?" he noted with no small amount of pride. "I couldn't be happier with how they turned out, don't you agree?"

Desiree struggled to keep from passing out. The android behind her had for sure snapped her collarbone. Although she herself was also an android, her series had been programmed to infiltrate humanity. Thus, she had been given a pain response in order to blend in. And right now her mind was being overwhelmed by such signals.

"The Master has asked for the child and the child he will have." Ravencroft watched her for a moment. "Tell me what you know about the UAP retrieval in Texas."

"UAP retrieval?" Desiree's vision was becoming cloudy.

Ravencroft shook his head. "I'm starting to wonder if your heart is still in this."

"It is," she replied weakly.

"I'm sorry, I can't hear you." He leaned in, cupping an ear.

She didn't say anything after that. There was no point. She could tell Ravencroft only wanted to toy with her, like a cat pawing at its meal. Her fate wasn't in question. Clearly, his mind had been made up before she'd even arrived.

Chapter 9

Special Agent Dwight Douglas pulled up to the three-story Wesley Heights townhouse and watched as a group of guests shuffled inside. He was here for Monique's engagement party. Staring down at the gift sitting on the passenger seat of his cruiser, he found himself struggling to remember the young man's name. Was it Jason? Jasper?

Creedence Clearwater Revival was on the radio singing about a bad moon rising when Douglas raised his hand and rubbed his thumb and index together. Immediately, the music shut off, followed by the car.

To say that his life had been turned upside down after Japan was the mother of all understatements. Yuki Nakamura, the founder of Daimyo Defense Systems, had turned out to be a two-hundred-year-old who had been waiting for decades to fulfill a solemn promise to none other than Isadora.

But, like any good magician, Nakamura had had other secrets up his sleeve, namely that his construction company was building a new home for the dispossessed remnants of the Council. And rest assured, the irony of the situation was not lost on Douglas. Japan, a country with one of the lowest immigration rates, was preparing to take in millions of offworld humans.

Council members and humans shared two important traits, that was true. One, they were *Homo sapiens*. Two, they had both been victims of the Drax industrial soul complex. That was how Douglas referred to it—how else would you describe a technology that extracted the life force from a human being and turned it into an energy source?

The Drax had tried doing the same to him—the soul extraction, that was—but he'd been spared by an intervention from the Council. So too had Isadora. And yet, since meeting with Dr. Shepard at Andrews, he hadn't seen either one.

Douglas' gaze flicked over to the gift again. He wondered whether getting it had been a mistake, not to mention bringing it here in person. The chances were high that the Drax were watching. There were no two ways about it, the paranoia was real. You couldn't shake hands with a prominent member of the community without wondering who was man and who was machine. Desiree had made very clear that if Douglas didn't fall into line and fast, Monique's life would be in danger.

But there were two things Douglas couldn't tolerate. One was a bad plate of ribs. The other was someone threatening his family, even if that person was his daughter Desiree. Finding out she'd been replaced by the Drax was hard enough. Having her threaten what was left of his family was something else. And yet she had showed up in Japan with a license to kill, an order she'd refused to carry out. He hadn't seen her since she'd appeared in the gleaming hallway inside Daimyo Defense Systems. Was it possible she'd had a change of heart? Was such a thing even possible for a Drax?

He had been shouldering the troubling secret of the intragalactic conflict for weeks before finally coming clean to Monique. Needless to say, she either hadn't believed him or hadn't wanted to. The subject had never come up again and she made sure to squash it whenever he got close.

The same thing was happening to the general public. After Dr. Yamada had leaked the reality of the Drax presence on Earth, the news had exploded, hitting major outlets one after another like some relentless creeping barrage. No doubt the Drax were crapping themselves from all of this new attention. The shadows were where they felt most comfortable. Sunlight was the best antiseptic. But never underestimate a determined party's ability to board up the windows. In this case, it was clear by the sudden shift in the media coverage that the alien narrative was out in favor of hoax and misidentification. Witnesses were brought on air only to be questioned, doubted and in most cases ridiculed. They were trying to put the toothpaste back in the tube and, shocking as it was, they appeared to be succeeding.

Given the disturbing nature of the revelation, it was no surprise the general public had leapt at the chance to deny it was real. Short-sighted as it might have been, it nevertheless provided a sense of relief, like waking up from a nightmare only to find it was all just a dream. Thank the Lord!

He was startled by a rapid knock at the window. It was Monique gesturing at him. "Dad, you coming inside or what?"

He grabbed the gift. It was wrapped in the cartoon section from Saturday's paper.

"Oh, you didn't have to," she said sweetly, leading him back to the house. She gestured to the red brick stairs that led up from the sidewalk and the smooth alabaster paint job on the façade. "So, what do you think?"

He studied the townhouse's exterior. "It's lovely," he replied, trying and failing to match her enthusiasm. "I'd kinda hoped you two would find a nice place outside the city, really far away."

She threw him a sideways glance. "You think I don't know what you're up to, always trying to chase me off?"

"I want you to be safe."

"Life isn't safe, Dad. Now, are we gonna stand out here and fight or are you gonna come inside and join the party?"

He stopped her at the front stairs. "Do me a favor." He handed her the gift. "Open this now. You know I'm not a big fan of crowds and attention."

There was a twinkle in her eye. "Of course." She tore at the paper and paused, studying a canvas carrying case. She opened it. "Oh, BBQ accessories."

Douglas grinned, oblivious. "It's a great set. Got your stainless-steel flipper and tongs. Figured Jason could get a head start on weekend cookouts."

"He's a fashion designer, Dad, not a short-order cook."

Douglas leaned in. "Well, it couldn't hurt the man to expand his repertoire a little, don't you think?"

Monique stepped in and hugged him. "I love you, even if you are a little clueless at times."

He cocked an eye. "I think there's a compliment in there somewhere."

Just then his phone rang. It was Junior Agent John Griscole. "Give me a second, honey, I gotta take this. I'll meet you inside." Douglas took the call.

"Agent Douglas?"

"I'm here, John. What's up?"

"There's been a murder."

"It's D.C. They happen every day. I'm at my daught—"

Griscole texted him an address. "It's serious, Douglas. I can't say anything more over the phone. How soon can you be there?"

Douglas glanced at the house and the muffled sound of festive voices from inside. Then back at his cruiser parked across the street. "I'll leave right away."

Chapter 10

Joint Base Andrews

The conference room was awash with chatter before Commander Bradshaw brought everyone to order. Shepard, Peters and the rest of the team, including Mateo, Dr. Mercer and Dr. Singh, were watching him intently. Also present were the three Delta operators, Alvarez, Jake and Nash.

Bradshaw folded his hands and set them on the table. "I'd like to open this meeting with a request for any intel on the current status of relations with the Council."

They looked from one to another before Shepard spoke up. "As you know, things are complicated. Let's just say that our standoff with Elder Gorian and his team inside the anomaly suggested they weren't entirely trustworthy. Both of our groups were after the source of the fifth force radiation and the Council seemed quite certain they should have it and not us."

"I seem to remember him saying humans were too dumb to use it properly," Jake offered as way of clarification.

Peters frowned. "I don't think that was exactly what he said, but I won't deny the spirit is pretty close."

"Then he showed up on Mars," Shepard continued, "and became our prisoner, before we opted to let him go."

"He seemed pretty happy about that last part," Nash said, nodding at the others around him.

Bradshaw cleared his throat. "I'm sure he was. But that hasn't really answered the question."

"The facility on Mars was completely destroyed," Shepard told him, "along with any of the crystals they'd hoped to retrieve. Thanks to Captain Mathis, we managed to secure the sole remaining specimen. For all we know, they're scouring the local star systems for other facilities. I'm guessing there's been no contact since we let Gorian go free?"

Bradshaw shook his head. "We've got enough to worry about with the Drax. One powerful alien enemy at a time is more than enough, wouldn't you agree?"

Peters nodded. "Absolutely, although we can't forget that Shepard's FBI contact also revealed the Council has millions of their compatriots in deep hibernation. The moment we defeat the Drax, God willing, it seems their plan is to resettle on Earth like some galactic immigration wave."

"Geez, Colonel Peters," Jake shot, his eyes shining. "I took you for many things, but never a xenophobe."

"Hey, I'd like to keep Earth for us humans. Sue me."

"All right," Bradshaw said, hoping to get them back on track. "If we find out where the Council's new base is located, perhaps we can send a delegation to see if they can't iron things out. I think we could use some friends right about now." He scanned the room. "Speaking of which, I've received word from the highest level that they're doing everything they can to nix the 'aliens among us' frenzy that Dr. Yamada set loose."

Shepard laughed. "Sounds to me like they want to put the genie back in the bottle. Good luck with that."

"I wouldn't be so sure," Bradshaw countered. "The Pentagon's threatened the major media outlets with a blackout on any future access unless they either drop the subject or ridicule it into the ground."

Alvarez raised his hand. "I can confirm what the commander is saying. Once the alien invasion story first dropped, the mainstream news was all over it. Pundits on both sides of the aisle losing their minds. Since then, they're mostly bringing on skeptics and treating UFO experiencers like mental patients."

"Maybe for the better," Mateo said under his breath.

Shepard turned to him. "Really?"

Mateo straightened. He clearly hadn't expected anyone to hear, let alone respond to, his flippant remark. "Let me put it this way. If I thought the average person could handle the truth, my opinion might differ. Besides, what's the general public meant to do with that sort of explosive information?" He waved his hands in a wide arc. "'An evil species of aliens is living among us, kidnapping folks at will and pushing our sun toward a supernova. Now get on with your lives and do your best not to freak the hell out.'"

Jake burst into a wild gale of laughter. "Man's got a good point."

"Listen, I'm not trying to be a jerk," Mateo went on, "but you see what I mean. Why bother scaring people senseless if there's nothing they can do about it? As far as I can tell, in such a situation, the only ones who might benefit are the Drax."

Peters aimed a finger at him in solidarity. "Another reason I don't trust the Council, by the way. Don't forget, Yamada, the one who spilled the beans in the first place, was one of their agents."

A cacophony of voices erupted at once.

Bradshaw raised a hand to settle everyone down. "Either way, we need to be aware the Pentagon isn't keen on the extra scrutiny. Congress has been asking questions and trying to throw their weight around. We're a matter of days from having to create another debunking project like Blue Book in the sixties. Something, anything to get them off our backs."

"Let's hope it doesn't come to that," Shepard said. "I'm all for truth, but I'm no absolutist. Even I recognize the damage that might do."

"Now, before we go too far astray," Bradshaw said, reeling them back once again, "I want to hand the floor over to Dr. Singh." He motioned to the scientist. "I understand you and your people have had a breakthrough with the Aurora UAP."

Singh put his glasses on and studied the tablet in his hands. "We've confirmed that the recovered craft was some sort of satellite circling our planet."

Shepard scratched her chin. "Can you say how long it was up there?"

"Given it crashed in 1897, the simple answer is no. But the idea of a non-human satellite orbiting our planet isn't all that far-fetched. Are any of you familiar with the Black Knight satellite theory?"

The faces around him were blank. "Is that a chess thing?" Jake asked.

Singh ignored the question. "In 1897, the eccentric engineer and inventor Nikola Tesla was conducting experiments in wireless radio transmissions. During one such trial, he claimed to have received signals that were completely different from anything he'd seen before. On most occasions, he got interference from thunderstorms and Earth noise. These new signals, however, were coming from orbit. But more than that, they were rhythmic and orderly. Keep in mind, his experiments took place sixty years before the first human satellite was placed in orbit."

Peters sat back. "Wow, that is pretty wild."

"No kidding." Singh clicked a button and an image appeared on the screen behind him. It was of a hangar with a wooden platform positioned in the center of an open space. Resting on that platform was the UAP. Singh used a laser pointer to draw their attention to the three blinking lights. "It didn't take long for us to figure out the red button released the hatch. Now, according to the female witness"—he checked his notes—"uh, Lena Lang…"

Nash's eyes went wide. "Wait a minute. Do you mean *the* Lena Lang?"

"You know her?" Peters asked.

"Are you kidding me?" Nash fired back.

Peters stared at him, growing more confused by the minute. "I'm being a thousand percent serious. Can you tell us how you know her?"

"*Paranormal Places,* man. She's only the host of one of the greatest shows on Earth. Granted, they've only done two seasons, but I make sure to TIVO every episode."

Alvarez shook his head in disgust. "Nash, you need to get out more."

"If I can continue," Singh said. "Lang claimed that after opening the hatch, a hologram addressed her."

Bradshaw folded his hands, intrigued. "What did it say?"

Singh shook his head. "She says she doesn't remember, but I suspect she might not be telling the truth."

"Wasn't her co-host brought in showing signs of a fifth force mutation?" Shepard asked.

"That's correct," Dr. Mercer acknowledged, seated to her right. "So far his signs are stable and we're contemplating how to remove the appendage growing from his neck."

Jake grimaced. "Poor guy."

"That's probably why she isn't talking," Shepard suggested.

Bradshaw shifted his attention her way. "Care to elaborate?"

"It could be she feels it's her only bargaining chip for getting proper care for her friend. She may be under the impression that once they've told all they know, they'll be considered expendable."

"Can't blame her," Mateo said. "If I was in her situation, I'd be thinking the same."

"While finding out what was said may prove helpful," Singh informed them, "it doesn't change what else we found. I'm going to let RUTH go over the next part."

"Thank you, Dr. Singh," RUTH's melodic voice said from the intercom positioned in the middle of the conference table. "The markings on the inner lid of the UAP erase all doubt the craft that crashed in Aurora, Texas, was Endarian. I have since compared the script inside with everything we recovered from the facility on Mars. The vast majority was instructions on making repairs and swapping out defective internal modules. There was, however, another section that made mention of the galactic forge."

This prompted a series of questions and RUTH spent the next few moments going into detail about what they knew thus far of the forge, its purpose and the immense power it possessed.

"Hold on a second," Peters said, sitting up. "Are you telling us this thing that crashed is a forge?"

"It does not appear to be, Colonel Peters," RUTH replied. "Although we believe it may be pointing us toward the forge's possible location. Dr. Singh, would you care to take over from here?"

"No, RUTH. You're doing just fine. Go ahead."

"Understood. While Dr. Singh and his team were unable to reactivate the holographic function inside the UAP, we have detected a periodic burst signal being transmitted every hour."

"A signal? But to whom?" Bradshaw asked.

"It appears to be targeting the distant dwarf planet of Eris."

Mateo cleared his throat with surprise. "Eris, as in the icy planetoid inside the Kuiper belt?"

Located beyond the orbit of Neptune, the Kuiper belt is home to a wide array of icy bodies. Among the millions of objects are the dwarf planets Pluto and Eris.

"That is correct, Dr. Vargas."

A look of concern flashed across Dr. Mercer's face. "If we do manage to get our hands on this forge, what's to say it will do what we hope it will? For instance, what if it blows up the sun instead? Something tells me it won't exactly come with an owner's manual."

"That's a valid point," Bradshaw said, scratching his chin. "To be frank, I have a concern of my own. Given the Drax and the Council were both searching for fifth force crystals, we can only assume they would love nothing more than to get their hands on ancient Endarian tech."

"If this forge even exists, you can bet your ass they're already searching for it," Alvarez added, anticipating where Bradshaw was heading.

Peters' gaze hardened. "All the more reason we need to get to it first."

Chapter 11

As soon as the meeting had adjourned, all present shuffled out, except for Shepard, who stayed behind. Bradshaw was still seated at the conference table, signing a handful of documents. He stopped and looked up at her. "Something I can help you with, Dr. Shepard?"

"I take it you're serious about heading to Eris?" she asked.

He sat back. "The risks are incredibly high, so it isn't my first choice. Then again, I think Alvarez made a good point—if we're looking for this forge, there's an excellent chance our enemies are too. Seems to me the risk of not going is far greater. Do you disagree?"

"No, that isn't why I'm asking. I'm assuming your plan is to send the same team that went to Mars."

Bradshaw nodded, a hint of aggravation on his face. "I hope you're going somewhere with all of this, Dr. Shepard."

"Yes, I am. I think Sam should join us."

There was a notable change in Bradshaw's otherwise calm demeanor. "You can't be serious."

"I get how it must sound, but his presence may prove invaluable."

"His presence? Strictly speaking, we don't even know what he is. Nor what he's capable of." A touch of color came to Bradshaw's cheeks. "I wish you could see how many strings I've had to pull just to keep his existence a secret from the top brass."

Shepard thought she understood just fine. "Any concerns you have that Drax infiltrators at the Pentagon might try and grab him are completely justified."

"They could take him or do much worse." Bradshaw paused for a moment, tapping his pen against the table. "I take it you heard about Sam's latest outburst? Dr. Mercer said everything in the room began to shake. And you want someone with those kinds of abilities, someone who may not be fully stable, on a crucial mission to the furthest reaches of our solar system?"

Her gaze fell. "Sir, with all due respect, how would you handle being poked and prodded every thirty minutes, living in a glass cage under twenty-four-hour observation? That's enough to drive anyone a little crazy, don't you think?"

"Point taken," Bradshaw grudgingly conceded. "Then explain this to me. If he's the asset you say he is, why on earth would you be willing to risk losing him?"

Swallowing, Shepard said, "By all indications, whatever's waiting for us on Eris was built by the Endarians. And although Sam has DNA from Colonel Peters and me, a big part of him is not human at all." Even as she spoke, she could see nothing she was saying seemed to be getting through to Bradshaw. A change of tactic was in order. "You're a student of history. Think back to America's westward expansion in the nineteenth century. Where would the US cavalry have been without their Apache and Navajo scouts? Likewise, we saw the same thing only a few years back in Afghanistan and Iraq where brave locals acted as guides and translators. I would argue it's far riskier to launch this mission without him."

One of Bradshaw's eyebrows twitched as he let out a long, ragged breath. "I'll think about it, Dr. Shepard. But don't get your hopes up."

•••

From there, Shepard made her way to the base hospital complex. Her clearance level had allowed her access to the video confiscated from the TV crew. Shepard had gone over the footage nearly a dozen times. After reviewing it, it was clear that the host, Lena, and at least one of the others had been speaking to someone or something. The question was who, a question that had not been resolved for a simple reason: the video showed the craft and the open hatch, but no hologram. For all intents and purposes, they might as well have been talking to a ghost. Or could it be that the dosage of fifth force radiation their bodies had been subjected to had made them hallucinate the entire encounter?

While Shepard was always keen to give people the benefit of the doubt, she also believed strongly in facts over feelings. Of course, the mitigating factor against the hallucination hypothesis or flat-out lies was that each of them had recounted the same conversation.

Shepard entered Lena's room. Centered by a single hospital bed facing a TV, it was nearly identical to what one might expect to see in any sterilized medical facility. It was only the hazmat suit Shepard was wearing that dispelled the normality of the situation.

"I'm Dr. Katherine Shepard," she said, smiling.

"Are we going to die?" Lena asked, clearly concerned by the protective gear her guest was wearing.

"Eventually, yes. Just like the rest of us mortals."

Lena fought back a grin. "You had me scared there for a minute."

"The good news is you weren't exposed long enough to do any permanent damage."

Glancing over Shepard's shoulder, Lena asked, "And John? How's he doing?"

"Less well," Shepard admitted, aiming to be as honest and transparent as she could. "But they're expecting a full recovery."

"I saw a finger growing out of his neck," Lena said, clearly disturbed.

Shepard moved right next to her bedside. "I can't imagine what that must have been like."

"Terrible." The fear wasn't there more than a second before it was replaced by something like desperation. "Has anyone reached out to my husband and kids? They must be worried sick."

Shepard assured her their families had been informed. "The complicating factor is that you and your crew were exposed to something potentially life-threatening. Not to mention the area where you found it has since been designated top secret."

"Was that spaceship giving off some kind of…"

"Radiation? Yes. And if I'm going to be honest with you, some people exposed to it have died. Which is why it's so important you answer all of my questions."

"Okay, fine. Go ahead."

Shepard smiled as she drew nearer. "Great. First off, I understand you were filming an episode for a TV show, is that correct?"

"*Paranormal Places*," Lena told her, the light from above framing her delicate features. "It's cheesy and hyperbolic, I know. Most of the time we just make stuff up for the ratings. Once we made our way into the cave,

I saw the glowing moss covering the walls and part of me wondered if our producer Alex Rivera had staged the whole thing—you know, to get a more natural reaction for the episode. But then the giant grasshopper thing showed up and the alien ship and the blue hologram that—"

"That's where I'd like to stop you for a minute," Shepard cut in. "About that blue hologram, none of it shows up on the footage you recorded."

Lena grew still, lines of confusion playing across her face. "I don't see how that's possible. Have you spoken to our director, Marcus? He was the one who filmed it."

Leaning in, Shepard asked, "Do you recall exactly what the hologram told you?"

Lena turned, glancing out the window for a long moment. "He said he was God."

"God?"

"Yeah. I don't know if he meant *a* god or *the* God. But I was just as surprised as you were."

"What else do you recall?"

"He asked if I was pleased by his form. I asked him who we were speaking to. And then suddenly I felt a jolt and it seems a bunch of stuff was put into my head, a conversation the others couldn't hear."

"What was it he told you?"

"That something called the Ascension was coming."

"What's that?" Shepard asked.

"I wondered the same thing. He told me there were three stages: Arrival, Awakening and Ascension."

Shepard bit her lip in thought. "Did he explain what he meant by that?"

Lena shook her head. "I wish he had. Do you think the world's about to end? With the sun swelling up like it has, the internet's going nuts with conspiracy theories."

"Conspiracy theories?" Shepard asked, playing dumb. "What kinds of things are you seeing?"

Pausing for a moment, Lena said, "Well, after that woman came forward claiming aliens were here on Earth, living under our noses, you can just imagine. Our ratings shot through the roof after that. I wouldn't be surprised if that was what convinced the production company to sign us on for a third season. The footage we got in Aurora will make us legends, so long as the military agrees to let us have it back."

Shepard smiled weakly, feeling bad for the woman. The Pentagon had an itchy trigger finger when it came to classification. She knew the odds of Lena getting back that film were slim to none. Instead of crushing her spirit, Shepard chose to gently redirect the conversation.

"Lena, do you recall the word 'forge' coming up at all in your conversation with the hologram?"

The woman's eyes traced up and to the left as she replayed the encounter in her mind once more. Seconds later, she shook her head. "Can't say that I do." Her fingers went to her temples as she squinted. "Although, since it happened, I keep getting these sharp pains in my head. Feels like an intense pressure that comes and goes without warning, as though he somehow dumped a whole lot more into my brain. But I'll be damned if I can remember any of it. The feeling is haunting me, like an itch you can never quite scratch."

"Give it time," Shepard said, intrigued.

Lena's eyes became grave. "Funny. That's what the hologram said."

Chapter 12

The Crescent Moon Hotel was about as seedy as they came. Nestled on the fringes of the bustling H Street Corridor, far from the gentrified shops and upscale nightlife, it stood as a rotting relic of the past. A damaged neon sign flickered, revealing a once-vibrant façade now faded from neglect. Nowadays, the predominant clientele were drifters and degenerates, folks who preferred to do their business at night away from prying eyes.

A host of police cars were parked out front. Douglas weaved past them and into a lobby that smelled of cigarette smoke and stale beer. The wallpaper was peeling at the corners, revealing layers of past renovations, echoes of a bygone era. Two officers were arguing with the clerk at the front desk, a portly man with a bad toupee and an even worse attitude.

Junior Agent John Griscole intercepted Douglas by the elevators. "Hey," he said, wearing a somber expression.

The FBI didn't show up for the average homicide, which made Douglas wonder what the hell was going on. "You're acting like a funeral director," he snapped. "Care

63

to fill me in on why the bureau's involved in what looks like a regular homicide?"

"We should go upstairs," Griscole said, leading him to the elevators.

"That where the body is?"

"Yeah. Sixth floor."

With a moan, the doors opened and both men got in. Griscole used his elbow to punch the button.

"Wise move," Douglas quipped. "There's no telling what you might catch in a place like this."

The doors opened to a mix of cops and FBI agents. On the outside, Douglas was a regular Cool Hand Luke, but on the inside he was nothing short of a mess. None of this was making any sense. Then a stray thought popped into his head.

You haven't heard from Desiree since Japan, have you?

He tried to push the errant thought from his mind. Moments later, they reached the room and entered. A crime scene photog was busy snapping shots of a woman slumped over in a chair. Douglas' heart did a little jig in his chest.

Then he saw her hair, fine brown and neatly kept at about shoulder length. It wasn't Desiree. A rush of guilty relief washed over him. He felt like a schmuck for being thankful. But his celebration didn't last long. A distinctive wedding ring on the dead woman's left hand caught his eye. He reached inside his jacket and removed a pen that he used to lift a clump of her hair, revealing her face.

"Oh, no," Douglas said, feeling his gut seize up in an excruciating knot of pain.

Griscole put a hand on Douglas' back. "I'm so sorry, Dwight."

Douglas took a step back on a pair of wobbly legs, staring down at the dead body of Agent Sue Keller. His head spun and through his shock a relentless barrage of questions began to form. At the forefront: what was she doing in a place like this? And, more importantly, who was it who had killed her?

He turned to Griscole, subdued rage in his eyes. "What do we know so far?" Little by little, decades of training were regaining control.

"She was shot twice. Both times with .45 ACP hollow-point rounds." Griscole moved closer to the body and carefully opened her blouse, revealing a ballistics vest with two small holes. "As you can see, Agent Keller came prepared, but the bullets went right through."

Douglas leaned over and located her service pistol. It was still in the holster and her right hand wasn't anywhere near it. "She was ambushed," Douglas said, a pit of rage boiling beneath the surface.

Stay cool, my man. You won't do Keller any good now if you lose your shit.

Instead, Douglas glanced around the room. The walls were stained with God knew what. The carpet was thin and in several places completely worn through. Calling this a seedy hotel was being far too generous. "The hell was she doing here in the first place? That's what I wanna know. Is there any indication she was working a case? Or do you think this was somehow personal?"

Griscole shook his head. "We've got a team back at FBI headquarters sifting through her case files and so far we're drawing a blank."

"Send me a copy of all of those files, will you?"

"Of course."

65

"I take it there are no witnesses?"

"We've been asking, but everyone denies hearing any shots."

"In a place like this? I can't say I'm surprised." Douglas sighed. "What about DNA or fingerprints?"

"No DNA, although we did get a few prints, mostly from the usual places—doorknobs and the like. I expect it'll take the lab a while to run them all down. It's a pretty high-traffic area."

"What about from the front desk? Anything there?"

Griscole shook his head. "No one here uses credit cards or their real names."

Suddenly a thought occurred to Douglas. "How long has Keller been here, do we know?"

Griscole checked his notes. "The last person to hear from her was her husband when she called him yesterday at one-twelve p.m."

Douglas checked the time. It was now close to ten p.m. the following day. "So she's been here for at least twenty-four hours."

Griscole nodded. "Maybe even a little longer. Why, what are you thinking?"

The truth was, two divergent thoughts were going through Douglas' mind at once. The first was that Keller likely wasn't a Drax, since the self-destruct mode normally kicked in within a few hours. The second was less a thought than a feeling of acute frustration. For obvious reasons, this was the one he decided to share. "If she'd just called me, I could have been here too to back her up."

"Hard to say, Agent Douglas. Maybe both of you would be lying here."

"Maybe so." Douglas surveyed the junior agent before him. "Anything else?"

"No, I don't think… Wait, yes, there is." Griscole pulled a sealed plastic bag from his coat pocket and handed it over. Inside was a scrap of paper torn from a legal pad. On it was written:

Cash. 5 p.m.

Douglas studied it intently.

"We matched the paper to a pad on Keller's desk, but that was about all. Mean anything to you?"

It was starting to look as though she'd come for some sort of payoff. That was the first thought that popped in, but one he didn't dare say out loud, especially if she was part of some secret off-the-books operation. Either that or she'd gone rogue on him.

Sue, what the hell were you doing in a place like this, dammit?

Douglas locked eyes with Griscole. "Has her work laptop been sent to forensics?"

"Not yet."

"Good." Then, waving the torn note, Douglas said: "Oh, and I'm keeping this."

"Uh, wait a second," the junior agent began.

But Douglas was already gone.

Chapter 13

Joint Base Andrews

The lab was a hive of murmurs and restless movement as the team filed in. Shepard led the way, her expression serious as she glanced around the cluttered space, taking a seat at the central table. Peters followed, his face set in its usual thoughtful frown, while Mateo and Nash discussed something in low tones, dropping into their chairs with synchronized thuds.

Alvarez entered next, his focus briefly caught by a new gadget on the side desk. He picked it up, examining it with a curious tilt of his head before Jake nudged him, whispering a joke that had Alvarez rolling his eyes but chuckling. Jake, ever the light-hearted one, tried to balance a pen on his nose, earning a mixture of amused and exasperated looks from his colleagues.

Dr. Rajan Singh stood before them. He clapped his hands once, the sound echoing in the high-ceilinged room, immediately drawing all eyes to him. "All right, everyone, let's settle down," he said, his voice calm but carrying. "We depart for Eris at 0600. That's exactly fifteen hours from now."

Singh flipped on the projector and an image of a distant, icy world filled the screen behind him. "Before we go, let's cover some essentials about our destination," he continued, adjusting his glasses. "Eris is named after the Greek goddess of discord and strife. This dwarf planet is about 2326 kilometers in diameter, making it slightly smaller than Pluto but significantly denser. It orbits at a remarkable distance, averaging about 68 AU from the sun, making it one of the most distant known objects in our solar system that we've directly observed."

Another click and the slide changed to display a model of Eris's atmosphere. "The air is thin, composed mostly of nitrogen and methane. It's also extremely cold, and the atmosphere may collapse and freeze onto the surface as Eris moves away from the sun. So, pack warm," Singh finished with a slight smile, trying to lighten the mood as he prepped the team for one of their most daunting missions yet.

"How long's our flight time?" Alvarez asked.

Jake's ears perked up. "Yeah, and what movie will be playing?"

Singh shook his head. "Utilizing the same Council craft that shuttled you to Mars, we anticipate the transit taking no more than thirty hours."

Nash's eyes went wide. "Man, that's not a short ride."

Singh laughed at the absurdity of Nash's comment. "Using conventional rockets, flying to Eris would take at least a decade."

"Snap!" Jake shouted, leaning back. "Let's hope those seats are reclinable."

As Singh carried on with his presentation, Peters leaned over to Shepard. "Any word on Sam?"

She shook her head. "Bradshaw has kept quiet. But I'm not surprised. I already know what his answer's going to be."

"Can you blame him?"

"Under normal circumstances, I'd agree with you." Shepard shifted, trying to get comfortable in one of the hard plastic chairs Singh had set out for them. "The only difference is what's at stake."

Peters' eyes flickered as he contemplated what she'd just said. "Our future?"

"Our future, our past and everything in between. If Sam can't somehow help us put an end to the Drax, then all I can say is we've been wasting our time. Time I could have spent at home with Ryan." Shepard bit her lip and Peters touched her back.

He was still consoling her when the lab door opened and in walked two guards who stood at attention at the door. Next to enter was Commander Bradshaw, followed by Dr. Mercer. Last in was a figure that took their breath away.

"Holy shit," Jake said, straightening in his seat. He pointed. "That can't be the kid."

The young man stared back at those assembled, his expression calm, almost neutral. He looked to be somewhere in his mid-twenties, but with none of the social skills of someone his own age.

"You'd be wrong, I'm afraid, Mr. Thompson," Dr. Mercer said, almost proud. "Everyone, I'd like to introduce you to Sam… uh…" She became quiet. "Well, he doesn't have a family name."

Bradshaw stepped forward. "This mission to Eris is the riskiest we've ever launched. Your failure will mean the human race is lost."

"Yeah, no pressure," Nash said, beads of sweat forming at his temples.

"It was for this reason that I agreed to allow Sam to join you," Bradshaw continued. "I know you'll make us proud. Don't make me a liar."

Sam shuffled over and sat next to Shepard.

She smiled at him. "How do you feel?"

"Hungry," he said.

There was an innocence that was hard not to like. Never mind that he had the power to control the fundamental forces of the universe.

Shepard reached into her bag and came out with a granola bar. "This should help." She tapped his knee and watched as he peeled back the wrapper and went to work.

Once his geological history of Eris was completed, Singh brought in Dr. Caldwell from engineering to discuss some of the equipment they'd be using.

Caldwell's excitement was palpable as he gestured to the upgraded MAGsuit displayed on a nearby stand. "Ladies and gentlemen, I present to you the latest enhancements to the Molecular Augmentation Garment Mark 2, specifically designed for the harsh conditions you'll be facing on Eris."

He waved his hand over the suit, highlighting its new features. "First and foremost, we've incorporated an advanced thermal insulation layer. This new insulation adapts to the planet's extreme temperature fluctuations, ensuring you remain warm and functional even in temperatures as low as -243 degrees Celsius."

Jake raised his hand. "So, it's basically a high-tech winter coat?"

Caldwell grimaced. "You could say that, but it's much more. The insulation works in tandem with an active heating system powered by the suit's energy supply. This system uses nanotechnology to distribute heat evenly, preventing cold spots and maintaining a consistent, comfortable temperature inside the suit."

Alvarez stood and walked over to inspect it. "How does it handle the battery drain?"

"The active heating system is incredibly efficient. It draws minimal power, and we've added an auxiliary unit to ensure you won't run out of juice when you need it most."

Peters pointed a finger at the boots. "What about traction on the ice? The gravity on Eris is about a tenth of what we're used to. We need to stay grounded."

"Excellent question, Colonel," Caldwell replied, having clearly anticipated it. "We've integrated magnetic traction control. These boots can anchor you to the ground, preventing slips and falls on the icy surface. The magnetic strength is adjustable, so you can fine-tune it based on the terrain."

Nash nudged Jake. "Looks like you won't be slipping and sliding all over the place this time."

Jake grinned. "Last time I took a tumble, I ended up legless." He rapped his knuckles on one of his metallic thighs.

Shepard nodded, impressed. "This sounds like exactly what we need. The conditions on Eris are going to be challenging, but these upgrades should help."

Caldwell smiled proudly. "That's the goal. We want to make sure you have the best possible chance of success out there. Any other questions?"

Jake raised his hand again, a mischievous glint in his eye. "Does it still recycle urine into drinking water?"

Alvarez elbowed him in the ribs. "Man, give it a rest."

Caldwell managed a small smile. "Yes, Jake, the waste management nanofiltration system is still in place. You can drink recycled water to your heart's content."

The team laughed, the tension easing slightly.

As the conversation died down, Singh stepped forward, carrying a sleek, futuristic weapon in his hands. The team turned their attention to him, curiosity piqued.

Singh cleared his throat and began, "In addition to the MAGsuit enhancements, we've developed a new series of personal protection weapons. Allow me to introduce the Photon Pulse Rifle."

He held up the rifle, and the team shuffled closer to get a better look. The weapon was sleek and elegant, with an ergonomic design and a digital display embedded in the stock.

"The pulse rifle shares the same power source as the MAGsuit, meaning you won't need to carry extra batteries," Singh explained. "This weapon uses concentrated photon pulse technology to deliver powerful and precise energy blasts."

Jake's eyes lit up with interest. "So, what can this bad boy do to targets?"

Singh smiled. "The pulse rifle delivers a high-intensity burst capable of breaching heavy armor and creating explosive impacts."

Alvarez whistled appreciatively. "I like it already."

"Will I get one of those?" Sam asked.

Jake laughed. "Yeah, that's a great idea."

Shepard turned to him. "You won't need one, Sam. We'll keep you safe."

Chapter 14

Washington, D.C.

Jason Henderson popped the tab on a Coke and leaned back until it was empty. He then drew his hand across his lips, sighing with an air of deep satisfaction.

"That first sip is always the best," the FBI IT specialist said, staring up at the face of a man who was anything but amused. Jason's demeanor changed at once. "Oh, sorry about that, Agent Douglas. Uh, yeah, about Agent Keller. I was really sorry to hear about her passing. She was an amazing asset to the bureau."

"That's why you're here," Douglas said, deciding to play nice. He motioned to the laptop and cellphone on the table before them. "Both of these belonged to Keller. I was told the initial scan of these devices didn't reveal anything important. I wanna look again with a fresh pair of eyes."

Jason nodded his understanding. This was normally where he'd launch into a long-winded diatribe about how the planet's ecosystems were collapsing, or how he'd seen a program on the sun last night and was certain we had less than a few weeks before it exploded, killing all life on Earth. Social graces were not Jason's forte. And yet, thankfully for everyone involved, he opted to skip the doomsday talk and focus instead on the task at hand.

In the meantime, Douglas was doing a computer search of his own. He'd gotten access to Keller's banking info, scrolling through a year's worth of statements. The scrap of paper had the word "cash" and "5 p.m." If this were a secret payoff of some kind, the first place to start was noting any unusual banking activity.

After finding nothing out of the ordinary—aside from multiple trips to the hair salon (Keller had been obsessed with keeping her roots covered)—Douglas contacted the FBI Asset Forfeiture Unit. When the FBI needed a suitcase of money for a sting operation, the funds were often sourced from money confiscated during previous drug busts.

"Eric, it's Dwight. Listen, do me a favor, would ya?" A pause. "I appreciate that, my friend. You have no idea how broken up we are over here. But the reason I'm calling is to follow up on something related to her case. Are you aware whether Keller had put in a request for funds from your department? Sure, I'll wait." Douglas moved the phone away from his mouth and turned to Jason. "Any luck?"

"I'm running the best data recovery software in the world and so far it's coming up blank."

"If Keller was trying to wipe her hard drive, she only managed to delete certain files," Douglas said.

"Looks that way."

Douglas clicked his tongue. "What if we try a different approach? How about you grab the files she created within the last six months and order them from newest to oldest, just in case she created some kind of backup folder."

Jason was in the middle of asking a follow-up question when Eric came back on the line.

"Yes, I'm here," Douglas said. "You've checked the registry and she's not on the list? And there haven't been any withdrawals of forfeited funds in the last month? I see. Okay, thanks, Eric. You hang in there."

"Hmm, I may have something here," Jason said, rotating the laptop in Douglas' direction as he drained the last few drops from his next soda can. "I did as you suggested and got a handful of files Keller created in the last week. Most of them appear to be admin stuff. The only one that looked remotely interesting was this." Jason double-clicked on a video titled "Jimmy Carmichael." It looked like a surveillance video of what appeared to be a naked man covered in dirt attacking the patrons of a gas station. The problem was, it had been taken at night and the quality wasn't great. From what they could see, the deranged man appeared to be swinging some kind of club at random people.

"Can you clean this up at all?"

The corner of Jason's mouth pulled taut. "Is the Pope Catholic?"

Douglas grimaced in reply.

Over the next few minutes, the IT guy began working his magic. Douglas stepped out for some air and when he returned, Jason was grinning broadly.

"It's not perfect, but this should do." They played it again and both men gasped. The nutcase wasn't covered in dirt at all. He was covered in blood. And that wasn't a club. It was a human arm, partially eaten.

Jason sat there, blinking. "What the heck did I just see?"

Drawing in a deep breath, Douglas said, "The product of a broken and deranged society, I'm afraid.

Maybe a better question is, who's Jimmy Carmichael? And why did Keller have this video on her laptop?"

A quick search of the local police database revealed that two weeks ago, a man named James P. Carmichael had been arrested for assault and possible murder. The cops were still trying to figure out who the arm had belonged to. In the meantime, Carmichael was being held at the Sunnybrook Psychiatric Institute in Maryland.

Douglas sat pondering how Keller and this demented cannibal might be connected when his phone rang. The number was private.

"This is Special Agent Douglas."

"I just heard," the woman on the other end said. Her voice was soft and filled with compassion. "I can't tell you how sorry I am."

"Who's this?"

"Don't you recognize the voice? It's Isadora. Can we meet?"

Douglas looked down at his phone in surprise. "When did you give up your usual habit of simply appearing next to people?"

He caught a subtle puff of air that might have been a laugh. Isadora wasn't one to let her hair down. "Even old dogs can learn new tricks."

"Listen, I'm heading to Maryland," he told her. "Care to tag along?"

Chapter 15

Outfitted in their MAGsuits, the team assembled just outside the giant doors of Hangar Six. This was where the engineering team had gone over any last-minute checks on the alien craft they would use on their journey to the outer edges of the solar system.

Standing next to Shepard was Sam. While he was a little on the gangly side, the suit itself had a way of tightening or loosening to fit just about any body type. A few feet away, Nash, probably the largest member of their group, tugged at his crotch. He stopped when he realized he was being watched.

"Gotta make sure my bits have breathing room," he said, a little too defensively.

Alvarez chimed in in agreement. "Big guy's got a point. Thirty hours in each direction with another thirty hours or so for the mission itself? No man can stand a wedgie for that long."

"Or woman," Shepard added, one eyebrow raised. Glancing beside her, she noticed Sam was biting his lip. "Nervous?"

His eyes met hers. They were dazzling, hard to stare at for too long lest you risked losing yourself. Two swirling black holes, infinitely deep.

Sam grinned and all that darkness went away. "I've never been on a ship like that before."

"Sure you have," Jake said, clapping him on the back. "You just don't remember. In fact, you're looking at the guy who lugged your sorry ass out of that Endarian facility on Mars seconds before it imploded."

"Oh, thanks, I guess," Sam offered sheepishly.

Jake waved his hands like he was helping a truck back up. "Keep it coming, my friend."

Nash leaned over. "He needs all the reassurance he can get. Jake's a walking masterclass on how not to be."

"Hey! The kid would do just fine if I took him under my wing." Jake paused for a moment while he adjusted the temperature controls on his suit. He punched the button repeatedly with no effect. "This damn thing!"

Sam raised a finger, turned it sideways and wiggled it.

"Oh, there we go," Jake said. "Now it's working." He caught sight of Sam's little trick and glanced back at the console on his wrist, confused. "Was that you?"

Sam shrugged. "Sorta."

"You some sort of voodoo priest or something? If so, please don't curse me. I got enough troubles in life."

Sam let out an awkward, stuttering laugh. And as he did everyone turned to witness something they'd never seen before. "It's not magic. It's science."

"Can you teach me?" Jake asked without a hint of sarcasm.

Sam shook his head. "I wouldn't know how. I can just do things. Except there's always a price to pay."

The young man blinked and Jake saw a swollen vein in his left eye.

79

"The alien part of me is just fine with it," Sam explained. "Not so much the human part. The forces of nature are like instruments. If my desire is strong enough, I can reach out and play notes. But whenever I do, my body fights back."

"It's like your immune system kicks in," Jake observed.

"And if I push myself too hard, I worry I might just die."

Jake turned back to the console, noticing it was working fine now. "Must be nice to be out of that glass cage."

Sam flashed a set of straight and impossibly white teeth, a sight that made sense given his rapid aging meant he'd hardly used them. "I'm not sure how I feel about being out," he said, staring down, deep in thought. "That cage, as you call it, is the only home I've ever known. Feels normal to me. Getting pestered all day long by those terrible people in white coats, that's the part I could never get used to."

Jake grew uncharacteristically serious for a moment. "I wish I could say I didn't know what you meant." The time he'd spent in the hospital after both legs had been seared off by a Drax plasma cannon made the kid's comment especially poignant.

"Where are you from?" Sam asked the Delta operator.

"Me? Oh, the Midwest. Small town. Not much to do there except get into trouble. Did a fair share of that in my day, before I smartened up and joined the military."

"Must be nice," Sam said, longing in his eyes.

Jake understood at once. The kid didn't have a place he could call home. He'd been born in a tiny glass box and now lived in a bigger version of the same. Jake was suddenly struck by a profound realization—privilege is invisible to those who have it, in the same way that walking around on a pair of biological legs was a privilege he'd enjoyed for close to three decades.

Commander Bradshaw appeared, his hardened gaze passing over each of them. "All right, folks. It's showtime."

The team members put their helmets on, sealing them shut. Shepard helped Sam with his. After that, they boarded the craft, taking a seat along the outer wall facing inward. In the center of the craft was the pilot's seat. Commander Foster, the hero who had brought them to and from Mars, would now be entrusted with flying them to Eris.

When everyone was in place, Foster closed the hatch and activated the electromagnetic power source. The inside cabin began to glow a series of faint, undulating colors, nearly all of them reminiscent of the aurora borealis. Shepard was certain the visual was just as breathtaking from the outside.

On her right, Peters winked and blew her a kiss. On her left, Sam's knee was bobbing nervously up and down. She reached out and laced her gloved hand into his. The act reminded her of her son, Ryan, and she did everything she could to chase the thought away. It wasn't fair to Sam. He wasn't a proxy for her dead son. And yet she appreciated his presence. He calmed her, despite the danger of bringing along a being of such unimaginable power.

As they sped up, the walls of the craft became translucent. Clouds whisked by. Then blackness and a large white orb came into view.

"Ladies and gentlemen," Foster said, his voice low and gravelly, "if you look to your left you should see our moon. If you need to, feel free to say goodbye. We won't be seeing her for a little while."

Sixty seconds later, Foster sent a final message to mission control and increased the throttle. The moon flicked away in a blur of speed. They were now hurtling through space at an almost unbelievable rate.

With the Earth rapidly diminishing in view, Shepard began to focus her attention on their destination—the icy dwarf planet Eris.

Not long ago, the Endarian craft they'd found in Aurora, Texas, had sent a beam of energy toward the Kuiper belt, for what purpose they didn't know. Would the forge be there when they arrived? Or would this entire mission have been a complete waste of time? In a little over thirty hours from now, they would have their answer.

Chapter 16

"These last few weeks have been pretty rough for both of us," Isadora said, her green eyes studying Douglas from the passenger seat of his cruiser. Her form-fitting black bodysuit creaked against the leather upholstery as she shifted slightly. He glanced over and grunted. She was beautiful, there was no denying it—a strange thought really, given that, in the strictest sense, neither one of them was biological anymore.

He also understood where her comment was coming from. She had recently discovered the Council's motives in liberating Earth were far less altruistic than they had first appeared. During Douglas' tour of Suwanose Jima, Yuki Nakamura had made that perfectly clear.

Even more startling, Douglas had learned that the past she thought she knew was nothing more than planted memories. Isadora believed she had been the wife of a Spanish nobleman five hundred years ago and that the Drax had swapped her for an android in the hopes of influencing her powerful husband.

Of course, after his return from Japan, Douglas had kept much of this to himself. There was no telling how she might handle being told the truth.

As they exited the highway, Douglas caught Isadora eyeing him with suspicion. "You've got that look about you again," she said, always observant. "Like you're in the middle of hatching something."

He glanced at her without responding.

"Caring means sharing," she continued, trying to get him talking. "Isn't that how the saying goes?"

A pained grin filled Douglas' face.

"Keller's still on your mind, isn't she?"

"Among other things."

"Spit it out."

Douglas shook his head.

"Don't you trust me?" Isadora asked, a touch hurt. "You know, if it wasn't for me, you'd still be in the dark. I helped you discover your true nature."

"I thanked you already, didn't I?"

Isadora laughed. "Probably not, but who's keeping track?"

She had a good point. "Any news from the Council?"

The change in her expression made clear she knew he was trying to skirt the subject. She decided to let him get away with it. "Last I heard Elder Gorian was still searching for another abandoned Endarian outpost."

One of Douglas' eyebrows rose. Nakamura had explained the fifth force to him and the power it contained to shape the physical world. He also recalled the old man telling him about Isadora's role in trying to stop the Council from messing with something that could destroy them.

"They think it's the only shot they have at beating the Drax," she said, doubtful.

"I was told the Council had millions in cryosleep, just waiting to be reawakened. Why not revive them and defeat the Drax once and for all?"

She shook her head. "You don't understand. Those still asleep represent all that remains from hundreds, maybe thousands of lost worlds. They were promised they would be reawakened only when the time came for resettlement."

"So the Council made a promise they can't keep. What changed?"

Isadora plucked out her new phone and began searching.

"You have a data plan for that thing?" he asked, surprised.

She smiled. "Of course not. This device is piggybacking off the network."

"Why does that not surprise me?"

Holding up her phone, Isadora showed him.

Douglas peeled his eyes from the road long enough to have a look. It was a medieval-looking image depicting a walled city. Above it was the sun along with dozens of strange-looking objects. "I don't get it. It looks like an old painting."

"It's a woodcarving called 'Celestial Phenomenon over Nuremberg,' created in 1561."

"Okay. So what?"

"At the time, the townspeople described an immense heavenly battle," she explained. "People thought they were experiencing the end of the world. Only what they didn't know was that they were really witnessing the largest battle between the Drax and the Council. Many thousands died. The Drax were victorious and the Council retreated in tatters. It's taken them centuries to recover. Then, just as things were looking up, the Drax located and attacked the Council's stronghold on the moon."

85

"Overwatch," Douglas said, shaking his head. "One loss after another. It's hard to imagine."

"It isn't a question of numbers," she went on to explain. "It's a question of technology. The refined Drahk'noth energy the Drax harvest from humans may be cruel, but the end product is incredibly powerful. Perhaps the only thing more potent is the fifth force. Hence why Elder Gorian and others are convinced it represents the only chance they have of victory."

Douglas couldn't help detecting a hint of doubt in her voice. "And you? What do you think?"

Isadora grew solemn. "I want the Council to avenge the wrong that was done to them. More importantly, I agree with their main objective. To eradicate the Drax once and for all."

Turning onto a narrow dirt road, Douglas waited patiently, certain there was more. It wasn't long before he was proven right.

"That being said, I've heard the myths and legends of what became of the Endarians. The fifth force is not to be trifled with. The cost of using such a thing is beyond any mortal's ability to control."

Something about her answer reminded him once again of his conversation with Nakamura.

Now it was her turn to read him. "There's something you aren't saying. There have been enough secrets during this long war. Isn't it time we all started being honest?"

He drew in a deep breath. "Yes, it is. When I was on Suwanose Jima, there was something I learned. Something I've kept to myself because I didn't know how to tell you."

Her eyes widened as she pressed an index finger to her chest. "Tell me?"

Douglas nodded. "Something that had to do with the jade necklace." He went on to explain what the old man had told him. Isadora had feared the Council might destroy themselves if they tried manipulating the fifth force, and she had gone rogue and stolen the artifact, hiding it with a young Nakamura for safekeeping. When the Council had finally caught up with her, she had refused to divulge its whereabouts. Rather than kill her, they had opted to reprogram her, inserting a batch of false memories. She wasn't the wife of a nobleman. Whatever she had been before this doomed mission might never be known.

Isadora sat in silence for a long time after that, staring out the window, her lips moving slightly. Finally, in a low voice, she spoke. "Are you certain about this?"

Douglas nodded, his features filled with sympathy. "The old man was truthful about everything else. I have no reason to believe he lied."

"So you're saying that not only was I robbed of my human body, I've also been robbed of my past?"

"I'm sorry," he said. "You wanted the truth. I remember not so long ago, I was sitting where you are. The truth hurts, but living a lie is so much worse. A wise man once said, 'In a time of deceit, telling the truth is a revolutionary act.'"

"Who was that, Nietzsche?"

"No, George Orwell."

Chapter 17

Maryland, Virginia

Storm clouds were gathering as Douglas and Isadora pulled up to Sunnybrook Psychiatric Institute.

The once-grand, three-story Colonial Revival building now showed clear signs of neglect—shutters were askew, and ivy crept up its sides, clinging to the remnants of its former grandeur. The entrance featured a set of white columns, now peeling. Above these, orderly rows of barred windows lined the facade, their glass reflecting the subdued gray light outside.

Over the radio came a breaking news story about riots in cities across North America as well as the European Union. A handful of small militant groups were calling for an end to the embargo on information about UFOs. Ever since the whistleblower Dr. Yamada had divulged the reality of the alien presence on Earth, the US military had been working overtime to pretend like none of it was real. Clearly, some believed she'd been telling the truth.

Regardless, Douglas had to remind himself of one simple fact—the leak had been part of the Council's master plan of sowing chaos. They had aimed to draw attention away from their plans for Earthly resettlement. Another black eye Isadora would need to contend with.

Douglas touched his index and thumb together, shutting both the car and the radio off at once.

Isadora threw him a funny look. "Wait, what did you just do?"

He laughed. "Long story. I'll explain later."

They got out and headed toward the entrance.

Passing through a set of double doors, they encountered an older woman at a desk. The blonde wig she wore was tied up, tucked away from a face filled with wrinkles.

Douglas pulled out his badge and flashed it. "I'm Special Agent Douglas and this is…"

Isadora caught the expectant look in his eye. "Uh, Special Agent Smith."

The woman eyed both of them with mild suspicion. "What can I do for you?"

"We're here to speak with a patient named Jimmy Carmichael."

She clicked the mouse of a computer that was older than most college freshmen. "Carmichael, James P. Fourth floor. Eval."

"Eval?" Douglas asked. "What ward is that?"

"Not a ward. Mr. Carmichael is still undergoing psychiatric evaluation. Once that's completed, then he'll be assigned."

They thanked the woman and headed toward the elevators, exiting onto the fourth floor. As they did so, they were assaulted at once by the tormented screams echoing along the barren corridor. Unfortunately, it was a sound Douglas was quite familiar with.

Every so often, the requirements of his job meant Douglas would visit a maximum-security prison. That was where the worst of the worst were held. The howls he heard emanating from the patients here were eerily similar.

"How dehumanizing," Isadora observed, a disturbed look on her face.

"Your first time?"

She nodded. "And hopefully also my last."

They reached a set of doors with the words "Evaluation" stenciled overhead. Pushing their way inside, they were greeted by a male nurse who looked desperately in need of a break. The name embroidered over his left breast pocket read "Cooper." Behind him was a long hallway with rooms on either side. Douglas explained who they were and why they'd come.

"Carmichael?" Nurse Cooper said in a raspy voice. A hint of fear flashed across his weathered features. "That guy's a real piece of work."

"Precisely why we need to have a word with him."

"Yeah, unfortunately, visiting hours are over." Cooper motioned to the clock on the wall. It read ten minutes after five.

"You don't understand," Douglas said, growing agitated. "We're following up on a murder."

"That's nice," Cooper shot back. "And I was meant to be replaced thirty minutes ago. Seems we both have our share of problems. Come back tomorrow between nine and five. Thank you."

"Not gonna happen. I'm afraid we need to see him tonight," Douglas insisted, leaning forward, his hands pressed against the nurses' station.

The move didn't seem to faze Cooper one bit, probably because the nurse's gaze was locked on Isadora and the pack of cigarettes she was fiddling with. "Hey, any chance I could bum one of those? Forgot mine in my locker downstairs."

"Sorry, we don't smo—" Douglas started to say before Isadora cut him off.

"Oh, these?" Isadora said, playing dumb. "I'd be happy to donate the whole pack. For a good cause, that is." There was a sly twinkle in her eye.

A light of understanding shone in Cooper's eye as well. He nodded and she handed over the pack, which Cooper slipped into the breast pocket of his teal-colored scrubs. "Third door on the right. I'll mark you down as a four-fifty arrival, in case anyone asks."

"You're the best, Cooper," Isadora said, smiling.

As they circled past his desk and into the corridor, Isadora was still looking rather proud of herself.

Douglas opened his mouth to speak. She raised a hand, preemptively silencing him. "You eat nasty BBQ meat. I smoke once in a while. So what?"

He considered that for a second before admitting defeat. "Touché."

They entered Carmichael's room to find a rather strange setup. The space—or cell—was divided in two by a glass partition. On one side was a desk and two chairs for visitors, or in Carmichael's case a psychiatrist. On the other was a cot next to a chrome toilet and sink.

Carmichael was lying down on his bed, eyes open, staring at the ceiling.

"Quite the setup you've got here, Jimmy," Douglas offered.

Carmichael blinked but otherwise didn't move a muscle.

Undeterred by the lack of response, Douglas said, "My colleague and I are here from the FBI. We're following up on the murder of Special Agent Sue Keller. Did you know her?"

The man uttered an unintelligible noise. His lips were moving as though he was speaking to himself. Was he talking gibberish or reciting a prayer? Douglas couldn't be sure.

"I understand you were brought in five days ago."

More mumbling. Douglas magnified his hearing, a trick Isadora had taught him.

"Noback. Noback. Noback."

"He keeps repeating it over and over," Isadora said, having just listened closely herself.

"Noback," Douglas repeated. "Is that someone you know? What about Agent Keller? Did you ever meet with her?"

"Nogoback. Nogoback. Nogoback."

Isadora sighed and crossed her arms. "This is going nowhere and fast."

Suddenly, the door opened behind them and a young nurse sauntered in. Cooper must have finally gotten that break he'd been dying for. "I'm sorry," she said, "but eval patients aren't meant to have any visitors."

Douglas flashed his FBI badge. "I understand, but this is extremely important. I have a few questions I need Mr. Carmichael to answer."

She looked surprised. "Good luck. This patient's been nonverbal since he arrived five days ago."

"Well, he's talking now," Douglas said.

"Fact, we can't get him to shut up," Isadora added, pointing.

"If he utters more than a bunch of word salad you'll be lucky," the nurse replied.

Isadora eyed the uniform she was wearing. "Hey, any chance you still have Mr. Carmichael's possessions?"

The nurse nodded. "Of course." She led them down the hall to a room with a series of lockers. She opened number twenty-eight. On the door was a list of the locker's possessions. "Bloody shirt. Bloody jeans. One sock, also bloody."

"A psycho *and* a minimalist," Douglas said, gritting his teeth. "Just our luck."

The nurse didn't nod in agreement, but Douglas could see she wanted to. "All the more reason to wonder why he's had so many visitors."

Douglas spun in her direction, surprised. "Visitors?"

"Well, in a manner of speaking," the nurse explained. "Other than you two, some guy has already come twice. Said he was a close friend."

"Does this man happen to have a name?" Isadora asked.

The nurse grew quiet as she searched her memory. "Uh, Simon something. Dash. No, that's not it. Simon Cash."

A lightbulb flashed in Douglas' mind with blinding ferocity. Keller had written down, 'Cash. 5 p.m.' But that wasn't for a payoff. Cash was the name of the contact she'd gone to meet.

Act 2

Endarian Prophecy

Chapter 18

Eris

Shepard came awake to an incredible sight. Commander Foster had the spacecraft hovering some thirty thousand feet over an icy planet.

The surface was an expanse of mottled gray and white, with patches of what appeared to be frozen methane and nitrogen glinting in the feeble glow from the sun. Below, jagged cliffs and deep, shadowy craters stretched out in every direction, the terrain marked by ancient, frozen ridges that seemed to have been carved by the hand of God.

"Have we arrived?" she asked, blinking.

Slowly the others began to stir.

The muscles in Singh's body tensed. "Look at those ridge formations. They must be millions, maybe even billions of years old, untouched by anything since their creation. It's absolutely gorgeous."

"The signal sent from the Aurora craft arrived at a point just beneath us," Foster told them as he studied the readout.

Peters cleared his throat. "Descend to five thousand feet so we can execute a flyover."

"Roger that," Foster said, tilting the nose of the craft downward. Within seconds they were in position. Already the planet's rugged surface was coming into sharper focus. Those ripples of ice now looked more like a mountain range.

From here, it took them nearly an hour to locate the Endarian structure, since much of it was covered over with layers of frozen methane. In the end, a good old-fashioned radar that the engineers had added to the craft's equipment list revealed what the unforgiving landscape had tried so hard to conceal.

"RUTH," Shepard said, awakening the AI. "Scan the surface for any signs of intelligent life, would you?"

"Sure thing," RUTH replied. Minutes passed before RUTH chimed in again. "I see no signs of organic life. However, I am detecting what appears to be an entrance."

Following her directions, Foster set the craft down a dozen yards from a giant set of double doors.

"They sure are a dead ringer for the gates of Babylon," Peters observed.

Shepard glanced over at Sam, who was fixed on the sight before them. "How are you feeling?" she asked.

"Strangely, I feel at home," he replied, unable to take his eyes off those gates.

Mateo peered out the translucent side of the craft. "Is there any chance RUTH can do a scan to see what's inside the structure?" There was the slightest hint of apprehension in the physicist's voice.

"I'm afraid not," Shepard replied. "The first question we need answered is whether we can even breach those doors." The facility on Mars had also been sealed by an impressive barrier. The key to opening it had been the jade pendant provided by Douglas and Isadora. That particular relic was no more, which meant it was only a matter of minutes before the team discovered if they'd come all this way for nothing.

His jaw clenched, Jake rubbed at his elbows. "I don't know, man, it looks really cold out there."

"Quit being a wimp," Peters chided him.

"Outside temperature readings are -350°F," Foster added, grinning. "That's a warm day here on Eris."

"Oh, damn!" Jake shouted. "I think just hearing that gave me frostbite."

"Now imagine the shrinkage," Nash said, chuckling as he undid his safety belt. "You may never be able to show your face again."

Even Alvarez, normally stoic during a mission, burst into wild gales of laughter.

Singh and Mateo exchanged a derisive glance. For some reason, soldiers were often just as eager to rib each other as they were the enemy.

Peters brought the men around. "How much juice do we still have on this thing?" He was referring to the craft they'd arrived in.

Foster examined the console. "Sixty-six percent."

"Then I think it's best we power it down to save energy."

The pilot agreed. "I take it we're all going in then?"

Peters nodded. "There's an extra pulse rifle for you, if that's what you're wondering."

Twenty minutes later, they opened the hatch and pressed out into the frigid, alien landscape. It didn't take more than a few steps to realize the challenge. Alvarez no sooner got started than he faceplanted into hard pack ice.

"You all right?" Shepard asked, helping him up.

"Yeah, fine. I just wasn't used to the low gravity."

"That's a good point," Singh said. "I suggest everyone activate your gravity boots."

Each of them tapped the control panel on their wrist and took a few tentative steps.

"Much better," Alvarez said, walking normally now.

They pressed forward, each astronaut cloaked in a gentle blue glow as the sun's distant rays danced upon the glistening ice sheets.

Upon reaching the gates, the party craned their necks, staring up in awe. Each door had to be well over a hundred feet high. Shepard marveled at the level of Endarian craftsmanship. The seam between each door was no thicker than a human hair. For several moments they scanned the surface, searching for some way inside.

The gates were etched with mysterious symbols, a fact not lost on RUTH, who was busy recording them using the team's helmet cams. This was both the eerie and incredible thing about her recent upgrades—not only was she smarter and far more capable, she could also be in all places at once.

A few feet away, Jake was knocking. "Hello? Anyone home?"

"Yes, there is," Sam murmured.

Shepard turned to him. "What did you say?"

He shook his head. "Nothing. I think I'm just tired and a little cold."

"Turn the heat up in your suit," she suggested. She was trying hard not to mother him, without having much success.

Old habits die hard.

"Oh, that's better," he said, grinning.

"The sooner we're inside, the happier I'll be," Mateo said, running his finger along the nearly invisible seam.

One of the grooves in the intricately designed entryway looked suspiciously like a handprint. Shepard pressed her gloved palm against it on the off chance something might happen. The fit was close, but no luck. She spun around to find Sam watching her, a smile on his lips. While everyone else was busy hunting for a way inside, he was just standing there. Her gaze flickered between him and the handprint.

"You want me to try?" he asked, his eyes tracing down to his open palm.

Shepard nodded.

Sam stepped forward tentatively and pressed his hand into the groove. It was a perfect fit. There was an expectant, almost excited look on his face. But like before, nothing happened. His features dropped.

"RUTH," Shepard called out, hopeful the AI might be putting the pieces together. "You making any sense of these symbols?"

"Yes, Dr. Shepard…"

But before she could finish, RUTH's voice was drowned out by a screeching and a grinding sound. Shepard and the others leaped back to see that the handprint was now glowing. So too was the palm of Sam's hand, slightly muted through the fabric of his MAGsuit.

"Open sesame," he cried, his eyes bright with anticipation.

Chapter 19

The grand entrance of the Endarian facility opened into a veritable cathedral of alien engineering. Towering pillars seemed to stretch endlessly into the darkened heights of the structure, each etched with intricate, ancient symbols both foreign and vaguely familiar.

The walls, made of a metallic alloy unfamiliar to human eyes, reflected a faint, eerie glow from the ambient light that filtered through recessed openings in the ceiling. Each one cast long shadows that danced across the floor.

From every surface, tiny multicolored lights blinked on and off, lending more weight to the feeling they had just stepped into a strange mixture of ancient and futuristic. They might just as easily have been in Egypt's Third Dynasty as in an alien compound billions of miles from Earth.

The team was dwarfed by the oppressive environment they currently found themselves in, and Shepard couldn't help feeling like an ant, trudging along some giant's kitchen floor. Soon, the team found themselves in a valley of sorts as they passed between the rows of pillars looming on either side of them.

Here they encountered a number of sealed containers, some stacked one on top of another. The units varied in size, some as large as small buildings, others more compact. Overhead, massive conduits and pipelines crisscrossed the ceiling, a testament to the sheer power it must have taken to keep this place up and running. If the Endarian facility on Mars was big, the one on Eris was colossal.

And yet for all of its impressive splendor, a closer look revealed noticeable neglect. Shepard stepped over more than one crack as her boots crunched over the frosty floor. She paused and bent down to observe three black lines spreading out from the fissure in the smooth surface. Peters joined her.

"What is that?" he asked, spearing the strange object with his light.

"Looks organic," she said, unsure. She went to nudge it with her finger before he pulled her hand back.

"Better not until we know what it is."

Shepard reached into her utility pack and extracted a scalpel and a vial. Using the knife, she cut off a two-inch length of the black, mold-like anomaly and sealed it for later study.

As they pressed on, the haptic feedback system of her MAGsuit—designed to provide a real-time sensory experience of the outside world—was working overtime to generate a scent from the environment. So far this place had no smell. Pressing further into the cold, silent depths, Shepard couldn't shake the feeling that this facility felt more like a tomb.

"Dr. Singh," RUTH said. "Would it be possible to have a look around?"

"Sure thing," he said, opening the case and releasing four quadcopters specially designed to operate in low-gravity environments. The engineers at Joint Base Andrews, working under Dr. Caldwell, had taken a page from NASA's recent *Perseverance* rover mission and optimized the team's copters for Eris' unique situation.

RUTH would now fly each drone simultaneously, mapping the area as they went, taking note of any landmarks that matched the objectives of their mission. At the top of that list was finding the galactic forge. With any luck, it would be out in the open, perched beneath a glowing sign, just waiting for them. If only life were ever that easy.

"There's something I should let you know," Peters said. "Something about the parameters of the mission."

To Shepard, the almost apologetic tone in his voice wasn't sitting well. She glanced over at him with trepidation.

"I had a meeting with Commander Bradshaw shortly before we left. His instructions were very clear. While our overarching objective is to locate and retrieve the forge, that isn't all we're here for."

"Oh, no. What dirty little job have they put you up to now?" she asked, trying hard to mitigate the venom that was dying to get out.

Peters' lips were pressed tightly together. "They want more samples of fifth force waste product."

"More crystals?"

He nodded. "All we have is the single specimen Captain Mathis brought back from Mars."

"And why was I not told?" she asked, feeling hurt and more than a little suspicious.

"It isn't personal, Shepard. You simply didn't have a need to know."

"And yet you're telling me now?"

"I figured you were bound to find out one way or another," he explained as they passed beneath the shadow of a nearby pillar. "Besides, I believe their

104

concern was that you'd kick up a stink before the mission even got underway."

She chewed on that quietly for a few moments. "Yeah, that sounds like something I might do. Just make sure we keep our eye on the prize. Crystals are all fine, but without the forge, we're dead in the water."

A moment later, RUTH fed the results of her initial scouting mission into their HUDs (heads-up displays). It appeared that once they exited this part of the facility, it broke off into two directions, one ascending, the other descending.

Peters checked the mission clock. "We may have to split up. This place is way more massive than we anticipated." He motioned to them one by one. "Alvarez, Foster, Nash, and Dr. Singh, you four take this far ramp here and explore the upper levels." He turned to the others. "Shepard, Mateo, Sam and Jake, you come with me."

"Into the basement?" Jake spat, his eyes wide. "Just my luck to get the short end of the stick. Why can't we all head upstairs?"

The pleading sound in his voice elicited laughter from Nash and even Mateo.

"Aren't you supposed to be special forces?" Mateo asked, confused.

"That's right," Jake shot back.

"Didn't you know? His call sign's Chickenheart," Alvarez said, grinning.

"Yeah, keep laughing," Jake said defensively. "The dangerous stuff is almost always in the basement. Am I wrong?" He looked from face to face as one by one they turned away and began sorting themselves into their respective groups.

"Oh, and Jake," Peters said, "you're on point."

Just then RUTH broke in. "There's something else you should know. In my analysis of the wall markings, I have already located fifty-seven mentions of the galactic forge. That is eleven point four times more than what was found on Mars."

"Finally a bit of good news," Mateo said, grinning broadly.

Shepard smiled as they got underway. This mission might not have been a waste after all. She turned back to see Sam standing by himself, staring up at the imposing architecture around them. "Hey, you coming?"

"Earth to Sam," Jake called out.

Sam remained still before finally snapping out of it. "Yeah, wait up."

Chapter 20

Shepard adjusted the light on her helmet as they followed a long, downward-sloping corridor. Mateo stopped to examine the walls. "They appear to be made from some kind of epoxy resin, reinforced perhaps with nano-scale carbon fibers."

And yet, despite their strength, the ravages of time and the elements had sought out the weakest points, exploiting them until cracks became gaping holes. That wasn't the issue concerning them the most. It was what they saw sprouting from those openings that was both unsettling and perhaps even dangerous. The same black fingers of mold Shepard had seen in the grand entryway covered nearly every inch of the corridor before them. Whatever it was, it seemed to have pushed through the cracks in the epoxy and spread like a vine scaling the side of a brick wall.

"I don't like it in here," Sam said, his arms tucked closely by his sides, careful not to let them even brush against any surface.

Shepard couldn't blame him. The mere thought of mold made her thankful for the MAGsuit and helmet she was wearing. The more layers between her and this stuff, the better.

Mateo moved his face closer to one of the openings before leaping backward. "Holy crap!" He raised a finger at the hole. "It's moving behind the walls."

Shepard could see a light up ahead. She spun and realized the way back was probably twice as far. "Keep moving forward," she said, grabbing Mateo by the arm. The physicist seemed to be stunned by what he'd just seen.

She was focused on reaching the light and doing her best to fight the overwhelming feeling of claustrophobia that was pulling the walls in all around her. She spotted movement on the ceiling, a long amorphous shape lowering itself just as a snake might lower itself from a low-hanging branch. Shepard's heart rate and pulse spiked. At the same time her mouth went dry with fear.

"You seeing this?" Peters asked, close behind Jake, who had practically broken into a run. It appeared their presence had awoken something.

A black hand slapped her visor, leaving a tarlike streak. She flicked it away and found that it was sticky. She let out a little cry.

"Stay calm, everyone," Peters ordered.

Just then Alvarez came over the radio from the team heading to the upper level. "Colonel, can you give us a sitrep? Do you need help?"

"Negative, Alvarez," Peters replied. "Continue your mission."

There was a pause before Alvarez said, "Roger that. Carrying on."

Even through her growing fear, Shepard realized calling in reinforcements would do them no good. All they could do was press on.

That was when Sam took a spill in front of her. He struck the floor and bounced halfway up. While the gravity boots were keeping them weighed to the ground, it didn't keep the top half from bouncing around like one of those inflatable clown punching bags.

Sam grunted as his body was yanked backward by the foot. He cried out in fear. Glancing down, Shepard could see a black tendril was wrapped tightly around Sam's ankle.

"Hold up," she called out urgently. "One of these things has got Sam."

Peters spun at once and raced back while Jake skidded to a stop, panting in place. Shepard closed both hands around the tendril's slippery surface and began to pull.

"Ouch, it's getting tighter," Sam cried out. His right leg was beginning to pulse with waves of faint blue energy.

Below that, she could see smoke rising from part of his MAGsuit. It appeared to be somehow burning through the fabric. Then another tendril snaked down from overhead and wrapped around Sam's right arm. He was suddenly being pulled in two different directions.

"Help!" he shouted, struggling in vain. Shepard removed the pulse pistol at her hip and placed the barrel center mass. She pulled the trigger and the black tentacle retracted with an audible hissing sound.

Peters did the same with his pulse rifle with similar results. Now free, Sam began to fall once again before Peters caught him.

"I think we better get out of here and quick," Mateo exclaimed, pointing behind them. All they could see was a dark mass heading toward them, silhouetted by the light in the distance.

None of them needed to be told twice. Single file, they tore down the corridor, the mass closing every second.

No sooner had they all escaped the tunnel than they reached a bulkhead. A large red switch sat on the wall. Shepard waited for Mateo to clear it before she punched the button. The black mass had just turned the corner when the bulkhead slammed shut.

Each of them stood, breathing heavily. This time Singh was the one to ask them over the radio, "What's going on down there? Are you all right?"

"The stuff on the walls," Mateo said, struggling to catch his breath. "Stay as far away from it as you can."

Shepard and the others were moving away from the bulkhead door.

"Are you kidding me?" Singh shot back. "That stuff is all over the place. Oh, wait a minute."

"What's wrong?" Peters asked, worried.

Alvarez came online. "Our slime seems to be behaving itself, at least for now. But we've come to a cracked doorway covered with alien lettering. Singh is getting RUTH to translate." A tense few moments went by before he resumed. "She's telling us it's the containment room."

"Hey, Alvarez," Peters said. "Share your video feed, will you?"

"Sure thing."

Suddenly, a tiny visual from Alvarez's POV appeared on their individual HUDs.

Peters' team watched as Alvarez and Nash pried the doors apart just enough for them to pass through. It was much darker inside, the lights from their helmets sweeping from left to right.

"Well, it appears this was where they stored the waste crystals," Singh said. The feed showed a series of empty canisters.

"Looks like whatever was here disappeared long ago," Nash said.

Alvarez's camera caught something in the corner.

"Hey, Al, turn back and rotate twenty degrees to the left, would you?" Peters asked Alvarez.

The marksman did so and speared an undulating black mass in the corner. It was the size of a Cadillac Escalade.

"Don't touch anything else," Peters ordered them. "Just back out of there, real slow."

"The heck is that thing?" Foster asked, sounding like a man who wished he had stayed outside in the freezing cold.

"Don't ask stupid questions," Peters barked. "Just do as I say."

Shepard paced back and forth, unable to keep the clawing terror at bay. They had traveled billions of miles intent on finding the galactic forge and instead they had found a nightmare.

Chapter 21

Washington, D.C.

Douglas was weaving through traffic on the I-395 going a hell of a lot faster than he ought to. To make matters worse, he was trying to tilt his phone, currently in the center console, at just the right angle.

"Let me help you," Isadora said as she tried keeping an extra eye on the road.

Douglas waved her away impatiently. "Griscole, can you still hear me?"

"Yes, Agent Douglas, go ahead."

"Keller wasn't paying someone off. She was meeting a man named Simon Cash."

"I see," Griscole said. Clearly he hadn't expected that either.

"But before we go down that road, what have you found out about Jimmy Carmichael?"

The sound of Griscole flipping through pages came through the phone. "Used to be a music teacher at the local high school. Got into a car accident about ten years ago. Broke both his legs and hurt his back. Began taking painkillers, the hard stuff—oxy, hydro, you name it. Eventually transitioned to street drugs once his prescriptions ran out."

"Does he have a fixed address?" Douglas asked.

"Not at present, no. He was evicted about two years ago and ended up on the streets."

Sitting next to him, Isadora was busy using the cruiser laptop to pull up info on Cash.

"We have any idea how these two might have known each other?" Douglas asked, veering past an eighteen-wheeler. "For all we know they worked together at Burger King."

"I'll see what I can find," Griscole replied.

Douglas hung up the phone right as Isadora shouted, "Bingette!" Her face was glowing like she'd just won the Publishers Clearing House sweepstakes.

"Who the hell's Bingette?" Douglas barked.

She laughed. "It's an expression. You know, like 'Eureka!'"

Douglas shook his head. "The word is 'bingo,' not 'bingette.' Anyway, fill me in. What'd you find?"

"Cash and Carmichael knew each other from school. Cash works for Safe Harbor Initiative in Dupont Circle."

"Safe Harbor Initiative?" Douglas said, his forehead rippling in concentration. "Sounds like a naval thing. He a dock worker or something?"

Isadora smiled. "No, it's an NGO. They've been around for about a decade."

"Yeah, but what do they do?" Douglas asked, switching back into the fast lane.

"I'm getting there, if you'll let me. Geez." Isadora pulled up the NGO's mission statement. "'At Safe Harbor Initiative, our mission is to provide comprehensive support and housing solutions for individuals experiencing a lack of shelter. We are dedicated to fostering a compassionate and inclusive community where everyone has the opportunity to rebuild their lives with dignity. Through innovative programs, advocacy, and partnerships, we strive to address the root causes of this epidemic and empower individuals to achieve long-term stability and success."'

Douglas grunted.

"What's wrong?"

"It's midday," Douglas said. "A guy like Cash isn't likely to be home. I say we hit his work first and see if we can't find him there."

Ten minutes later they were pulling up to the offices of Safe Harbor Initiative. Douglas was unashamed to say it looked exactly how he expected. The stark, utilitarian facade looked like something out of Stalinist Russia, a drab concrete frame punctuated by large and often cracked windows. Sheltering the homeless wasn't at the top of anyone's list of priorities, which explained the sorry state of the premises.

Under normal circumstances, Douglas might have called ahead to set up a meeting with a manager, but he worried that might give Cash a heads-up that the authorities were onto him. In this case, the element of surprise would be vital.

He and Isadora parked out front and headed inside. Here they encountered a group of purposeful young people. Both the men and women wore their hair at shoulder length. All the men sported facial hair of various styles—beards, goatees, and sideburns were essential, with bushier being better. For the women, shaved armpits were grounds for immediate expulsion. Both men and women apparently sourced all their clothes from the same thrift store.

These were not people obsessed with the latest fashions or the most expensive cars. That much Douglas had figured out the moment he saw the kinds of transport parked out front. Most of the employees at Safe Harbor motored to work in beat-up jalopies or rode on second-hand bikes.

While they might not have a million Instagram followers or popular vlogging channels, it was clear they'd decided to pour their energy into something far more meaningful. They had an elevated purpose and it showed in the way they carried themselves. They radiated an almost addictive vibrancy, especially in their eyes, which were bright and dazzling to a person.

An attractive young woman with blonde pigtails and a wide smile bounced over to them. "Hi! My name is Rachel. I'm the outreach coordinator here at Safe Harbor. How can I help you today?" Her blue eyes sparkled with compassion.

Douglas flipped open his badge and introduced himself and Isadora. "We're here about an employee of yours. A Simon Cash." He was glancing over the woman's shoulder, searching the faces for one that looked like the picture Griscole had sent him.

"Simon?" Rachel said, drawing a blank.

Just then a wiry man in his early thirties came over, clad in orange shorts and a light blue t-shirt. If Douglas and Isadora had been part of the fashion police, rather than the FBI, he might have needed to effect an arrest. The man put out a hand attached to a thin and cleanly shaved forearm. "Chad Winters," he said, grinning. His teeth were near perfect. "I'm the assistant director here. I understand you're looking for Simon."

"That's right," Douglas said, growing a little impatient with the flight attendant routine. "Is he here?"

"He goes by the nickname Si," Chad explained. "That's why Rachel wasn't sure who you meant." He slid

115

a hand into his pocket. "Simon hasn't been in for a few days…"

Douglas straightened. "If you don't mind, young man, I'll ask that you keep your hands out of your pockets."

The blood drained from Chad's face and he did so at once, letting the arm dangle limply by his side. "Yeah, so I can get you his home address if you'd like." Without waiting for an answer he called out to Rachel. "Go grab Si's address, will you? Thanks."

"What exactly do you do here?" Isadora asked, glancing around at the beehive of motion behind him. "I read on your website it was something to do with the homeless."

Chad winced. "We don't use that term around here."

"You mean homeless?" Douglas asked, confused.

Another pained expression. "Yes, we prefer the unhoused."

Douglas wanted to laugh, but bit his lip instead. "So tell us what you do here at Safe Harbor then."

That winning smile was back. "Of course. We're a nonprofit that specializes in finding permanent and sustainable living arrangements for the unhoused of Washington."

"So you're local?" Isadora asked.

"Right now we are, but we do have plans to expand to every major metropolis in the country over the next ten years."

Sorry to burst your bubble, friend, but the human race won't be around in ten years, was another stray thought Douglas opted to keep to himself.

Rachel bounded over a moment later with a scrap of paper that contained Simon's address.

"Thank you," Chad said as they turned to leave. "Oh, and if you find him, do you mind telling him to give us a call? Cheerio!"

Chapter 22

They had no sooner pulled up to Cash's duplex apartment than Douglas' phone rang. The caller ID flashed "Dr. Green." She was the county's medical examiner, an energetic woman in her early fifties with a penchant for dark humor and a surprising passion for collecting antique books. The last time the two had spoken, Senator Miller's body had spontaneously combusted. And it had nearly razed the medical examiner's office to the ground.

"Dr. Green," Douglas answered eagerly.

"Still out on the streets driving people crazy?" she asked, her voice harsh, but marked with a hidden tenderness.

"Only the ones who deserve it. What's up?"

"I received Agent Keller's remains yesterday," she said, her tone shifting to a more somber note. "Wanted to update you."

"Please tell me she didn't burst into flames," Douglas said, only half-joking. Keller had been one of the few folks he trusted. To find out she'd been a Drax all along might be more than he could handle.

"No need for the fire department, thank God," Green replied. "But I'm afraid it's just as bad. Keller wasn't just shot. Both of her arms were broken in several places." Green paused, presumably checking her notes. "Her humerus on her left and radius on the right suffered compound fractures. Also, she had half a dozen broken ribs. She didn't just sit there and get ambushed. Keller put up one hell of a fight."

Douglas clenched his jaw, his eyes darkening. "So she was overpowered."

"Badly," Green confirmed. "Despite her training, she was no match for whoever or whatever did this."

"That also explains why she didn't go for her gun."

Green agreed. "With two broken arms, there wasn't much she could do."

Douglas winced, his mind racing. "Thanks for the update."

"Anytime, Douglas," Green said, her voice softening. "Stay safe."

He ended the call and glanced at Isadora, who was watching him intently. "Keller didn't go down easy," he said, a note of admiration in his voice. "She fought back, hard."

Isadora nodded, her expression grim. "Whoever did this has to be strong. Really strong. Sound to you like some sort of Drax assassination unit?"

He shrugged, not entirely able to eliminate the possibility. "But it's not really their style. Those skinjobs like to catch you out in the open. And they don't generally use human weapons. Not when they can carve out your insides with a plasma blaster."

The troubled expression on Isadora's face hung for a moment.

Douglas took a deep breath, his gaze shifting back to the townhouse. "Let's go see what Cash has to say." He got out of the car and headed around to the trunk. Once there, he pulled out his Remington V3 semiautomatic shotgun and racked it. "You packing?"

She threw him a disapproving look. "What do you think?"

He laughed. "Next time you can just say yes."

They headed to the front door and knocked. When there was no answer, Douglas peered through a nearby ground-level window. "Not seeing any movement inside. Wait here while I go around back."

Douglas reached the wooden gate with a digital padlock. He stared at it for a moment, wondering if his little trick would work. Rubbing his fingers together, he saw numbers flashing across the screen. A second later, it popped open. He found the sliding back door ajar. Withdrawing his pistol, he entered through the kitchen, calling out Simon's name.

The stench was the first thing to hit him—an overpowering blend of rotting food and stale air. Empty takeout containers and dirty plates were piled high in the sink, creating a breeding ground for flies that buzzed near the overflowing trash can. The countertops were covered with crumbs and sticky patches, remnants of meals long forgotten. The once-white linoleum floor was stained with mysterious spills, and the refrigerator door was plastered with faded magnets and yellowing notes.

"Looks like the maid took the month off," Douglas muttered, wrinkling his nose in disgust. He wondered about the quantity of food. All this seemed like a lot for someone who lived alone.

He crossed the room and unlocked the back door to let Isadora in. She stepped inside and immediately covered her nose with her sleeve. "What died in here?"

"Get used to it," he said, glancing around the cluttered kitchen. "It may only get worse."

120

They moved through the duplex, searching the main floor. The living room was no better. Empty beer bottles and soda cans littered the coffee table, and a layer of dust coated the worn-out furniture. A sagging couch faced a large, outdated television, its screen smudged with fingerprints. The walls were bare except for a few crooked picture frames, their glass cracked and splintered.

"Nothing up here," Isadora said, peering into a hallway closet crammed with old clothes and mismatched shoes.

Douglas nodded, his senses on high alert. Then he heard it—a faint, muffled sound coming from below. He motioned for Isadora to follow him. They reached the basement door, which was fortified with multiple dead bolts and other locks.

"What's down there that Simon doesn't want getting out?" Douglas wondered aloud, his expression grim. He snapped his light under the barrel of his shotgun.

Isadora's eyes narrowed as she examined the heavy-duty locks. "Whatever it is, it can't be good."

Douglas took a deep breath and began unlocking the door, each click echoing ominously through the silent house.

Douglas and Isadora flicked on their flashlights and began descending the creaky wooden steps. Each step echoed through the confined space, amplifying their apprehension. As they reached the bottom, the noise from before was suddenly gone, leaving an eerie silence in its wake.

The unfinished basement was cluttered with piles of old clothes, meticulously separated into types—jackets, sweaters, shorts, long pants, socks. Douglas and Isadora exchanged puzzled glances, their flashlights casting long shadows across the jumbled heaps.

"Did this guy rob a thrift store?" Douglas muttered, his beam sweeping over the assorted items.

"Or maybe he's the world's most prolific couponer," Isadora suggested, her brow furrowing as she scanned the room.

Their flashlights revealed more surprising finds: boxes of packaged food stacked neatly in one corner, rows of toiletries lined up on a rickety shelf, and even several sleeping bags rolled up and tied with string. The basement seemed like a labyrinth.

Isadora shook her head in disbelief as she picked up a new pack of socks. "It's like he's stocking up for an apocalypse or something." She stopped, tilting her head to listen more closely.

"These are all things a homeless person might need," Douglas noted.

"Don't you mean the unhoused?" Isadora said, grinning. A muffled thud sounded somewhere in the distance. Her head snapped to one side. "You hear that?"

Douglas turned. "Where's it coming from?"

She moved her light across the wall, revealing a wooden shelf crammed with more items. "I think it's behind here," she said, stepping closer.

Douglas joined her, his eyes narrowing as he studied the area. Seconds later, he spotted it—a faint seam indicating the outline of a door. "Good catch."

Together, they pushed the heavy bookcase aside, revealing a door secured with multiple padlocks. Douglas pulled out his phone to call in backup. "We're gonna need some help down here."

As he dialed, Isadora's curiosity got the better of her. She started unlocking the dead bolts one by one, her nimble fingers working quickly.

"Isadora, wait—" Douglas began, but it was too late.

The last lock clicked open, and the door creaked ajar, revealing a dimly lit room. The walls were lined with shelves, each one cluttered with more supplies. But what caught their attention was the series of makeshift beds arranged in a row, each one occupied by a figure lying motionless under a thin blanket.

Douglas and Isadora exchanged a wary glance. "What the hell is this?" Douglas whispered.

Isadora moved closer, her flashlight beam revealing the gaunt, hollow faces of the people lying on the beds. Their eyes were open, staring blankly at the ceiling, and their skin had a sickly, pallid hue.

"They look like they're in some kind of trance," Isadora said, her voice barely above a whisper.

Douglas' stomach churned as he took in the scene. "We need to get these people out of here."

As he spoke, one of the figures stirred, letting out a low, guttural moan. Douglas and Isadora froze, their eyes locked on the person struggling to move.

"What's wrong with them?" Isadora asked, her tone filled with a mixture of fear and concern.

Just then, the sound of footsteps echoed from above. Douglas and Isadora exchanged a tense glance.

"Looks like we're not alone," Douglas muttered, his gaze shifting to the room they had just been in.

Suddenly, a figure appeared silhouetted in the doorway. Douglas speared him with the beam of his flashlight and saw it was Simon Cash. Before he could say a word, Simon lunged at them with a ferocity that took Douglas by surprise.

123

"Simon, stop!" Douglas shouted, but Simon's attacks were relentless.

His first act was to knock the shotgun out of Douglas' hands. It scattered to the floor and slid under one of the cots. In the small confines of the room, the fight was intense. Simon's strength was unbelievable. Even Douglas and Isadora, both enhanced with android strength, struggled against his furious blows. They couldn't go for their secondary weapons without risking the lives of the prisoners lying on the cots.

Simon's fists connected with Douglas's ribs, sending him crashing into a stack of boxes. The air left Douglas's lungs in a painful rush, but he managed to roll to the side as Simon's next blow shattered a crate behind him. Douglas tried to regain his footing, but Simon was on him again, a blur of fists and fury.

Isadora lunged at Simon, aiming a precise strike at his midsection. Simon grunted, barely flinching, and spun, delivering a bone-rattling punch that sent Isadora reeling into a metal shelf. The impact knocked cans and supplies to the floor with a clatter.

"Simon, you don't have to do this!" Douglas shouted, dodging another powerful swing. "We just want to talk!"

But Simon was beyond reason, his eyes wild with rage. He slammed Douglas against the wall, the force of the impact reverberating through the room. Douglas's vision blurred, but he fought to stay conscious, grappling with Simon's powerful arms.

Isadora recovered and drew her energy baton, its sleek surface gleaming ominously in the dim light. She activated it, the tip glowing with a deadly yellow energy. She lunged at Simon, aiming for his side.

But Simon was quicker than she anticipated. He twisted her arm with a speed and precision that belied his berserk state. The baton slipped from her grasp, and in a swift, brutal motion, he turned it against her. The energy baton connected with her torso, and Isadora froze, paralyzed, her body locking up as the energy coursed through her.

Douglas watched in horror as Isadora collapsed, her limbs stiff and unresponsive. The baton clattered to the ground, its glow fading. Simon stood over her, breathing heavily, his eyes now locked on Douglas.

Douglas barely had time to brace himself before Simon lunged again, his fists swinging wildly. Douglas ducked and grabbed a metal bedpan from a nearby shelf, swinging it with all his might. The bedpan cracked against Simon's head, but it only seemed to enrage him further. Simon roared and got his hands around Douglas' neck, squeezing with a vise-like grip.

Douglas struggled, feeling the life drain from him as Simon's grip tightened. Spots danced before his eyes, and he fought to break free, but Simon's strength was overwhelming. Just as darkness began to close in, rough hands grabbed Simon from behind and yanked him off.

It seemed another figure had entered the fray. Douglas could only make out the silhouette of a woman, her form lit by the dim glow from his fallen flashlight. She moved with precision and strength, tangling with Simon in a flurry of motion. She dodged his wild swings and landed a series of quick, calculated strikes.

Simon fired off a number of desperate punches, but the woman dodged them with ease, her movements fluid and controlled. She swept his legs out from under him with a swift kick, and Simon fell hard, his head cracking against the concrete floor. He lay stunned, and she moved in quickly, delivering another strike that knocked him out cold.

Douglas gasped for breath, his vision slowly clearing. He saw the woman standing over Simon, breathing heavily. She picked up one of the flashlights from the floor, illuminating the room. The emaciated figures on the cots cowered, their eyes wide with fear and confusion. Isadora began to regain movement, rising slowly and groaning in pain. Douglas raised his light from the unconscious Simon to the figure now standing before him and saw who it was.

"Desiree?" he asked, confusion etched across his face. "How did you know we were here?"

She glanced at him, her expression serious. "Keller stumbled onto something big. I wasn't able to get there in time to help her, but I tracked her movements. It led me here."

"Is this your...?" Isadora asked, her voice shaky as she regained her footing.

"Daughter, yes," Douglas replied, his voice tinged with a mix of relief and confusion.

"But this isn't what you think," Desiree told him, her eyes darting to the cowering figures and then back to her father. "There's more going on here than you realize."

In the distance, the sound of sirens began to wail, growing louder with each passing second.

"I can't stay," Desiree said urgently. She turned to Isadora, her eyes filled with a mix of warning and resolve. "And neither should you."

Both women fled, their footsteps echoing up the basement stairs and out of sight, leaving Douglas to wonder what the hell he had gotten himself into. He turned back to Simon, still unconscious on the floor, then to the terrified figures on the cots. Flipping Simon over, Douglas put two pairs of cuffs on him. Given the man's unusual strength, he wasn't gonna take any chances.

Shining his flashlight around the room, he shuddered at the gaunt, hollow faces staring back at him. "You're safe now," Douglas assured them, although judging by the spaced-out expressions, there was no telling if they understood a word he said.

He moved quickly, helping the prisoners to their feet and guiding them toward the stairs. As they ascended, Douglas began to take in the weight of the situation. Desiree's warning echoed in his mind. Whatever was happening was not what it seemed. What had she meant by that?

They reached the ground floor just as the first police cars pulled up outside, their lights flashing in the darkened street. Officers spilled out, guns drawn, and rushed toward the house.

"I'm a federal agent," Douglas called out, raising a hand holding his I.D. "These people need immediate medical attention." The looks of shock on the officers' faces was sudden and palpable.

The cops hesitated at first, then lowered their weapons as they checked his I.D. "Are there any others?" one of them asked.

"I'm not sure, but the perp is downstairs, handcuffed," he told them.

Douglas stepped out into the blinding swirl of police lights. He would let the local cops process the scene. But as soon as he could, he wanted to have a word with Simon.

Chapter 23

Eris

Shepard and the others pushed deeper into the complex, eager to put as much room as they could between themselves and whatever had attacked them in the tunnel. And yet here too the once-pristine corridors were marked with the same black fungal spores. It seemed to be everywhere. At least now they knew not to get too close or antagonize it.

At last, they settled on a large, dimly lit room filled with an assortment of containers, many of them stacked higher than a man. A quick check confirmed this was one of the few locations not completely overrun with the strange lifeform.

Shepard and the others took a seat in order to regroup and plan their next steps. Glancing at her boots, she saw they were sitting in a line of powder. She reached down and flicked it with her finger. It appeared to be a thick concentration of dust. On a whim, she scooped some into a sample tube and slotted it away.

Next to her was Sam, who was rubbing his ankle.

"Are you hurt?" she asked, moving closer.

Sam grimaced. "It burns a bit."

Seeing what was going on, Mateo headed over. He lifted Sam's leg, examining it. "Looks like it cut right through the MAGsuit's outer layers," he said, shifting Sam's ankle from left to right.

Shepard held her wrist console next to Sam's until they synced. That way she could get a reading on his suit. "Oh, boy," she said, worried.

"What is it?" Peters asked, looming over them.

"Seems Sam's suit was breached during the attack. Thankfully, the self-sealer activated before he could decompress."

"Breached with what though?" Mateo wondered.

The markings around Sam's ankle gave the distinct impression the suit had been melted.

"Some form of acid perhaps?" Shepard suggested. "A defense mechanism. You were shining a light at it. Maybe it got spooked."

"Spooked?" Jake said, not at all convinced. "Mateo was the one poking at it. Why'd it latch onto Sam?"

A good question none of them had an answer for.

"What about you, RUTH?" Peters called out. "We're open to any insights you might have."

"I'm still collating," the AI replied. "However, I have been reviewing the footage of the waste storage room on the upper level." She was talking about the video Alvarez had taken before backing away from a giant glob of black goo undulating on the wall. "Upon closer inspection, it appears that each of the containment chambers was pried open and emptied."

"So someone got here before us," Jake said, throwing his hands in the air. "I'll bet the forge isn't here either. We crossed billions of miles for nothing."

"That doesn't appear to be the case," RUTH corrected him. "Judging by the way the storage units

129

were bent open, I would hypothesize it was done by the same black organism seeping from the walls."

Shepard leaned back. "Wait a second. You're suggesting the mold stole the crystals?"

"Not stole," RUTH amended. "Consumed."

Shepard and Peters exchanged a troubled glance.

"Are you saying that it doesn't just feed off fifth force radiation," Mateo began, "but has eaten the power source itself?"

Jake's face tensed. "That's like eating raw nuclear waste."

Shepard stood and paced around. While worrisome, that wasn't the part that frightened her the most. "I hate to even say it, but what RUTH is saying makes sense. These things are hungry for crystals. And there's no telling how long they've gone without a meal." Her eyes settled on Sam. "We all saw how even though Mateo was antagonizing this thing, it went after Sam."

"That's right," Jake said, his eyes wide. "And when he cried out in pain and the room shook, it went for him even harder."

"I see," Peters said, rubbing his hands together in thought. "With him being a conduit for the fifth force, whatever this thing is, it's drawn to him."

"Drawn?" Jake said, shaking his head. "You make it sound like this thing's looking for a date when the truth is, it wants to eat him."

Shepard reached into her sample case and pulled out the one with the mold she'd collected in the grand entrance. The black fungus lay limp in the tube. She held it next to Sam as all of them watched. Within seconds, it came to life, pressing itself against the edge of the glass closest to him.

"I told you it wanted a piece," Jake said, disgust on his face.

"I can feel it inside of them," Sam said, his eyes leaving the sample tube and passing over each of those present.

"What do you mean by that?" Shepard asked.

"What you're calling the fifth force," he said, looking like a young man with a terrible curse. "When it started to move, I felt something inside. Like it could suddenly see me."

Just then Alvarez came over the radio. "Folks, I hope you're sitting down, because I got something here you're not going to believe."

"Please tell us it's something good," Peters said apprehensively. "We could use a little positive news right about now."

"Well, let's just say that after we hightailed it out of the containment chamber, we kept looking around, hoping to find a stash of crystals. Instead, we found this." Alvarez bent over, focusing the camera on a blinding blue light.

"It's too bright," Peters barked, annoyed. "The image is all washed out. Back away a little more, would you?"

"Sure thing." Alvarez did as ordered, brushing away a layer of frost. Slowly the edges of a glass container came into focus. Azure mist swirled inside the transparent enclosure, obscuring what was inside.

A fresh batch of crystals, perhaps? Shepard wondered.

Moments later, the mist briefly cleared, revealing the face of a man staring back at them. At first glance, the man seemed human, but something was off. He had two eyes, a nose and a mouth, that much was similar. But the shape of his head was elongated, the forehead

131

unnaturally smooth and sloping in a way she had only seen in ancient cultures that practiced head flattening. She had studied the Peruvian elongated skulls extensively, noting how the cradleboard technique had been used to shape the skulls of infants.

It was less than a second later that the magnitude of the discovery hit her. The figure they were looking at was an Endarian. And he appeared to be alive.

Chapter 24

Peters turned to RUTH. "RUTH, can you provide us with a map of the facility? We need an alternative route to reach Alvarez's team."

The AI responded immediately. "One moment, Colonel. I'm accessing the facility's schematics now."

As they waited, Shepard glanced around at her team. Jake was fidgeting, his eyes darting nervously around the room. Sam was trying to stay calm, but the tension was palpable. Mateo was busy checking his equipment, while Shepard herself felt a knot of anxiety tightening in her stomach.

"RUTH," Peters said, his voice cutting through the silence. "What do you have for us?"

A holographic map flickered to life on their HUDs, illuminating a series of corridors and passageways. RUTH highlighted a path in blue. "This route should bypass the majority of the mold-covered areas and lead you to the upper levels where Alvarez's team is located."

Jake looked visibly relieved. "Thank God we don't have to go back through that tunnel."

Sam nodded, his face pale. "I don't want to go through that again."

Peters gave a reassuring nod. "All right, everyone, check your weapons. We don't know what we might encounter on this new route."

Shepard unslung her pulse rifle and checked the energy levels. Jake did the same, and Mateo nervously fingered his own weapon, trying to steady his trembling hands.

"Alvarez, this is Peters," the colonel said over the radio. "We've got an alternative route mapped out. We're on our way."

"Copy that, Colonel," Alvarez replied. "We'll hold our position until you arrive. Stay safe."

Peters took point, motioning for the team to follow. "Let's move out. Stay close and stay alert."

The team moved in a tight formation, their steps careful and deliberate as they navigated through the facility. The mold seemed to be thicker in some areas, its tendrils reaching out like sinister fingers. Shepard's heart pounded in her chest, every shadow and movement putting her on edge.

They moved down a narrow corridor, the walls closing in around them. The faint light from their helmets cast eerie shadows, and the ever-present mold pulsed with a sickly glow.

"RUTH, keep an eye on those tendrils," Peters ordered. "Let us know if you detect any significant movement."

"Understood, Colonel," RUTH responded. "Monitoring the mold for any signs of activity."

Jake, bringing up the rear, muttered under his breath, "Why did it have to be mold? Why couldn't it be something less creepy?"

Shepard and the others continued down the narrow corridor, their steps echoing in the oppressive silence. As they approached an open doorway, Shepard's heart skipped a beat.

A milky-colored tentacle lay across the corridor, resembling a sleeping anaconda. Its tip, however, was black like the mold, and it moved slowly, groping around as if searching for something.

"Hold up," Peters whispered, raising his hand. "Look at that, would you."

They came to a halt, eyes widening as they took in the sight. Mateo pointed upwards, his voice tense. "There are more of them hanging from the ceiling."

Shepard followed his gaze and saw similar creatures suspended above them, their translucent bodies swaying gently. The tips of their appendages were also black, the same as the mold, and they seemed to pulsate with a life of their own.

Sam stood frozen, his eyes wide with terror. The ground around him began to tremble, the air filling with energy. His fear was triggering the fifth force. And with that, the appendages began to stretch in his direction, as though they could sense a nearby meal.

"Sam, stay calm and keep moving," Peters said firmly, but with a touch of reassurance. "We can't stay here."

Shepard moved closer to Sam, placing a hand on his shoulder. "One step at a time." She wasn't sure what might happen if the kid lost it. Would there be some kind of explosion? Or would the surge in fifth force energy summon all of the creatures at once?

Reluctantly, Sam nodded, taking a deep breath and forcing himself to take a step forward.

Drawing his pulse rifle, Peters aimed at the creature's center mass. The tension in the air was palpable as he squeezed the trigger. The pulse rifle discharged with a bright flash, and white liquid squirted out from the tentacle. It retracted quickly into the room, squealing in pain. Surprisingly, the other appendages hanging from the ceiling retracted as well, vanishing into the darkness.

They pressed on, navigating through the corridor with heightened caution. The threat of encountering more of these things loomed large, but they moved with a sense of urgency. As they neared the end of the corridor, the walls opened up into the grand entrance, the chamber with the towering pillars they had seen earlier.

"We're nearly there," Shepard said, her voice steady despite the anxiety gnawing at her insides.

They made their way across the vast open space, careful to step over any cracks in the stone floor. Finally, they spotted the ramp leading to the upper levels.

Relief swelled in their hearts when they spotted the lights from the other team, bobbing like beacons in the darkness.

"Alvarez, this is Peters," he called out over the radio. "Hold your fire. We're coming up on your position."

"Copy that. We see you," Alvarez replied with a grateful breath. "Aren't you lot a sight for sore eyes." He spotted Sam limping a little. "They get you too?" Alvarez pointed to a slash mark across Nash's helmet.

"Yeah, well, they don't want your fat ass. It's the kid they're after," Jake said, motioning at Sam.

Singh looked confused. Shepard explained what they suspected was going on.

"When Peters blasted one part of it," Mateo told them, "the others retracted as well."

"Which means what?" Nash asked, slinging his pulse rifle.

"What if what we've been seeing," Mateo began, "what we thought was mold, was really just the tip of something much larger?"

Shepard crossed her arms. "You're saying this may all be part of a single organism?"

"It's only a hypothesis," Mateo answered.

"While I see what you mean, it does seem unlikely," Foster said. "It would need to be enormous."

"Mold doesn't have a brain or a central nervous system," Mateo said. "An octopus, on the other hand, has both of those things and can move each of its many arms independently."

"I don't see how it really matters," Nash said, readying his weapon. "I catch sight of another clump of that stuff and I'm opening up on it, no questions asked."

Shepard wasn't so sure. "I hate to burst your bubble, Rambo, but if this thing is a single organism, then each time we interact, it learns something new about us. It seems to be relatively dormant right now, and I'd like to keep it that way."

"Yeah, why awaken the kraken?" Jake asked, sounding miffed at Nash's cavalier attitude. "Ever hear the expression 'muck around and find out?'"

Nash squinted. "'Muck around?' Really?"

"The kid," Jake said, motioning. "I'm trying not to turn him into a degenerate like us."

"What's a degenerate?" Sam asked, curious.

"Ignore them," Shepard said, before turning back to the others. "Now, about that frozen Endarian…"

Alvarez led them back to what he called the cryochamber. Next to the grand entrance, this was by far the largest and most intricately decorated room in the facility. Against the far wall were two cryounits. One was in use, while the other stood empty, its lid raised. Facing that was a strange-looking device.

It looked like a giant robotic eye that had been cut in half, a blend of ultramodern with the archaic. The object's sleek, metallic surface was punctuated by intricate, glowing circuits that pulsed with a rhythmic energy. Yet interwoven with these futuristic elements were components that looked almost ancient, their surfaces worn with time and perhaps usage.

Shepard drew closer, taking note of the Endarian symbols etched into the device's outer edge. "RUTH, you getting this?" she asked.

"Of course, Dr. Shepard."

She turned to find Sam staring down intently at the man in the cryochamber. The sight seemed to be stirring something deep within him.

"He an uncle of yours or something?" Jake asked.

"Shut up," Alvarez admonished him.

The comms specialist shrugged. "What do I know? The kid looks like he's in a trance."

He may very well be, Shepard thought, circling around, *but a kid he is not.* In just the short time it had taken for them to venture to Eris and explore the facility, Sam had changed once again. Rather than a young man of twenty-one, he now looked more like someone in their early thirties.

Sam laid his hands on the curved glass and grimaced in pain. It was unclear whether he was having a physical or emotional moment, seeing one of his kind for the first time.

Singh moved in and put a hand on his back to comfort him. No sooner had the scientist's palm touched Sam's back then he recoiled as though shocked.

Mateo ran to his side. "Dr. Singh, are you okay?"

Singh waved him off, massaging his injured hand. Through all of that, Sam hadn't moved a muscle. Perhaps he couldn't be moved. None of them were entirely sure what was happening.

A faint blue light began emanating from Sam's visor.

"He's glowing," Jake yelled, suddenly alarmed.

A tense voice called out from the doorway to the chamber. It was Nash and he had his pulse rifle leveled down the oncoming corridor. "Looks like we're getting some company." He patched in his video feed. Slithering at them along every surface of the corridor were dozens of blackened, slug-like creatures.

Shepard panned upward and gasped. More were coming in through cracks in the ceiling. Dark fingers pushed through openings, feeling along the soft surface, blindly seeking out the source of the nourishment they seemed sure was not far away.

"He's drawing them in," Peters said, reaching down to pry Sam's arms from the capsule. A bolt passed between them, tossing him backward.

Near the doorway, Nash opened fire. "Take that, you sons of bitches."

Soon, pulse rifles were going off all around them. From every direction, tentacles lashed out. Singh cried out as one grabbed him by the wrist and pulled him across the floor. Jake dove through the air and stomped it with his foot, firing at what remained until it retreated.

A door to a neighboring room began to bulge from an enormous weight. Shepard watched as the metal strained and then finally gave way. Dozens of thick appendages spilled into the chamber, cutting through the objects and people. One rose up before Commander Foster and wrapped around his neck, lifting him off his feet. Dropping his rifle, he clutched at his throat, no longer able to breathe.

Weaponless, Singh shouted, "Shoot it!"

Shepard raised her rifle, struggling to avoid shooting Foster, who was being tossed around like a child's doll.

"Almost there," she said under her breath right as she gained a clear shot. Suddenly, the rifle was knocked from her hands. It now dangled by her side, attached by the strap. Disoriented, she spun to see a thick, milky arm swing through the air and impact her chest. She flew ten feet and struck the ground, skidding another dozen or so.

Scrambling to her feet, she saw each member of the party engaged in a losing battle, often surrounded by dozens of these things. Foster's limp body hung in the air, as though dangling from a noose. She raised her rifle again and this time made a clean shot. The tentacle released the pilot, who fell to the ground slowly in the unusually light gravity. That suggested his boots had been disengaged, which could only mean one thing.

The appendage that had sent her flying was moving toward her again. She spun and fired several rounds, spraying milky blood with every impact. Screeching, the arm retreated.

She ran to Foster's side, turned him over and realized with horror that he was gone.

Soon they were all fighting a retreating battle, heading toward Sam, who was still poised over the frozen Endarian. Except now he was glowing even brighter, casting off soft hues of green and yellow. He looked like a living aurora borealis.

Slowly and then all at once, the air in the room was sucked in towards him before it exploded in a dazzling burst of energy. The team members were thrown to the ground, but the creeping fingers of mold and sinewy appendages detonated, spraying out clouds of milky vapor.

In the process, Sam was blown back several feet.

"No," Shepard cried, hurrying to his side. Moments later, the others joined, covered in the nasty remnants of their attackers.

"He's unconscious," Alvarez said, pushing in for a better look. A few feet away, Mateo was tending to Singh, who appeared to have an injured arm.

"Hey, kid," Jake said. "Quit messing around and wake up."

Shepard checked his vitals by syncing consoles. "He's not breathing and his heart has stopped."

Peters touched the side of Sam's helmet, nudging it slightly. "Come on, son. Don't give up on us."

Tears formed in Shepard's eyes. She couldn't lose another child. Not like this. She racked her brain, wondering how they might jump-start his heart.

"Yo, goofball, wake up!" Alvarez shouted.

As though in response, Sam's eyes snapped open and he drew in a hungry breath. All of them recoiled in shock.

"Back off. Give him space," Peters urged.

Shepard helped him sit up and caught the strange look in Sam's eyes. He was staring at something behind them. They turned at once to find the cryocapsule open. And standing next to it was the Endarian.

Chapter 25

Washington, D.C.

The interrogation room was a stark, oppressive space, its gray walls and fluorescent lights creating an atmosphere of unrelenting tension. In the center was a cold metal table and two rather uncomfortable chairs. Cameras nestled up in the corners recorded every moment.

"Are you in the habit of scooping the homeless up off the street and locking them in your basement?" Douglas asked the man seated across from him. There was anger in his heart, you might even say rage, but he was doing what he could to remain calm.

Simon Cash scanned him briefly with sharp eyes and then glanced away without saying a word.

The cops had sent in three different detectives before Douglas had arrived and each one had come out shrugging. *The guy hasn't said a peep since they brought him in.*

Douglas opted for a different approach. "This is some kind of sexual fetish for you, isn't it?" Douglas asked, derision in his voice. "It's probably why you got the job at Safe Harbor. Hiding amongst a bunch of do-gooders, waiting for an opportunity to exploit people. You're a real sicko, you know that?" Douglas flipped through his pages, glancing up long enough to see the sharpness of his words had left a mark.

Simon's eyes had narrowed. Like he wanted nothing more than to take another swing at the FBI agent. The two sets of cuffs locking his hands to the table meant that wouldn't be possible, a fact Douglas was thankful for. That last tangle hadn't exactly gone well for him.

"Five men and one woman," Douglas said, checking the roster of victims they'd fished out of Simon's basement and the list of possible charges. "Kidnapping, false imprisonment, possible sex trafficking—all felonies, I might add. You know, if you don't start giving us what we want, they could put you away for life."

Simon flinched. "You haven't the foggiest idea what you're talking about."

Douglas stiffened. "No? Then tell me where I'm wrong."

"They weren't prisoners."

The FBI agent grinned. "Just roommates? Is that it?"

Simon shook his head before it slumped. He was shutting down again.

Quickly, Douglas tried to keep the pressure on. "And what about Agent Keller? They say she put up quite a fight before you shot her twice in the chest."

Simon's eyes darted around.

Glancing down at Simon's hands, Douglas could see they were scuffed. But at this point it was impossible to say for sure when that had happened. During his struggle with Keller? Any good defense lawyer could just as easily say it had happened when they'd fought in the basement.

"You're so wrong it's painful," Simon said.

Douglas leaned back. "Is that so?" He produced the plastic bag with the note on which Keller had scribbled *Cash. 5 p.m.* "This was you, wasn't it?"

143

"You're in way over your head and you're just too dumb to realize."

"You killed my partner, you son of a bitch!" Douglas shouted, rising out of his chair and grabbing Simon by his shirt and shaking him.

"I didn't kill anyone," Simon protested.

Douglas released his grip and straightened Simon's shirt. "But you were intending to meet her, weren't you?"

Simon nodded.

"And according to you, you never made it. What happened? Did you miss your bus?"

Simon's eyes studied Douglas before darting around nervously. "It wasn't safe."

"At the hotel?"

"Anywhere." He raised his chin, sniffing the air. "You smell like one of them."

Douglas' eyes grew wide. "One of what?"

But Simon had shut down again, this time for good.

Realizing he'd gone as far as he could, Douglas left the police station after that, feeling an ache in his side, like a punching bag that had taken one too many shots. He was getting too old for this. Didn't matter he wasn't human anymore, least not in the strictest sense. Or maybe he needed some new parts, the way Isadora had swapped out her leg for a new one after they'd been jumped by those Council assassins.

He was a few feet from his car when he felt a hand close down on his shoulder. He drew his weapon and spun, only to find Desiree staring back at him. His face softened. "You got a real death wish, young lady."

She smiled. "Can you give a girl a lift?"

"I know you don't need a ride anywhere, but hop in. I'm about to meet up with Isadora and I'm sure she can't wait to thank you."

This time Desiree let out a full burst of laughter. "I'll believe it when I see it."

Chapter 26

Eris

The cryochamber's silence was shattered as the Endarian stepped forward from the open capsule. His elongated, smooth head and alien features were striking, making him look both familiar and otherworldly. He wore a golden robe, embroidered with a series of intricate designs. Perched on his unusually shaped head rested a silver-colored circlet, giving him a regal appearance.

Shepard and her team stared in awe, their reactions a mix of fear, curiosity, and something like reverence.

Peters' face, however, was etched with concern, his grip tightening on his weapon. "Could he be a threat?" he whispered to Shepard.

The Endarian looked on, his enigmatic gaze passing over each of them.

"A threat? I don't think so," Shepard said, taking a tentative step forward. "Look at him. He's just as confused as we are."

Mateo's curiosity got the better of him, and he moved closer, studying the alien figure with keen interest. "Incredible. An actual Endarian. Can you believe it?"

Sam, still groggy from his earlier ordeal, struggled to sit up. Jake, on the other hand, was visibly fearful, his eyes darting around the room as if expecting another attack.

Alvarez kept his weapon trained on the alien, ready to react at a moment's notice. Nash, weary and uncomfortable, shifted his weight from one foot to the other, while Dr. Singh, despite his injured arm, looked elated, a wide smile spreading across his face.

The Endarian began to speak, his words a series of unintelligible sounds that echoed through the chamber. The team exchanged confused glances, unable to comprehend the alien language. Seeing their confusion, the Endarian paused, then tapped a button on his chest. There was a brief hum, and suddenly, his words became clear.

"This is a restricted area," the Endarian told them, his voice smooth and resonant, tinged with wisdom and authority. "Who are you? And do you possess the proper clearances?"

They looked at one another.

"What clearances?" Mateo asked.

"When an alien asks if you have the proper clearances," Jake said, exasperated, "you say yes."

"Why are you here?" the Endarian inquired.

Shepard searched the faces of those around her before speaking up. "We are from Earth. We've come seeking the galactic forge."

The Endarian's expression shifted to one of worry and perplexity. "The forge? How long have I been asleep?" He turned to the cryounit, his eyes narrowing as he read the indicators. "Many thousands of years," he muttered, the weight of the revelation heavy in his voice.

147

Peters, sensing the Endarian's distress, softened his tone. "We found this facility and followed the signals here. We've encountered many dangers, but our mission is crucial. We need the forge to save our world."

The Endarian's gaze moved to the empty pod beside his. "My brother... Aloine was also stationed here. He left for Earth many years ago, but it seems he never returned." His voice was filled with sorrow. "We were the last of our kind here, tasked with guarding the forge and its secrets."

"Do you have a name?" Shepard asked.

"Yes," he said, nodding. "Although not one you could pronounce. For simplicity, you may call me Thalor. In our language, it means 'keeper of secrets.'" He motioned to the empty pod. "His name is Aloine. In my language it can be broken down thusly. 'Al' is the giver of wisdom. 'Oine' is he who stands firm. Aloine."

"It sounds as though duty is important to your people," Peters said, with a growing sense of empathy and understanding.

"A civilization cannot survive without duty and those willing to carry it out," Thalor replied. "The Endarians as a people are bound by a code of ethics. We were sworn to a stringent ethos. Creation is the highest form of divine expression." The being glanced down, observing the carnage at his feet for the first time. A grimace formed on his features. "What happened here?"

"We were getting our asses kicked," Jake said matter-of-factly. He wasn't one for decorum or reverence, even when standing before a god-like being. "Then golden boy over there blew the place apart with a burst of blue light."

That last part Thalor found particularly intriguing. His gaze worked its way past Shepard and Peters until it found Sam. Then all at once his expression shifted into something resembling surprise. "You are not like the others."

Sam rose, struggling to steady himself. "I'm not sure what I am, to be honest."

Thalor grinned and punched another button on his chest. A hologram appeared, depicting what had taken place in the moments before Thalor awoke. They all watched as Sam leaned over the cryopod and let out a burst of energy, killing the creatures and knocking everyone down. When it was done, Thalor nodded. "The fifth force courses through your veins in a way I've not seen before. Have you been outfitted with any augmentation units?"

The blank stares plastered on all of their faces made clear they didn't have a clue what he was talking about.

"I see," Thalor said.

Singh, despite his injury, mustered up the strength to say, "Your brother… Aloine. We may have encountered a hologram of him on Earth before his ship sent a signal here. He spoke of an Awakening and an Ascension."

The Endarian's eyes widened. "My brother, for all his power, believed in what you on Earth like to call 'fairy tales.'" He looked at the team with a mix of sadness and derision. "Tell me, what is the state of Earth? Why do you seek the forge?"

Shepard took a deep breath, preparing to explain the dire situation they faced. "Our sun is destabilizing, and it's part of a plot by a malevolent force known as the Drax. The forge and the power it possesses may be our last hope of reversing the damage and saving the solar system."

"One of which this facility is a part, I might add," Singh said, perhaps hoping Thalor possessed some level of self-preservation.

The Endarian's expression grew grave. "The Drax. They were a warlike people who were wiped out."

"Not all of them," Peters informed him.

This news seemed to intrigue the Endarian. "Is that so?"

"The Drax are mostly synthetic lifeforms now," Shepard explained, "led by a disembodied consciousness who calls himself the Master. They seed *Homo sapiens* on any habitable planet they can find and harvest them for a potent energy they call Drahk'noth."

The Endarian tsked. "Refined dark matter. Yes, I'm familiar with it. A crude and cruel form of energy, extracted from the torment of others. This Drahk'noth, as you call it, was outlawed long ago. Back when my people still governed this galaxy." He swallowed, unable to hide the sadness overcoming him. "This was the basis of my brother's fever dream. That the ancient prophecies were true."

"Prophecies?" Shepard said, her words tinged with mystery and a touch of hope.

"That the Endarians' own hubris would lead to their demise, but that one day they would be reborn in a new form. The revelation spoke of three stages. The first was named Arrival, when the instigator would appear. My brother was certain it spoke of him. This was why he left for Earth. And yet I think he was mistaken."

"The Drax?" Peters blurted out. "You think they were the instigators?"

"'And you will know him, for he will have no form and possess no voice.'"

"The Master," Shepard said, her mind racing.

150

"'When that comes to pass, it shall usher in a new Awakening and then the Ascension.'"

The chamber was still as the Endarian completed reciting the prophecy.

"The chosen one," Shepard repeated, turning to Sam, who looked overwhelmed.

"It's not me," he said, his hand waving before him.

"Could it be true?" Alvarez asked, almost hopeful.

Thalor's eyes found Sam and then fell. "I do not know. My people's abuse of the fifth force proved to be our undoing. It did not matter how many warned of the damage being done. The waste crystals continued piling up in an unsustainable way. It was merely a question of time before concentrated pockets of radiation began distorting the space-time continuum and with that the minds of billions of Endarians. As much as I long for the vast empire we once had, I fear the same pattern would once again take hold. The allure of its power is too great. And it is for this reason that I cannot give you the forge."

Chapter 27

"Now you wait just a minute," Peters protested. "We've come too far for you to simply deny us out of hand."

"The decision is final, I'm afraid," Thalor said, walking past them to the strange device Shepard had noticed earlier. He put his hand on it. "I assume some of you have already figured out that this is the object you seek."

Mateo took a step forward, lips parted in surprise. "That's it? I had no idea."

The forge was ten feet tall and half as wide. Standing nearby, Shepard thought it looked more like a cross-section rather than a fully intact unit. Even from here it was apparent there was a space in the center of the forge where a lone occupant was meant to stand. At the base was a single stirrup where one might place a foot and dangling from the ceiling was a handle.

"I don't understand," Shepard said. "Where's the rest of it?"

"The mirror image was taken by my brother, to be hidden somewhere of his choosing," Thalor explained. "This was done to mitigate the temptation of using it."

"If the forge is so terrible," Singh asked, perplexed, "why not simply destroy the infernal machine?"

Thalor hesitated.

"It's against your code, isn't it?" Peters said. "You're from a civilization of builders. You make things. And you avoid destruction whenever possible."

"Very noble," Nash said, nodding.

Jake wasn't having it. "Sounds like weak sauce to me."

"We mock what we do not understand," Thalor replied, clearly miffed at Jake's remark.

"Tell me more about this ethos of yours," Shepard said, genuinely intrigued. "Is this the path taken by all intelligent life in the galaxy?"

Thalor nodded. "Eventually, yes. The teachings of Meloiria were passed down millions of years ago by the prophet for whom they are named. The first tenet: 'Knowledge is the path to enlightenment.' The second tenet: 'To preserve the spark of life is to honor the divine.' The third tenet: 'Maintain balance in all things.' The others, I've already mentioned."

Shepard looked thoughtful as she watched Thalor run his hand along the forge's carved Endarian symbology. "And what if the divine is disobeyed?" she asked innocently.

Thalor's eyes widened. "That is the greatest of all shames. Such codes are not meant to be broken lightly."

"And yet you break them at this very moment," she said, her gaze finding his and remaining firm. Peters moved in and put a hand on her shoulder to quiet her, but she shook him off.

"How so?" Thalor asked, a hint of disbelief and even anger in his voice.

"You said the forge must never operate again because its destructive consequences ran against your philosophy to do no harm. Can't you see that by

153

allowing the Drax to destroy Earth, the spark of billions of lives will be extinguished, along with the forge itself?"

"That's right," Mateo said, jumping in. "You said yourself that creation was the highest form of divine expression. By helping us, you're not only preserving the forge, you're preserving the potential for all the life and creations that will come from humanity."

"More than that," Shepard added, "you will avoid dishonoring the divine and, by extension, yourself."

Thalor's normally serene features looked suddenly troubled as he sought to reconcile the contradiction. "I don't see how that can be right." He pressed a hand to the circlet on his head, mumbling as he moved past them, exiting the chamber.

"Great job," Jake said. "Now you pissed him off."

Shepard crossed her arms. "I had to try," she said, disappointed. Glancing over at Commander Foster's body, she lowered herself to the ground. Everything had happened so fast she hadn't had time to register the pilot's death. "We should get him back to the ship."

Nash moved over to Foster's side, laid him on his back with his arms crossed and said his goodbyes. "He looks so peaceful."

Alvarez stood behind Nash, staring down at the body. "What if we get Sam to talk to Thalor? You saw how the Endarian reacted when he saw him."

Sam was shaking his head. "I'm not sure what I'd say. I may be part-Endarian, but I know nothing of the culture."

"You knew enough to detonate the mold before it got us," Alvarez countered. "Maybe your intuition is stronger than you think."

Jake stood staring at the forge. "What if we just took it?"

"Are you insane?" Peters said, disgusted. "We're better than that."

Furrowing his brow, Jake said, "You sound just like Thalor. Maybe you two should get a room."

"Maybe if you actually stood for something other than yourself, you might not be such a dick."

Shepard moved between them. "The two of you threatening to brawl isn't helping. Thalor told us his brother brought the other half of the forge with him when he left Eris. Maybe we should look for that. Fifty percent of a forge is better than no forge."

Singh's face scrunched in dismay. "As I'm sure you already know, the solar system's a heck of a big place. Aloine might have it hidden anywhere. We could spend the next million years searching without finding a thing."

"Listen, I'm open to a better idea if you have one," Shepard snapped. "But so far all we have is laying on more persuasion, which didn't work in the first place, or stealing the damn thing. And to both of those, I say, 'No, thank you.'" She grew quiet, wringing her gloved hands. "What about you, RUTH?" she asked in something of a Hail Mary. "Tell me you've got something brilliant for us."

"I'm afraid not, Dr. Shepard," the AI said with notable dismay. "Otherwise, I would gladly have volunteered it."

"All right, folks," Peters said, no longer able to hide the defeat in his voice. "On that cheery note, gather your things. We head out in two minutes. Jake and Nash, you carry Foster."

"Body duty," Jake sighed. "Why am I not surprised?"

Feeling down, the team headed out of the cryochamber and down the corridor to the grand entrance. Thalor was nowhere in sight and it was just as well. He had let them down in the worst possible way. They had crossed billions of miles only to be told no. Worse still, they had lost perhaps the most crucial member of their team, Commander Foster, the very man who had saved them on Mars after the facility was destroyed—and the only one who had any inkling how to navigate the ship to return home.

She could almost hear Jake's irreverent voice. *Maybe we shoulda called ahead. And saved ourselves a trip and a boatload of heartache.*

Imaginary Jake had a point.

Soon they crossed the threshold, pushing out into Eris' bitter cold. Despite their state-of-the-art protection, within seconds, fingers and toes grew numb. Each of them increased the heat in their suit as they pressed on, their boots crunching the hard-packed Eris snow.

They were no more than fifty yards from the craft when Nash called out from the rear. They spun to see him waving his hand. "You can't make this stuff up," he said, motioning to the giant gates looming behind them.

In the distance, Thalor had just emerged from the facility. He wore no protective suit except for the shimmering energy field surrounding his body. In his hand was a tube about a foot long and from it ran another globe of energy. Suspended inside was the half section of forge he had initially denied them.

As he drew closer, Shepard could see a look of serenity had come over the Endarian. It was clear her words had rattled something loose within him.

Just then the look on his face changed again. This time, peace was replaced by surprise as he glanced up.

A large explosion detonated in front of them. The shockwave struck the team, throwing them to the ground. Shepard raised herself up long enough to see that their UFO was now a flaming wreck. Debris rained down around them. She scanned the chaos, searching for any sign of her teammates amidst the smoke and fire.

"Thalor, run!" she shouted as the gravity of the situation began to dawn on her.

A smaller blast landed next to the Endarian, knocking him to the ground. Down too went the baton he'd been using to levitate the forge. With a thud, the device tumbled onto its side, cutting a groove in the hard snow and ice. That was when Shepard spotted the triangular ship hovering overhead. The same kind that had docked with their Galaxy transport plane on Earth so long ago.

"The Drax," she heard Peters say under his breath, his voice seething.

A yellow energy beam enveloped the forge. The device seemed to shake for a moment before it was pulled up and into the Drax ship. Seconds later, the triangular craft streaked away and was gone.

Chapter 28

Back in the grand entrance, Alvarez and Peters set Thalor down on the stone floor. It was clear he was far too wounded to be moved anymore. Purple liquid ran from the corners of his mouth and eyes.

A quick check confirmed everyone else was accounted for and unhurt. In spite of this glimmer of good news, Shepard couldn't help feeling a terrible burden of guilt settling over her. If she hadn't convinced Thalor to help them, he might still be alive.

The Endarian reached out and took her hand. "Put aside any feelings of guilt," he told her. "Soon, I will join my ancestors." He paused, struggling to breathe.

Had they simply left, the Drax would have eventually showed up and taken it anyway. Surely they too had been aware of the signal beamed from Earth to Eris. The responsibility was not Shepard's own. And yet why was it she still felt so bad? Perhaps it was losing the final member of a dying race.

Thalor's trembling hands went to the sides of his elongated head. There they fumbled as he attempted to remove his circlet. She and Peters helped him.

"You will need this," he told them, "to operate the forge. Without it, the device is useless."

Shepard turned it over in her hands, marveling at the craftsmanship. Beneath the surface was a network of what looked like circuitry. When she examined the front, she saw a recess. She asked him what it was for.

"That is for the power s-source," he stammered, coughing up more blood.

Peters caught her eye. "A crystal?"

Thalor nodded.

Shepard turned back to him. "And the other half of the forge, where is it?"

The Endarian's face was once again peaceful.

"Thalor?" she asked, touching his cheek, hardening in the freezing Eris wind. But his eyes would not open again.

They carried him back to his pod and reconvened at the grand entrance.

"How much food and water do we have left?" Peters asked, his survival instincts kicking in.

They had been consuming a high-calorie liquid diet supplied within their suits. It tasted rather terrible, but was more than enough to sustain them over the flight there and back as well as sixty hours on the ground.

The batteries powering their suits could go on for more than a few weeks. That wasn't the issue. They would likely die of dehydration long before their batteries ran out.

Singh checked his consumables gauge. "I'm down to forty-five percent."

Checking her own, Shepard saw she was at fifty-three percent.

Peters had the others do the same. Most were in the forty to fifty percent range. The only variations came from Sam, who was at nearly seventy percent, and Nash, who was at seventeen.

159

"How the hell is yours so low?" Jake said in shock.

But the heavy weapons operator was having none of it. "You try clocking in at well over two hundred pounds and living off of a diet of liquid Soylent Green."

He was referring to the classic Charlton Heston film. In it, Heston discovered the food source for his seemingly utopian society came from recycled human corpses.

"Yeah, I'm suddenly not so hungry anymore," Mateo said, wincing.

The fear on Singh's face betrayed the severity of their situation. "We need to find some way of getting home. RUTH, can you send a signal to Earth?"

"Unfortunately, that will not be possible, Dr. Singh."

"But you did it on Mars," Jake said, sounding desperate. "Why not now?"

"On Mars, I had access to a satellite that was in stationary orbit around the planet," she explained. "On Eris, there is no such satellite."

"So we're screwed," Alvarez said, taking a seat on the hard floor. The light had gone out of his eyes. He bore the appearance of a man who had surrendered to his fate.

Shepard was not yet ready to give up. The idea that the Drax had won was unfathomable after everything they'd been through. She glanced over at Peters. He had laid his weapon at his feet and looked about ready to join Alvarez. Next to him was Sam.

"Seems I got you roped into this mess as well," she said, shaking her head in disgust.

"Are you kidding?" Sam replied, grinning weakly. "I'd swap this for that fishbowl I was living in any day."

Just then movement caught their attention. A shadow approached. Could the mold have somehow

160

returned? Peters scrambled to collect his weapon. Except this particular shadow had come from the howling, frozen wastes outside.

The figure stopped before them, flanked by two similar-looking individuals. Brushing particles of snow from his shoulder, the figure grinned. "Seems the shoe is on the other foot now, doesn't it?" Elder Gorian exclaimed, nauseatingly proud of his own wit.

A wave of relief washed over them.

"But how did you know we needed saving?" Shepard asked.

He shook his head. "We didn't. But our sensors detected an enormous burst of fifth force energy from Eris and we decided to investigate."

"That FFE spike must have been when Sam here was pulling his magic trick," Jake volunteered.

Gorian raised an eyebrow. "This can't be the child," he said, clearly confused.

"It's a long story," Shepard said. "We'll explain it all on the way home."

Chapter 29

Washington, D.C.

The dimly lit bar, aptly named "The Dugout," was a sports bar in the Northeast part of the city. With dark wood paneling and deep red leather booths, it exuded a cozy, laid-back charm. Above the bar, a flat-screen TV displayed a baseball game: the Mets against the Pirates, tied at the top of the ninth. Framed jerseys and sports memorabilia adorned the walls. Small groups of people were scattered about, nursing drinks and sharing good conversation and the occasional burst of laughter.

Douglas, Isadora and Desiree were sequestered in a booth in the back corner, sipping on a trio of draft beers.

"I don't see why she has to be here," Isadora said, her palms pushing against the edge of the table, as though the act might somehow get her further away from the woman seated across from her.

Desiree's eyes narrowed. "The opinion's mutual, trust me."

Douglas put up his arms, feeling like a referee in a sports match that was about to get heated. "Ladies, can we try and be civil? At least until we hear what Desiree has to say."

"She's one of *them*," Isadora snapped, not letting it go.

"The gratitude is incredible," Desiree said.

"She's saved our asses not once but twice," Douglas reminded her.

Isadora turned to him, incredulous. "So you think she did it out of the goodness of her heart? That's how the Drax operate. Lull you into trusting them and them bang." She slammed the table. The bartender and some of the other patrons looked over, alarmed.

"You wanna cool it?" Douglas barked.

Desiree started to get up. "Look, maybe this was a mistake."

"Damn right it was," Isadora said, waving her away.

"Hold on," Douglas called out, beckoning her back. "I know we have something of a complicated history. On the outside, you're my beloved daughter. But on the inside, you're"—he paused—"something else."

"I'm no different than you," Desiree said.

Douglas tilted his head. "I'm not so sure about that."

Desiree's brow furrowed. "Really? What's that supposed to mean?"

Lifting his right hand, Douglas did a subtle little dance with his fingers. Just then the channel on the TV changed to a sitcom.

Desiree turned and watched as the patrons began yelling at the bartender. Flustered, the man took the remote and switched it back to the game, only to have Douglas flip it over to the sitcom once again.

"Okay, really? What the hell, man?" someone shouted.

"Keep going," Isadora said, "and you're gonna start a bar fight."

Douglas laughed. "We aren't the same, you and I."

163

"Cute party trick," Desiree said, sliding back into her seat.

"I aim to please."

"If we're gonna do this," Isadora said grudgingly, "then let's get it over with."

Douglas crossed his arms. "In Japan, you were sent to kill us. Why didn't you?"

Taking a sip of beer, Desiree let it sit in her mouth for a moment before swallowing. "You know, just taking a sip of beer is a masterpiece of engineering for humans just as much as it is for us. It involves over fifty pairs of muscles and the coordinated effort of multiple body parts, including the mouth, pharynx, larynx, and esophagus."

"Thank you, Professor," Isadora said. "Yes, swallowing is complicated. Now get to it."

"That's precisely my point," Desiree countered. "Our bodies—organic or synthetic, take your pick—are masterpieces of engineering, each one mostly the same and yet subtly unique. The more this thought began to take root, the harder it was to shake. Then I compared that to the Drax's mission statement. We seek to harvest humans in order to gather the energy we need. And one day when they start to catch on, we destroy them all. But don't be fooled. Only the Master and his immediate entourage travel alone to the next planet."

"You mean he leaves millions of Drax behind to die?"

"Die?" she said with what looked like a sneer. "How can something die if it was never truly alive? And as for the few who might beat the odds and attain some level of consciousness—well, 'tough titty,' said the kitty."

"Damn, that's cold," Douglas said. "Even for this Master, whoever he is."

164

"To my people, he's something of a deity," Desiree tried to explain. "It's only recently that I've even allowed myself to speak his name."

Isadora's gaze met Desiree's. "And this god of yours, where is he?"

Desiree shook her head at once. "I don't know. It's a secret few are privy to."

"And if you had even an inkling," Douglas began, "would you tell us?"

Desiree's hesitation didn't last more than a split second, but it was enough. "I'd like to say yes, but while I detest what my people have done, I also know that without the Master, each of us would immediately cease to exist."

"You're linked to him?" Isadora asked, worried.

"In a manner of speaking we are. He doesn't see what we see. But there are spies everywhere. Sometimes in the places you'd least expect it."

"Come work for us," Douglas said, leaning forward.

"For the FBI?"

He shook his head. "For the Thalasians. In a remote capacity only."

Desiree's features became set. "You want me to become a spy."

Douglas nodded.

"I'm not sure," she replied. "I'm already taking a huge chance speaking with you now. Ravencroft has tortured me and threatened to do worse if I give him any reason to be suspicious of me again."

"This Ravencroft fellow sounds like a real charmer," Douglas said, putting it mildly. He decided to shift gears. "What can you tell us about Simon Cash?"

"Not much," she admitted. "Although I'm fairly certain the people working for that NGO aren't what they seem."

Intrigued, Douglas pressed further. "What's that supposed to mean?"

"I overheard Ravencroft discussing them once, but I never got the full context of the conversation."

"Are they Drax?" Isadora asked.

Desiree shook her head. "Not a single one of them."

"That's pretty uncommon, isn't it?" Douglas wondered.

"Uncommon? It's almost impossible. There's hardly an organization on Earth that doesn't have at least one Drax infiltrator. From what I do know, the people at Safe Harbor aren't socially conscious as much as they are fanatical."

This piqued Douglas' attention. "We were just there. They seemed polite and friendly."

"Maybe a little too friendly?" Desiree asked.

Isadora nodded. "Yeah. You could see them all smiling and saying the right thing, but they came across as…"

"As fake as a three-dollar bill," Douglas said. "I assumed it had more to do with the virtue-signaling aspect of their chosen profession."

"Finding homes for the indigent?" Isadora said, confused.

"Don't get me wrong. It's a worthy cause," Douglas admitted, trying to dig himself out of a hole that was growing deeper by the minute. "But it's one thing to stand behind a good cause and another for that to breed a sense of superiority." He turned to Desiree. "Now when you say 'fanatical,' what exactly do you mean?"

166

"They follow the director with something resembling blind devotion," Desiree explained. "His word is the gospel."

"Does this prophet have a name?"

"He must, but I don't know it," Desiree replied.

"But you're saying they're the ones who killed Keller?" he asked, struggling to have it all make sense.

Desiree nodded. "Yes. They caught wind of Cash's meeting with Agent Keller and got there first, attacking her in the hotel room. Simon must have arrived after and seen something or someone in the lobby that spooked him."

"And what exactly was their motive?" Douglas wondered.

"They're planning some kind of big operation. To deliver to the Master something he wanted very much."

"And they're one hundred percent human?" Douglas asked, double-checking.

Desiree sipped at her beer before setting it down on the coaster. "From what I know."

"Which makes them something we haven't seen yet," Isadora said.

Douglas let her words wash over him. She was precisely right. It was a dirty little word he hoped to never use when referring to a member of the human race. "Collaborators."

"Oh, there's one more thing," Desiree said.

Douglas held his breath. "I'm scared to ask."

"Something else I heard from Ravencroft. The Drax have gotten their hands on part of a powerful weapon and they're stepping up their plan for the final destruction."

"How long do we have?" Isadora asked, the muscles in her face tightening.

167

"It was years," Desiree told them, finishing the last of her beer. "But now it could be a question of days."

Chapter 30

Unknown

Ravencroft entered the gloomy chamber, a sense of dread weighing heavily on him as he anticipated the upcoming meeting. The cavernous room, illuminated by a ghostly glow, seemed to be alive, with walls that pulsated in rhythm with the Master's consciousness. At the center of the room, suspended above a pedestal, was the dark sphere that housed the Master's pure consciousness, a complex web of conduits and hoses snaking out from it like the limbs of some great, slumbering beast.

He advanced slowly, flanked by two of his Drax Praetorian Guards. The guards carried the gleaming, intricate half of the galactic forge. Ravencroft's heart pounded as he approached the sphere, bowing deeply, his gaze fixed on the ground.

"What is this you have brought me?" The Master's voice reverberated through the chamber, deep and commanding.

Ravencroft straightened, his voice quivering. "My liege, this is a device of unimaginable power, capable of amplifying the fifth force. I present this to you in the hope that it will bring you contentment."

The Master's presence seemed to grow, the very air around them thrumming with his scrutiny. "Is there more?" The question was both inquisitive and critical, cutting through Ravencroft's nerves like a blade.

"Yes, of course. I neglected to mention the Endarians disassembled it. We are currently in the process of tracking down the other half."

A silence fell over the chamber, heavy and oppressive. "So you present me only half a gift. Is that what I'm to understand?" The Master's voice was colder now.

Ravencroft could feel the tension in the room tightening like a noose around his neck. He bowed even lower, desperation creeping into his voice. "I beg your forgiveness, my liege. We will recover the other half. I swear it."

The Master's displeasure was almost palpable, a wave of dark energy that sent a shiver down Ravencroft's spine. "And what of the child? Do you have him too?"

Swallowing hard, Ravencroft answered, "Not yet, my liege, but we will very soon. We have planted a new mole within the humans' crash retrieval team. They will help us secure the child."

There was a pause, a moment that stretched into an eternity. Then, at last, the Master seemed to relent. "Good. But remember, Ravencroft, failure is not an option. Bring me that child, along with the remaining piece of the forge, or face the consequences."

The threat hung in the air, unmistakable and terrifying. Ravencroft bowed even deeper, his voice a whisper. "Yes, my liege. I will not fail you again."

As he withdrew from the chamber, Ravencroft was distinctly aware that his life hung in the balance. The

Master had given him a second chance. It had also been made clear that there would not be a third.

Chapter 31

Joint Base Andrews

Shepard stepped off the track and bent forward, her hands on her knees, trying to catch her breath. The moon was out, illuminating the night sky with a ghostly glow. One or two other late-night exercise nuts nearby were also doing laps.

Apart from a brief conversation with Gorian, she'd slept for most of the way home. And no sooner had they landed than she'd changed into her workout gear and hit the track. It sure beat staying in her quarters sulking. And there was no shortage of melancholy to go around. Foster had died, along with Thalor, perhaps the last remaining Endarian on the planet, and it was all because of her. If that wasn't bad enough, the Drax had swooped in like a bat out of hell and snatched the prize from their very grasp. The whole thing made her mad enough to see red.

She spotted someone walking toward her.

"Couldn't sleep either?" Peters asked, stooping to lace his shoe.

"I'm not in the mood to be cheered up, Peters," she snapped.

He raised his hands. "I was about to tell you the same thing. But this is part of what we do. Not every mission ends in a resounding success, you know."

"We traveled to the edge of the solar system and what do we have to show for it?" she said, her lips forming a thin line. "I'm just so pissed right now I could scream."

Peters stepped forward. "Then go for it."

"What?"

"You heard me. Let it all out."

She shook her head. "No, it's late."

"Stop making excuses and belt it out. Go on."

Shepard shouted something unintelligible.

Peters shook his head in disgust. "Really? That was pathetic. Go on, do it for real now."

Next came a scream.

"Better," he said. "But still pretty sad. Never mind. I thought you had it in you, but clearly I was wrong."

Drawing in a massive breath, Shepard bellowed. She looked over and saw Peters' eyes were mostly whites.

"Wow, that was something else."

She smiled. "Don't forget, my bite is bigger than my bark."

"Stop," he said, pointing a finger at his lips. "I promised I wasn't here to brighten your mood."

"I'm still angry, if that's any consolation."

He moved closer. "Well, here are a few reasons you shouldn't be." Lifting a hand, he began counting on his fingers. "Our lives, for one. We now know the other half of the forge is out there somewhere."

She considered this. "With our luck, the Drax have already destroyed it."

173

"Then you don't know the Drax as well as I thought you did. Can you really picture them wrecking a device that holds the power of all creation?"

"No, I suppose not."

"Glad we agree. Plus, I wasn't finished with my list. The Drax may have stolen part of the forge, but they didn't get their hands on Sam."

Yes, that was something to be thankful for. "That's unusually sloppy of them. They're androids, after all. Aren't they supposed to be deadly efficient?"

Peters drew in a long breath. "You know, I thought about that for a large chunk of the journey home. I couldn't for the life of me figure out why they ignored him. For all intents and purposes, Sam is a grown man. A wildly inexperienced one, but a man nonetheless."

"Sure, but what's your point?"

"The last time Ravencroft or any other Drax laid eyes on Sam, he was a baby. And that was all of, what, a few weeks ago?"

Her green eyes flashed. "Of course. That makes perfect sense." She spotted two familiar figures standing beneath an oak tree. "Excuse me for a moment," she said, heading in their direction. "You know you could have just called," she said to Douglas when she arrived.

"Hey, don't look at me," he said. "This was her idea. If we didn't see you out here, we were going to throw pebbles at your window."

Shepard laughed. "I'm sure the MPs patrolling the base would have loved that. I'm assuming you heard about Eris."

Both of them shook their heads. She filled them in.

"Elder Gorian?" Isadora said, a look of surprise etched on her face.

"I suppose he was repaying the favor."

"Does that mean humans and the Council are back on good terms?" Isadora asked.

"Depends on what you mean," Shepard replied, growing serious. "Most of the leadership in the US government is either ignorant of the Council or they're Drax agents who hate them. But so far he came through when it mattered. In my books, that means a lot."

Douglas then proceeded to inform Shepard about the case they were working on and its possible links to the Drax.

"Collaborators," she said, struggling over the word the way an old man might struggle against a long flight of stairs. "Imagine betraying your own species in the hopes of securing alien table scraps."

"To be honest," Isadora said, "we're not entirely sure what these people are up to or why. After speaking with a Drax double agent, we also learned that following the final destruction, the Master flees to safety, letting his loyal androids perish in the supernova. So if these turncoats think they've won themselves a ticket to the next star system, they've got another think coming."

"About that forge you mentioned," Douglas said. "Any word where the other half is?"

She shook her head. "Not yet, but we're working on it."

"I only ask because our contact said the Drax had pushed up the destruction date. Perhaps they expect to have both portions of this forge in the near future."

Isadora nodded. "I would also caution you about being extra vigilant. I suspect our contact's warning might also mean Drax sleeper agents will be stepping up their efforts. Don't be surprised if it comes from areas you least expect."

Chapter 32

The following morning, the atmosphere in the conference room was oppressive. The overhead fluorescent lights cast a harsh glow on the polished table and the walls, giving the space an almost clinical feel. As Shepard and her team shuffled in, the weight of their recent mission hung over them like a dark cloud.

Commander Bradshaw stood at the front of the room, his posture rigid, his jaw tight. Shepard couldn't help but feel a knot tighten in her stomach as she recalled the abrupt awakening she had experienced earlier that morning. First Lieutenant Connor, Bradshaw's executive assistant, had summoned her with an urgent call, yanking her from a sound sleep into a state of immediate alertness.

As they took their seats, Shepard noticed the series of stern faces glaring at them from the screen behind Bradshaw. The Joint Chiefs of Staff, led by General William Hayes, were visibly displeased. Hayes, in particular, looked like a storm cloud ready to burst, his face flushed with anger and his eyes boring into each member of the team.

Bradshaw began to set the scene, his voice steady but laced with an underlying tension. "Ladies and gentlemen, we are gathered here to discuss the recent mission to

Eris and its subsequent fallout. As you know, the objective was to retrieve the galactic forge and—"

General Hayes cut him off abruptly, his voice a bark that echoed through the room. "Enough, Commander Bradshaw. We all know what the objective was. What we need now is accountability."

Shepard flinched, feeling the heat of the general's gaze on her. Hayes continued, his anger palpable. "We lost a decorated officer, Commander Foster, who sacrificed his life in service to his country. Moreover, the only operational alien UAP in the Air Force's possession was destroyed. And the forge, the very purpose of this mission, was stolen right out from under your noses. I call that a resounding failure."

Jake, unable to hold his tongue, piped up, "Sir, with all due respect, only one half of the forge was lost—"

Bradshaw whirled on him, his face a mask of fury. "Lieutenant, if you can't keep your mouth shut, I'll have you demoted so fast your head will spin." The harsh reprimand echoed in the room, silencing Jake and casting a shadow of fear and uncertainty over the rest of the team.

The tension in the room was almost tangible, and Shepard's mind raced as she tried to anticipate the next wave of the generals' ire. The team had barely survived their encounter on Eris, and now they had to face the fallout from their own command.

General Hayes continued his tirade, his anger only seeming to intensify. "And another thing. Taking Sam along was not only reckless, it was irresponsible beyond measure. He's an Endarian, for God's sake! And he's a child, rapidly aging or not. What were you thinking, endangering him like that?"

177

Bradshaw spoke up, his face a mask of steely resolve. "That was my decision, General. I gave the order to bring him along. The responsibility for that falls squarely on my shoulders."

Hayes's eyes narrowed, his voice dripping with disdain. "I expected more from you, Bradshaw. You were supposed to be the voice of reason, the guiding hand. Instead, you let this mission spiral out of control. You will face disciplinary action for this, rest assured. The time and place will be of my choosing, but for now, you need to smarten up. Fast."

The tension in the room was suffocating. Shepard could feel the frustration and anger radiating from her teammates. They had risked everything, and now they were being chastised as if they were mere children.

"And furthermore," Hayes continued, his tone unyielding, "I'm shutting down the crash retrieval program altogether."

Shepard's eyes widened in shock. Isadora's words from last night were ringing in her head. Isadora had warned that pushback would come in ways they least expected. Even so, Shepard couldn't stay silent any longer. "General, that's a terrible idea. Don't you see? It's precisely what the Drax are counting on. If we stop our efforts now, we're giving them the upper hand."

The general's gaze shifted to her, cold and unrelenting. "What I see, Dr. Shepard, is a team that just got their asses handed to them. A mission that ended in failure and loss. And now I'm dealing with the repercussions." He paused, his expression hardening even further. "Congress is breathing down my neck. Half the senators want to be read in on the details and share everything with the public. The other half, those who know anything, want to keep it tightly under wraps.

178

We're caught in a political crossfire, and your failure has only made things worse."

Shepard felt a mix of desperation and anger. The stakes were higher than ever, and the consequences of their mission's failure were unfolding before her eyes. She glanced around the room, seeing the same frustration mirrored in the faces of her teammates. They were warriors, fighters who had faced unimaginable dangers, but now they were being reprimanded by the very people they were trying to protect.

As Hayes's words hung in the air, the reality of their situation settled heavily on them all. They were being torn apart from within, their efforts undermined by those who were supposed to be their allies. And without a doubt, the Drax were in there somewhere, pulling on the strings from behind the scenes.

Shepard's mind was racing, still reeling from the barrage of accusations and the abrupt shutdown of their mission. "What's going to happen to Sam?" she asked, her voice trembling slightly.

Hayes's expression remained unchanged. "Sam, the headgear, and the crystal fragment recovered from Mars will all be transported to Raven Rock Mountain Complex. There they will undergo further testing."

Peters, despite his military training, was unable to contain himself any longer. "What about the rest of the forge? If we don't act fast, the Drax will surely find it first, and then the human race is done for."

"Calm down, Colonel," Hayes snapped, his eyes flashing with irritation. "We're already laying the groundwork for a new team."

Alvarez shook his head, murmuring under his breath, "There isn't enough time for all that. Can't they see?"

179

Shepard's mind was a whirlwind of thoughts. The implications of what Hayes was saying were staggering. "When will they be moved?" she asked, trying to steady her voice.

"Within twenty-four hours," Hayes replied, his tone final. "I suggest each of you take that time to reflect on your performance and prepare for your next assignment, whatever that may be."

With that, the link to the Pentagon was cut and Bradshaw stormed out.

The room fell into a heavy silence. The weight of the situation was pressing down on them all. The implications of the Drax getting their hands on the remaining part of the forge were dire. Shepard could see the worry etched into the faces of her team members. They had faced incredible challenges together, but this felt like a betrayal from within.

Peters clenched his fists, his knuckles turning white. The frustration of the situation was unmistakable, but he knew better than to challenge Hayes further. He glanced at Shepard, seeing the same resolve in her eyes that had carried them through so many dangerous missions.

Jake, usually so full of bravado, seemed deflated. The loss of the mission and the rebuke from their superiors had taken its toll on him. Nash, still grappling with the reality of their situation, looked down, his face a mask of uncertainty.

Alvarez's murmurs grew louder, his frustration boiling over. "They're making a mistake. They can't just shut us down like this."

Mateo placed a reassuring hand on his shoulder, trying to calm him. "We'll figure something out. We always do."

But Shepard knew they were in uncharted territory. The stakes had never been higher, and the margin for error had never been slimmer. The Drax were out there, and time was running out.

Hayes's words echoed in her mind as they left the room.

I suggest each of you take that time to reflect on your performance and prepare for your next assignment, whatever that may be.

The team dispersed into the corridor, each member lost in their own thoughts.

"Well, that went better than I thought it would," Jake said, trying to look on the bright side. "With the way things turned out, we could have been court-martialed."

"The mission failed," Alvarez shot back. "It's not like we broke any laws."

Peters peeled away from the group and stomp down the hallway. Shepard chased after him. "Where are you going?"

"Who cares?" he snapped.

Shepard recoiled. He'd never spoken to her like that before.

He stopped and removed his hat. "Look, I didn't mean to raise my voice. It's just I've served in the military for more than half of my life and I've never been removed from an assignment."

"It hurts, I know," Shepard said, taking him by the shoulders. He tried to move away, but she held him firm. "But this is important. We didn't just get fired from Arby's for handing out too many onion rings. Something isn't right."

"What do you mean? We messed up."

"Sure, we did, but disbanding the entire crash retrieval program, Peters? Doesn't that sound a little heavy-handed? A reprimand, a serious dressing-down, either one of those is to be expected. But to scrap the whole thing? Nah, I don't buy it."

"You think the Drax are behind this?"

She nodded. "Of course. Why wouldn't they be? Maybe they finally got someone high enough in the chain of command to make a difference."

Peters seemed to consider the idea. "Someone whispering in General Hayes' ear, maybe?"

"Don't be afraid to think a little bigger. Could be Hayes himself. Or maybe even the president."

"So, what do you suggest, then? An appeal?"

She shook her head. "To whom? Besides, military bureaucracy moves at a glacial pace. By the time the paperwork got printed the sun would be about ready to explode."

He fixed her with a stern look. "I hope you're not considering anything illegal."

She blinked. "Who, moi?"

Chapter 33

Washington, D.C.

Douglas sipped at his Coke, wiped his lips with the back of his hand and then set the drink back in the console cupholder. "What do you suppose an NGO that seeks to house the homeless needs with a place that big?"

A bit of research had led them to a warehouse just outside Washington, owned and operated by Safe Harbor. They were parked far enough away they wouldn't be noticed, especially at night.

"Lots of stuff," Isadora replied. "Could be furniture. Clothing. You name it."

He checked his watch. Eleven p.m. "A little late to be moving clothes around, don't you think?"

Isadora was staring at him as he took another sip.

Douglas grunted. "Any particular reason you're giving me the stink eye?"

"The what?" Her face contorted in confusion.

"The stink eye. You know." He glared at her intently with one bulging eye.

She smiled. "That's your third Coke."

"So?"

"So, you're gonna rot your insides. Being synthetic doesn't mean you can treat your body like a trash can."

Douglas leaned back and leveled a pair of binoculars. "You're starting to sound like my ex-wife."

"Ha! You should be so lucky."

Another moving truck with Safe Harbor rolled by and went around the back of the building.

"There could be people in there," he surmised.

"Why would the Drax be involved in some human trafficking ring?"

He shrugged, leaning over to get his backup weapon out of the glove compartment. "Maybe they chop them up and turn them into food."

She glanced down at the snub-nosed energy weapon.

"The one I got from Alan," Douglas explained. "That conspiracy crank I met with in Virginia. She's petite, but has a nice kick. Reminds me of someone I know." He winked and she pursed her lips in a look of annoyance.

They exited the cruiser and hurried across the street, trying to reach the main structure of the warehouse before another delivery truck showed up. They moved along the side of the building until they came to a single metal door. Next to it was a biometric scanner. Isadora kept walking.

"Where you going?"

She spun. "To look for a way in that doesn't have top-level security. Unless you plan to give it the stink eye."

Douglas shook his head and rubbed his index and thumb together. "Behold, ye of little faith." A second later, the screen flashed green followed by the click of the door unlocking.

Isadora was impressed. "You must be great at birthday parties."

He smiled, pulling the door open. "I'm a hit."

They entered into what looked like an office area. The hallways were dimly lit. It seemed everyone had gone home for the night. A long corridor led to a pair of metal push doors.

As they went through, the warehouse opened up before them, vast and sprawling. The air was cool and carried a faint, musty odor, a mixture of old fabric, cardboard, and a hint of disinfectant. The ceiling was high, with exposed beams crisscrossing overhead, giving the place an industrial feel. Rows upon rows of towering shelves stretched out in all directions, creating a labyrinthine maze that seemed almost impossible to navigate.

The shelves were packed with various items, meticulously organized. To the left were stacks of neatly folded clothing. On the right were towers of dried food and toiletries. Further into the warehouse, furniture was stacked haphazardly in a designated area. Old wooden chairs, battered sofas, and mismatched tables were piled on top of each other.

As they ventured deeper, the sound of their footsteps echoed in the stillness. The sheer scale of the operation was impressive.

Isadora paused to examine a pile of neatly folded blankets, running her fingers over the soft fabric. "This place never ends," she muttered, glancing around.

Douglas nodded. He was starting to wonder if they were wrong and Safe Harbor was exactly what it claimed to be, a charity to help the poor and the indigent. And yet the lack of activity within the warehouse itself suggested otherwise.

"You hear something?" he asked.

She stopped to listen. "Nothing."

"Exactly. Why is it so quiet? We saw, what, four, maybe five trucks enter in the last hour and yet there isn't a person in sight. Whatever they were delivering, it wasn't pallets of soap and onesies."

"What's a onesie?" Isadora asked.

"You don't wanna know." They pressed on to the loading bay. The garage door opened just as they arrived and a packing truck backed onto a platform. Yellow lights began flashing.

"It's some kind of lift. Come on," Douglas said, hurrying down a set of stairs and onto the platform. They slinked toward the back of the truck and rolled the sliding door up a few feet, slipping inside. Isadora flicked on a flashlight, revealing three rows of giant glass tubes, seven feet tall and three wide.

Douglas rapped at the surface. It looked like some sort of funky aquarium but without the water and the fish.

From inside the truck, they jostled around, feeling the vehicle begin to descend on the lift. The faint hum of machinery filled the air, and the clattering noise of the lift descending echoed around them. A few moments later, the truck came to a stop with a jolt.

Isadora raised the back door slightly to peer out. Her eyes widened at the sight before her. "We're in the loading bay," she whispered, her voice tense.

Douglas leaned in, looking over her shoulder. The loading bay was a stark contrast to the quiet warehouse above. Bright fluorescent lights illuminated the area, revealing a long corridor with rooms on either side. People were bustling about, most of them dressed in white lab coats with protective helmets. The air was filled with the hum of activity and the occasional murmur of conversation.

Isadora's gaze shifted to a pair of security guards dressed in blue, their eyes scanning the area with a vigilance that made her stomach knot. One of them withdrew an inhaler from his pocket and brought it to his lips. For a moment, he seemed to twitch. His partner took it from him and did the same. "What is this place?" she wondered, a deeply unsettling feeling coming over her.

"We need to move, now," Douglas urged.

She nodded, her jaw set. They slipped out of the truck, moving swiftly and quietly towards a break room off to their left. The room was empty, the hum of a vending machine and the faint smell of coffee lingering in the air. On the wall, a row of lab coats and helmets hung.

"Let's gear up," Douglas said, grabbing a lab coat and helmet. They dressed, hoping to blend in with the sea of white coats outside. The fabric of the lab coat was stiff and smelled of antiseptic.

Isadora adjusted her helmet, making sure her face was mostly obscured. "Do we have a plan?" she asked, her eyes meeting Douglas' gaze.

"Blend in, find out what these cats are up to, and then get the hell out in one piece," Douglas replied, his voice calm. He drew in a deep breath, steeling himself.

They stepped back into the corridor, trying to exude the same confidence and purpose as the others. The white coats and helmets provided a sense of anonymity, but they knew it wouldn't last long if they didn't find what they were looking for quickly.

They passed a group of three scientists, their white lab coats pristine and their expressions focused. One of the men in the group glanced at Isadora, a polite smile crossing his lips. She forced a smile in return, trying to blend in. But then his expression shifted, his brow furrowing as if he were trying to place her face. Douglas noticed the change and nudged Isadora.

"Keep moving," he muttered under his breath.

They continued down the corridor, the sound of their footsteps mingling with the distant hum of machinery. On either side, rooms with large observation windows lined the walls, their interiors filled with various pieces of equipment and personnel. Douglas' instincts kicked in, sensing they needed to get off the main thoroughfare before they drew any more attention. Spotting an open door to their left, he pulled Isadora inside, the door closing behind them.

The room they entered was lit by rows of overhead lights that cast a sterile, golden hue. They were immediately stunned by what they saw. Those same glass tubes from the truck, now filled with a clear, gelatinous liquid, stood in neat rows. Each tube contained a naked person, suspended in the viscous fluid.

Douglas moved in for a closer look, his breath catching in his throat. Those inside the tubes were wearing helmets that covered their entire faces, making it impossible to see their features. Pipes ran from the tops of the helmets, snaking out of the containers and connecting to a complex network of machines that beeped and hummed with quiet efficiency.

"What the hell is going on here?" Isadora whispered, her voice filled with horror and disbelief.

Douglas shook his head, equally disturbed. "I don't know, but it's not good." He reached out and placed a hand on the glass, his fingers leaving smudges on the pristine surface. The emaciated man inside was motionless, his body eerily still in a form of suspended animation.

Isadora moved to another tube, peering inside. "They look… alive," she said, her voice quivering slightly. "But what are they doing to these people?"

Douglas's mind raced as he tried to piece together the scene before them. "Experimentation, maybe," he offered, thoroughly disturbed. "But for what purpose?"

"Look at this," Isadora said, pointing to a small control panel next to one of the tubes. Douglas moved closer, scanning the readouts and data displayed on the screen. It showed vital signs, brain activity, and other metrics that he couldn't fully comprehend.

"They're monitoring everything," he said, his voice grim. "It's like they're trying to control them or… I don't know."

Douglas caught sight of a particularly thin woman in a nearby tube, her skin wrinkled, either from age or being submerged for so long, he couldn't tell. As he approached, he saw her body begin to twitch. Moments later her legs began pumping as though she was running. The display at the base of her tube showed her vitals spiking. A few moments later she stopped.

"Over here," Isadora called out. This time a thin man with sores all over his body was flailing about, swinging his arms as though trying to defend himself.

"Are they dreaming?" Isadora asked, perplexed and looking unsettled.

Douglas glanced back at the helmets. "No, not dreaming. They're in sensory deprivation tanks and being fed visuals. But why? To stimulate them?"

Each of the individuals in this room all looked the same. They were sickly thin, often with cut or needle marks on their arms and legs. They were addicts, perhaps lifted off the street by Safe Harbor with the promise of a warm meal and a place to stay. But many addicts avoided such offers because shelters didn't allow them to drink or do drugs, and so many stayed on the streets. But Douglas suspected Safe Harbor took a different approach, likely promising them the freedom to use even at the NGO's facility. If it was a choice between the mean streets or a warm room, who could turn down such an offer? Little did they know they'd soon be hooked up to a nightmare machine designed for some nefarious purpose.

"We've got to get these people out of here," Isadora said, scanning the control panel.

Douglas recalled the long corridor with rooms on either side, presumably each one housing a similarly horrifying experiment. He was looking at a panel of his own, wondering the same.

"I see a button that says 'purge,'" Isadora shouted. "Should I press it?"

Douglas wasn't sure how they'd be able to whisk all these people away. At the same time, he couldn't imagine leaving them here.

"I'm hitting it," Isadora said, making an executive decision.

A red light above the sensory deprivation chamber began flashing at once.

"The water's not draining," she said, growing worried.

The woman inside began to convulse. Douglas punched at the glass with no effect. This was no aquarium. It was a thick shock-resistant acrylic. He stood back and leveled his weapon just as the woman's body grew still.

"Wait a minute," Isadora said, studying the screen, her eyes wide.

Douglas lowered his weapon and moved next to her. Three words blinked on the display.

Drahk'noth extraction complete.

Chapter 34

"What's going on here?" Isadora asked, staring at the woman's lifeless body in the tank. Douglas could see the guilt eating at her over hitting that button.

"You couldn't have known," he said, trying to reassure her. "This isn't like any other extraction facility I've seen. First off, normally it's part of a replacement, swapping out someone with social status with a Drax doppelganger. Sometimes they wait till the subject is older and gather even more potent Drahk'noth."

Isadora couldn't peel her eyes away. "Except in this case, they're snatching homeless off the streets and putting them in these tanks. But why?"

"It's like foie gras," he said. The blank expression on Isadora's face told him he needed to elaborate. "It's a delicacy born from the cruel practice of force-feeding ducks and geese in order to fatten their livers, which are then used to make a paté."

"Thanks for the cooking lesson," Isadora said. "But what does any of this have to do with these poor people?"

"Emotional trauma stimulates dark matter in the brain, helping to refine it," Douglas explained, searching one of the consoles for additional clues. "The more brutal the experiences, the more powerful the resulting Drahk'noth."

Her eyes widened. "So they're putting these people in isolation booths and piping in nightmarish experiences?"

"That's right. Eventually, they lose track of their bodies and start believing the images they're seeing are real."

"Which is why we saw them acting out inside the tank." She brought her hands to her face and gasped.

"Yeah, sick, isn't it? I suppose once they feel the person has reached a sufficient level of trauma, they harvest them, along with an even more powerful form of refined dark matter."

Just then the doors swung open and two startled-looking security personnel came in. "Oh, we weren't expecting anyone in room seventeen." His eyes moved past Isadora to the limp body suspended in liquid. "Was there an accident?" He stepped forward to check the console. That was when Douglas and Isadora began to head for the door.

"Wait a minute," his partner said, cutting them off.

Douglas and Isadora tried to make a break for it, but the guard by the door grabbed Isadora's arm with a vise-like grip. She struggled, her muscles straining against his iron hold, but he didn't budge. Douglas rushed to help, only to be met with a powerful punch that sent him flying across the room. He landed hard on a table cluttered with medical instruments, metal clanging and scattering as he hit. Dazed, he shook his head, trying to regain his senses.

Meanwhile, the second guard was advancing. Isadora kicked the first guard between the legs. He doubled over, his grip finally loosening. But before she could make her next move, the second guard was on her. They exchanged blows, Isadora flipping back with agility and grace, while the guard charged at her with brute force. She struck him multiple times, each blow aimed with deadly precision, but to her growing horror, they seemed to have little effect. His resilience was unnerving.

Douglas groaned, pushing himself up from the table. He saw the first guard regaining his composure and heading for a red emergency button on the wall. Panic surged through him. If that alarm was triggered, their mission would be over.

He fumbled for his energy pistol, his hands shaking from the impact of the punch. His vision blurred slightly, he managed to draw the weapon and aim it at the guard who was heading for the alarm.

A blast rang out and sliced a clean hole the size of an apple through the guard's head. The other, seeing what happened, put his hands up. From behind, Isadora landed a side kick to the back of his neck, sending him to the ground, unconscious.

Before they could move the two men, Isadora dug her fingers into the dead guard's head wound, feeling around. She was looking for a Drax cerebral device.

"Anything?"

She shook her head. "No, they're human. But their strength and agility… I don't understand."

Douglas bent down and fished an inhaler out of the dead guard's pocket. "We saw both of them using this earlier."

"That's right," she said, curious what it meant.

"I've never seen an asthmatic share his pump. I have a feeling something else is going on."

For now, they dragged the men behind the furthest tube. With any luck, it would be a while before anyone found them. Exiting the room, Douglas spotted a flashing yellow light in the distance. It looked like the fresh tubes had been offloaded and the truck was about to head topside. They hurried over, making it only moments before the lift began to ascend.

Once outside and heading to the cruiser, Douglas immediately dialed the local FBI headquarters.

Agent Griscole picked up. "Douglas, that you?"

"Yeah, listen, I got a situation here," Douglas began.

"Director Matthews needs to have a word and pronto."

Douglas looked down at his phone and saw a slew of missed calls. He swore. "Really? Can't it wait?"

"I wish it could."

"Okay, fine." Douglas hung up and dialed the director. He didn't care that it was well after midnight.

Surprisingly, a fresh voice answered. "Matthews here."

"Sir, you wanted to speak with me?" Douglas said. "I should tell you beforehand, I'm in the middle of something huge."

"It's always something huge with you," Matthews barked. "I was informed today that you've been investigating Agent Keller's murder."

"That's right, and—"

"And nothing, Special Agent Douglas," came the director's bellowing voice.

Sometimes Douglas swore there were two men inhabiting Matthews' body, one louder than the other. A single Matthews was bad enough, but now he was getting both barrels and had to pull the phone away from his ear.

"You think you're running your own little fiefdom over there, don't you? That you can just do whatever

195

your heart pleases. In what universe is an FBI agent ever supposed to investigate his partner's death?"

Douglas went to speak but was cut off again. Instead, he and Isadora slid into the cruiser.

"The answer is never. And yet here I am today getting briefed and what should come up? As of this moment, I'm taking you off the Keller case and handing it to Griscole and Farnsworth."

"They're two junior agents," Douglas protested, starting the car.

"Yes, but how else do you expect them to gain any experience?"

"Sir, with all due respect, I'm the only one with the necessary background for this case. Keller was onto something big when she was killed and I've been following up on her leads. In fact, just tonight we—I mean, I alone went to a warehouse filled with kidnap victims who are being kept in enormous vats."

Matthews wasn't buying it. "Please tell me you had probable cause and a search warrant. I don't wanna hear you just broke in and snooped around."

Douglas became quiet.

"You're lucky you even have a job at this point. Don't make me change my mind," Matthews said before hanging up.

Douglas cursed and threw his phone. It bounced off the dashboard and then the window, and flew into Isadora's waiting hand. She set it down in the center console.

"What about calling the cops and having them raid the place?" she asked.

Douglas shook his head. "Matthews is right. Without probable cause and a search warrant, we never should have been in there. And by the time we get one, Safe

Harbor will have plenty of time to clear the place out. It'll be like they were never there."

"So you're off the case then?" Isadora asked, disappointed.

"Says who?"

She threw him a strange look. "I could hear him yelling at you, Dwight."

"Who, Matthews? Nah, he'll come around."

"But he could fire you."

"At this point, the stakes are too high to worry about unemployment lines."

"You could end up homeless and picked up by Safe Harbor and thrown into a vat."

He shook his head, laughing sardonically. "Wouldn't that just be my luck?"

Chapter 35

Shepard knocked on the door to Mateo's room and found it open. The scientist was gathering clothes from the closet and depositing them in a suitcase next to the bed.

"Hey, you're not leaving, are you?"

He stopped long enough to furrow his brow before dumping a collection of button-down shirts into his suitcase. "What's it look like? You heard General Hayes. He's disbanding the crash retrieval group."

"Hold on," she protested. "Have they officially dismissed you?"

Mateo stalked back to the closet. "No, but I'm dismissing myself. I've been part of enough projects to know when they no longer have a pulse. Besides, I'm sure I can convince the University of Buenos Aires to take me back so I can continue the research Ben and I were working on before he…"

Shepard touched his shoulder, feeling his pain. She knew what it meant to lose a colleague, someone so close. "But what research could you possibly do that would be more important than saving the planet?"

Mateo gathered more shirts.

"Oh, I get it," she said, the pieces falling into place. "You wanna head home to Argentina and live out the few remaining days you have left before it's curtains for all of us."

He stopped, a cardigan slung over his shoulder. "And what about you? Sticking around where you aren't wanted, pushing your nose into everybody's business?"

"Yeah, well, I've made a career out of being annoying. But I'd rather be bothersome than a quitter."

She could tell that last one stung. Mateo clearly didn't have an answer.

"Look," she said, easing forward, her hands up as a peace offering. "I didn't come here to fight. Maybe I freaked out a little when I saw you packing to go. It doesn't matter what the generals say, we're a team, and we can't let ignorance, military bureaucracy or even Drax infiltrators divide us. I'm here because I have a plan to find the other half of the forge and I need your help."

"Plan?" he asked, trying his best to sound as uninterested as possible. "What plan are you talking about?"

"It starts with you heading over to medical and getting Lena."

Mateo raised his chin. "The TV woman? Is she still here?"

"Of course. She belongs to the US government now." Shepard laughed, although there was a hint of truth there.

"And you think Dr. Mercer will just let her go?"

"Fill out a temporary twenty-four-hour discharge form," Shepard advised him. "Tell them you want to run some experiments on her, which is not a total lie."

"And where will you be?"

"In the lab, trying to sweet-talk Singh into helping us."

Mateo looked skeptical. "So let's just say I'm successful and I bring you Lena. What then?"

Shepard tapped the center of Mateo's forehead. "The Endarian craft she encountered in that cave in Aurora planted something deep inside her subconscious."

"Your plan is to hypnotize her?"

"No," Shepard said, smirking. "Something far more straightforward. We're going to read her thoughts."

Chapter 36

An hour later, the four of them convened in the lab. Seventy-five percent of those assembled were either totally confused or doubtful any of this would work.

"Are you certain we should be doing this?" Singh asked, fiddling with the sensor cap.

Lena was far less enthusiastic. Crossing her arms, she said, "You do understand I've been held in that hospital bed for the better part of a week? When this gentleman showed up, I thought you were taking me home."

"My name's Mateo."

"Pleasure meeting you," Lena said curtly. "Now, will someone tell me what the hell is going on? Otherwise, I walk through that door and straight past the front gate."

"I don't recommend that," Singh said. "Those guards are armed to the teeth and aren't afraid to pull triggers."

Shepard wondered if a little woman-to-woman might do the trick. "We managed to get you out of quarantine in order to help us unlock whatever's hiding in your subconscious. We spoke earlier, if you remember, and it was clear a lot more happened during your encounter than you can recall."

Lena's eyes found the cap in Singh's nervous hands. "And you want me to wear that thing?" she asked, fearful. "Is your plan to electroshock me? Dr. Mercer's already done more than enough torturing lately."

Shepard smiled weakly. "The reason for the cap is because we need to record your brain waves as we ask you questions. Our AI system, RUTH, can then analyze that data and make an educated guess what might be locked beneath the surface."

Lena let out a loud and rather impressed laugh. "You've got to be kidding me."

"Put a different way," Singh interjected, "the EEG headset captures brainwave patterns. This information is processed to identify sequences corresponding to specific thoughts. The processed data is then fed into RUTH, who will attempt to translate your brainwaves into coherent text based on recognized signals and contextual understanding."

"And this is a thing?" Lena asked, taking a seat.

"It's a nascent field. So the success rate isn't great," Mateo admitted. "Last I checked it was in the forty to fifty percent range."

"Let's get started, shall we?" Shepard said as Singh moved in and fitted the cap over Lena's hair. He then attached the dry electrodes to key areas of her skull.

"And if I do this, you'll consider letting me go?"

There was a vulnerability in Lena's voice that tugged at Shepard's heart. "Think of it this way. You know how ever since you saw that hologram, you've been haunted by this terrible feeling, like an itch you can never scratch?"

Lena nodded. "It's been driving me crazy."

"Well, if this works, you'll be free of that nagging sensation."

Lena's features began to settle.

"Now, don't move," Singh told her as he turned the machine on.

The needle on the front display began tracking back and forth.

"RUTH," Shepard said. "You getting any of this?"

"Of course, Dr. Shepard," RUTH replied. "I can also tell Lena has a sharp, inquisitive mind."

"I'm also a scientist," Lena said. She tried turning around. "Is that your AI?"

"This will work best if you just remain still," Mateo instructed her.

Singh increased the voltage.

"Now, Lena," Mateo continued, "I want you to close your eyes and return to that day in Aurora. I want you to relive it as though it were happening for the very first time. I want you to feel the hot Texas wind on your face. Smell the tall grass and then the dampness of the cave."

Zeros and ones were filling the screen on a display above the machine. Slowly those began resolving into a series of amorphic shapes.

"Keep it up," RUTH said. "An image is taking shape."

"They appear to be symbols," Singh observed, studying the screen.

The lettering was thick at the body, tapering at the edges. Shepard recognized the Endarian script at once. "RUTH, this making any sense to you?"

"Yes, Dr. Shepard," the AI replied. "I am compiling and translating as the letters come in. However, they are not all in the proper grammatical order. This could be related to the brain's associative way of storing information."

The brain tended to link new information with existing knowledge, creating networks of related concepts.

"Some of it's starting to come back," Lena said, excited. "I can see myself traveling through space at a high rate of speed. I see a name. Aloh. No, Aloine. I see him arriving on Earth throughout the millennia, each time on a mission to awaken humanity. To free them from their bondage. To impart wisdom wherever he could. He was acutely aware of an evil presence on our planet, but also recognized he was part of a dying race and could do little to stop them. If humans wanted any hope of overthrowing their oppressors, they would need to put aside their petty bickering and band together. After each visit he would return to his outpost on an icy planet and sleep. But the last time he came to Earth, he never left. He's still here."

Lena's eyes were filled with tears. "I don't know what's come over me," she said, quickly wiping them away. "I'm not normally a very emotional person."

"That was the fifth force surging through your body," Singh explained.

"Did you see where Aloine put the forge?" Mateo asked.

"What forge?" Lena said, still rattled.

Shepard put a hand on her shoulder. "A large machine, about the size of an MRI, but cut down the middle."

Lena shook her head. "I didn't see anything like that."

Shepard swung back to the AI. "What about you, RUTH? Have you finished translating the Endarian script?"

"Yes, Dr. Shepard, and if I could, I would like to make a handful of additions to Lena's statement. It appears the craft discovered in Aurora was merely a portion of a larger ship, likely the one Aloine used to reach the Earth. It remained in cloaked orbit for thousands of years, acting as a satellite, relaying data back to Eris, until a malfunction caused it to fall from the sky."

Shepard couldn't stop thinking of what Lena had said earlier—the bit about humans putting aside their petty differences and banding together. In a world that felt more and more tribal every day, it was hard to imagine such a miracle occurring.

"If I may make a bold suggestion," RUTH said, interrupting the brief moment of silence, "it appears there is still the location of the forge to contend with. There is one, albeit risky, method that might be employed and we have all three ingredients currently on the base."

"Go on," Shepard said, seeing where this was heading.

"If Sam were to wear the circlet given to us by Thalor," RUTH began, "and if the circlet was outfitted with the crystal fragment we retrieved from Mars, perhaps he could interface with Lena and extract the last remaining bit of information that is eluding us."

Shepard's eyes lit up. "RUTH, you're a genius, you know that?"

"Yes," came her stoic reply. "I'm well aware."

Chapter 37

Washington, D.C.

Agent Douglas pushed open the door to the interrogation room, his footsteps brushing against the industrial carpeting. The fluorescent lights cast a harsh glare over the room, illuminating Simon Cash, who sat handcuffed to the metal table in the center.

Douglas settled into the chair across from Simon, setting a folder down on the table with a practiced motion. He studied Simon for a moment before speaking. "Still not ready to talk, I take it?" Douglas asked, expecting the silent treatment.

"You wouldn't believe me even if I told you."

"I went by Safe Harbor's warehouse last night," Douglas said.

Simon looked up, a faint light of hope in his eyes.

"Those folks down there, well, they're about as sick as they come. I also know you have a lot more to say, but the cat's got your tongue."

Simon glanced down at his hands, splaying out his fingers. "Someone's been spreading rumors that I'm in here on charges of pedophilia," he said, his voice strained. "Had to defend myself."

Douglas arched an eyebrow, flipping open the folder to review the charges against Simon. "That's not true," he said, glancing up from the papers. "These charges have nothing to do with that."

Simon let out a bitter laugh. "Of course not. But it doesn't matter. Once a rumor like that starts, it's a death sentence in here."

Douglas leaned forward, his eyes narrowing. "Why's someone spreading these rumors?"

Simon's jaw tightened. "It's obvious, isn't it? They want me dead."

"Who wants you dead?"

"Elijah."

Douglas frowned, flipping through the file to find more information. "Elijah Morant? The director at Safe Harbor?"

"That's him," Simon replied, his voice laced with a mixture of fear and hatred. "He may be the director, but they call him the Deacon."

"Deacon?" Douglas wondered out loud. "He some kind of ordained minister?"

Simon made a puffing sound. "He fancies himself ordained. Thinks he has a direct channel to God. I kid you not."

"So he's crazy?"

"You could say that." Simon brought his hands to his chest and leaned in. "You said you went to the warehouse. Did you see the tanks?"

Douglas nodded. "And I know what they use them for too."

This shocked Simon, forcing him upright in his seat. "How so?" He sniffed the air. "You *are* one of them, aren't you?"

"Not exactly," Douglas said. "But you're close. So why does this Elijah want you dead so badly?"

"That's easy. He's branded me an apostate. He and I were friends before all this started. He was a radical at university. Wanted to change the world. Became convinced a war between good and evil was being waged in the shadows and that human souls were the prize. Of course, I thought he was crazy. Then one day a sitting US senator paid our humble little charity a visit, a guy named Ravencroft. Said he was interested in the work we were doing and wanted to support our efforts to house the homeless."

Douglas' face became grave. "Go on."

"Well, soon Elijah began disappearing for long stretches, spending more and more time away from the NGO. When he was present, all he'd talk about was the Elohim and how they were real and on Earth and that it was his job to save humanity from itself."

"You saying he sees the Drax as some sort of deities?"

Simon drew a blank. "Drax?"

"An android race, commanded by a disembodied consciousness," Douglas explained. "The energy you're extracting from those innocent people, it's what the Drax use to power their technology."

"Elijah did say they were refining energy. And that he saw it as his mission in life to create the best product he could."

"By tormenting people?" Douglas said, disgusted.

"We were serving a higher ideal," Simon said, ashamed. "At least that's what I thought we were doing. But soon, something changed and Elijah was sending less and less of this refined energy to the people you call the Drax."

Douglas was puzzled. "Why's that?"

"Because at some point Elijah consumed some of it, mostly out of sheer stupidity and a touch of curiosity. It made him sharper, stronger, way more agile. Soon, he was insisting we all partake."

Douglas fished the inhaler out of his pocket and set it on the table.

Simon's eyes flashed with desire. "Get that away from me. Can't you see I'm trying to get clean?"

"Is that why you hid those people in your basement?"

Simon nodded. "I had to do something. I couldn't let him just torture people and then murder them."

"What about James Carmichael?"

A tear rolled down Simon's cheek. "We grew up together. But Jimmy developed his own addiction—meth—and ended up on the streets. When Safe Harbor picked him up and put him in one of those tubes, I guess I finally snapped out of it, all the lies and indoctrination. I threw it all away and freed who I could and fled."

"But Jimmy escaped?"

"That's right," Simon said, his bottom lip quivering. "Drugs will do a number on your brain, but nothing will destroy it more quickly than even a few days in one of those isolation chambers. Elijah realized the key to creating a better, stronger product was depriving his victims of any sensory input except the ones he piped in through the helmet. And over time, as his greed and sadism grew, the terrifying scenes he subjected them to became worse. Imagine living out your worst nightmare twenty-four seven until your body finally gives in and dies."

"So he's helping aliens subdue the human race because he thinks they're gods?"

"To be honest," Simon said, "I wouldn't be surprised at this point if Elijah saw himself as a god. Which is why he wants the crystal."

That last bit caught Douglas' attention. "Come again?"

"Elijah said Ravencroft had told him about a boy and a crystal, both possessing an incredible power. That got Elijah thinking. What if he managed to get his hands on that crystal and used it to create the most powerful Drahk'noth ever made? That's what he calls it."

"But how exactly does he plan to get his hands on it?" Douglas asked, increasingly worried.

"Ravencroft told him about a mole working for the US government—someone they'd recently swapped out, whatever that means—and that this person would feed them information on the best time to strike."

"Did this mole have a name?"

Simon squeezed his eyes shut for several seconds. "Damn. No, I can't remember."

Douglas' heart was doing backflips in his chest. He stayed another few minutes, but Simon was still drawing a blank. "Listen, I'm gonna have you moved to a safer facility and see if I can't convince the DA to drop these charges." Douglas stood to leave. "Reach out if you remember anything else."

Simon nodded.

Douglas was closing the door behind him when Simon shouted the name, relieved at last to have dug it out from the dusty confines of his mind.

"Dr. Mercer!"

Chapter 38

Joint Base Andrews

Beads of sweat rolled down Dr. Singh's forehead as he maneuvered the robotic arms inside the glovebox. Clenched in one gripper was the circlet. In the other was the crystal. "We may only get one shot at this," he told them.

Behind him, Shepard, Peters, Sam, Lena and Dr. Mercer all looked on with keen interest. The box itself would shield them from the fifth force energy emanating from the crystal, although there was no way to tell what would happen once the two were combined.

Slowly, Singh brought the two closer. As he did, Shepard could see thin tendrils of blue energy streaking between them. This grew stronger in the seconds before contact. Then came a clicking noise.

"The connection looks clean," Singh said, elated.

Relief spread through them.

"Now comes the tricky part," Mercer offered, eyeing Shepard.

"Thank you for bringing Sam down to the lab," Shepard said.

Mercer smiled. "Anything for the cause."

Sam and Lena then sat opposite one another. Any signs of nervousness on Sam were far less obvious than the noticeable change in his appearance. Tufts of gray hair had begun to form at his temples. The skin around his eyes was puffier and showing signs of wrinkles. And his hairline was slightly more swept back than it had been yesterday. Of course, no one said anything, but surely they all noticed it. Jake was the loudmouth who couldn't help but say whatever was on his mind. His absence from these proceedings saved everyone what might have been an awkward moment.

Singh took some more readings. "Fascinating!"

"You seeing something, Doc?" Peters asked.

"Merging with the circlet has made the crystal totally benign."

"Meaning?" Shepard asked.

"It means it isn't spewing out fifth force radiation," Singh explained. "It's as though the circlet is absorbing its power."

Dr. Singh slipped on a pair of specially insulated gloves designed to handle volatile materials. The gloves were made from a combination of advanced polymers and embedded with microcircuitry to shield the wearer from any harmful energy emissions. Carefully, he lowered the circlet onto Sam's head.

The moment the circlet made contact, a faint blue glow emanated from it, spreading across Sam's forehead. His eyes fluttered, and he seemed to tense momentarily. Shepard stepped forward, her concern evident.

"How's it feel?" Singh asked, his voice tinged with worry.

Sam gave him a thumbs-up, his eyes focusing again. "I'm okay," he reassured him, the glow from the circlet reflecting in his eyes.

212

Lena, sitting across from him, looked equally worried, her hands fidgeting in her lap. Singh observed closely, making adjustments to the equipment.

Sam took a deep breath and reached out, placing his hands on either side of Lena's temples. The moment his fingers made contact, Lena's body grew rigid, her eyes widening before they closed, succumbing to the connection.

Sam's mind delved into Lena's thoughts, flitting through a series of memories. The first was a scene of Lena as a child, playing in a sunlit garden, her laughter echoing in the air. The warmth and innocence of the memory filled him briefly before he moved on.

The next memory was of Lena graduating from university, the pride on her face evident as she accepted her diploma. The excitement and hope of youth surged through him. He then saw her first day on the job at the TV show, her nerves masked by a determined smile.

As he continued probing, the memories shifted, becoming more vivid and intense. He saw Lena exploring the UFO cave in Aurora, Texas, the glowing moss illuminating the dark space. The encounter with the Endarian hologram replayed in his mind. The whole time he could feel Lena's awe and fear.

Suddenly, the scene changed. A vast jungle stretched out before him, the air thick with humidity and the sounds of exotic birds. Rising from the dense foliage was a majestic pyramid, its stone steps weathered by time. Sam focused on the details, trying to extract more information as he relayed what he was seeing.

"Pyramid," Peters wondered, breathless. "Could that be Egypt?"

"No," Sam replied, shaking his head slowly. "Central America. A name… Ixchara."

Shepard felt a sudden and intense wave of anxiety wash over her.

"You all right?" Peters asked, noticing the change in her demeanor.

"Yeah, fine," she fibbed, trying to keep from reliving the terrible memories of her experience in Central America. It had occurred years ago and yet it still felt as fresh as if it happened yesterday.

The others exchanged glances, the significance of Sam's revelation starting to sink in. Sam released his grip on Lena, who slumped back in her chair, breathing heavily but unharmed.

"Ixchara is an area of Guatemala," Peters told them, breaking the silence that had settled over the room. He glanced around, his expression serious. "I had a retrieval mission there years ago."

Dr. Singh carefully removed the circlet from Sam's head, placing it back in the protective box. He hurried over to the computer, fingers flying across the keyboard as he pulled up satellite imagery of the area. The screen flickered to life, displaying a detailed map of the Guatemalan jungle with the known ruins highlighted with red markers.

While Singh worked, Shepard moved to check on Sam and Lena. Lena looked a bit rattled but seemed to be feeling lighter, as though a weight had been lifted from her shoulders. "How are you feeling?" Shepard asked.

Lena managed a weak smile. "Strange, but… better. Those memories aren't haunting me anymore."

Sam, on the other hand, was visibly weakened. His breathing was shallow, and his skin had taken on a pallor. Shepard placed a hand on his shoulder. "You did great, Sam. Just rest now."

Her phone buzzed in her pocket, and she glanced at the screen. It was Douglas. Before answering, she turned to Dr. Mercer. "Would you mind getting Sam and Lena some water?"

Mercer smiled, an expression that didn't quite reach her eyes. "Of course," she said, and walked out of the room.

Shepard answered the call, trying to keep her voice steady. "Douglas?"

"Shepard." Douglas' voice was breathless, urgent. "You need to listen to me. Drax infiltrators at the Pentagon are setting a plan in motion to kidnap Sam and to steal that crystal you brought back from Mars."

She switched the phone to her other ear. Nearby, Peters and Singh were scanning satellite imagery. She lowered her voice. "What are you talking about?"

"You're gonna have to trust me on this," he told her. "I was just speaking to an informant. He said the Drax have even managed to insert an imposter into the crash retrieval team."

Shepard's heart was racing. "Did they give you a name?"

"Dr. Mercer. Do you know her?"

Shepard's eyes widened. She glanced toward the door, her heart pounding. Just then, Mercer returned with a tray of glasses. Shepard struggled to keep her expression neutral, even as her mind raced.

"Got it," she said, ending the call.

Mercer set the tray down, her eyes narrowing slightly as she studied Shepard. "Everything all right?" she asked, a hint of suspicion in her tone. "You look a little peaked."

"That was the hospital. The blood test I ordered has just come back." Shepard smiled weakly.

215

"I hope it wasn't anything serious."

"Thankfully, no," Shepard replied, forcing a smile.

"I'd be happy to have a look, if you'd like."

"That won't be necessary. Doctor said I should be back to normal any day now. That reminds me. How's your mother doing these days?"

Mercer's smile faltered for a fraction of a second. "Oh, Mom. She's just fine."

The blood in Shepard's veins turned to ice. Mercer's mother had died two years ago.

"Fascinating," Singh shouted from over by the computer. He stood up with a printout, waving it in the air. "There's a fifth force hotspot in the area Sam identified. It's subtle enough we would never have found it without his help."

Just then each of them got a text. The convoy had arrived to transport Sam and the artifacts to a safe location.

Chapter 39

Shepard tried to maintain her composure as her mind raced. She needed to tell Peters about the mole, but Mercer was right there, watching her every move. She caught the colonel's eye, trying to signal the urgency, but he was preoccupied. "I have to go meet with Bradshaw about the convoy," he said, oblivious to her silent plea. "Whatever it is, it's going to have to wait."

Shepard's heart sank. If she let Sam get on that convoy, there was an excellent chance the enemy might get him. And yet she was also distinctly aware the Air Force might not believe her intel. They didn't know about Douglas and his investigation. She had to think fast.

"Sam," she said, helping him to his feet. "Let's get you back to the hospital to get your things."

"I can handle it," Mercer interjected, stepping forward. "You have more important things to do."

Shepard felt a surge of panic. "No, I insist. He needs my help."

Mercer's eyes narrowed as she sensed the tension. "I said I'll take care of it."

The situation escalated quickly. Shepard stepped between Sam and Mercer, her body tense. "You're not taking him anywhere," she said, her voice shaking with resolve.

Dr. Singh and Lena exchanged confused looks, unsure of what was happening. "What's going on?" Lena asked as she stood, holding her elbows.

Shepard turned to them, desperation in her eyes. "Mercer is a Drax! They're trying to steal Sam!"

Mercer's face twisted with indignation. "You're delusional, Shepard. You need to calm down."

Before Shepard could react, Mercer grabbed her arm, twisting it painfully. Shepard cried out in agony, struggling to break free. The room erupted into chaos as Singh and Lena tried to intervene, their voices a cacophony of confusion and concern.

In the midst of the turmoil, Sam's eyes flashed with fear. Summoning what little strength he had left, he reached out and touched Mercer's solar plexus. A burst of blue energy surged from his fingertips, sending Mercer flying backward across the room.

Dr. Singh stared in shock, unable to process what he had just witnessed. "What the hell…?"

Shepard seized the moment, grabbing Sam and making a break for the door. "Come on, we need to get out of here!"

They fled down the hallway, their footsteps echoing in the deserted corridor. Behind them, Mercer struggled to her feet, her eyes burning with fury and hatred.

As they reached the exit, Shepard's mind raced with the seriousness of what she'd just done. She had to protect Sam no matter what. They rounded a corner and stumbled into an empty lab room. She quickly shut the door behind them, leaning against it to catch her breath.

Sam slumped against the wall, his face pale and drawn. "I don't know how much longer I can keep this up," he admitted, his voice barely a whisper.

Shepard knelt beside him, her expression filled with concern. "You've done more than enough, Sam. Just hang in there a little longer."

Suddenly, the door handle jiggled, and Shepard's heart leaped into her throat. She braced herself, ready for another confrontation, but the door didn't open. Instead, she heard the faint sound of footsteps receding down the hallway.

"They're looking for us," she whispered, her eyes darting around the room for an escape route.

Sam nodded weakly. "We can't stay here. They'll find us eventually."

Fishing out her phone, Shepard called Isadora. It rang twice and went to voicemail. She tried Douglas next with no better luck.

After Shepard helped Sam to his feet, they moved toward the back of the lab, searching for another exit. They found a small door that led to a maintenance corridor. It was dark and narrow, but it offered a way out.

"Come on, this way," Shepard urged, guiding Sam through the door.

They crept down the maintenance corridor, the air growing colder and damper the further they went. Pipes and conduits lined the walls, their surfaces slick with condensation. The sound of dripping water echoed around them, adding to the sense of unease.

"Where are we going?" Sam asked, his voice trembling.

"Anywhere but here," Shepard replied. "If the Drax get their hands on you, it's game over."

After what felt like an eternity, they emerged into a storage room filled with crates and equipment. Just then Shepard's phone rang. It was Peters.

"What the hell are you doing?" he thundered.

Fighting to control her emotions, she struggled to fill him in.

"A Drax?" He sounded skeptical. "I don't know. How could she have gotten past our detection methods?"

"Who knows?" Shepard shouted. "Let's save the postmortem for later. Right now we need to figure out how to keep Sam safe."

She could hear on the other line that Peters was having a hard time. She was asking him to disobey direct orders.

"Can't you see that some of the Joint Chiefs have been compromised? If we follow that order, then the Drax will win and we lose."

"Come to Commander Bradshaw's office and we can work this all out."

A tear fell from Shepard's eye. Sam, sitting next to her, wiped it away. He was a much older man now, but somehow, she still saw him as a child.

Another call came in. This time it was Isadora. "I'm sorry, Devon. But I need to do this, even if that means I do it without you." Shepard clicked to the other line without waiting for an answer. "Hello, Isadora."

"You spoke to Douglas, I assume," Isadora said, her voice calm and soothing, but nevertheless filled with the gravity of the moment.

"Yes, and I need your help."

"Meet me in the usual place."

"The usual...?" Shepard began to ask, but the line was already dead.

They took the first exit outside. Not far away was the track where she exercised every day. Whenever Isadora and Douglas showed up on base, they always appeared among a grove of old trees.

"We're almost there," Shepard said, encouraging Sam. Channeling such a powerful force clearly took a toll.

When they arrived, they dropped to the ground. From here, she could see the base had become a zone of frenzied activity. Vehicles filled with military police were everywhere. Clearly, they were trying to lock the place down, which left Shepard to wonder how Isadora intended to get them out.

Close to thirty minutes passed before Isadora appeared behind them. "Ready?"

Shepard clutched at her heart. "You trying to give me a heart attack? Where did you come from?"

"Follow me," Isadora said, staying low.

Shepard and Sam did so for no more than ten yards before they came to a patch of discolored grass. Isadora reached down, grabbed hold of something and grunted as she heaved open a door. Beneath that was a ladder.

"You waiting for a royal invite?" Isadora asked, motioning them into the opening. One by one they scaled down to a concrete tunnel.

"What is this place?"

"A service tunnel under the base," she explained, her voice floating down the dim, cavernous passage ahead of them. "It's huge, and if we go this way, it opens into an abandoned section of the Washington subway system."

"They're connected?" Shepard asked, her boots crunching on the gritty floor as they trudged along, the hum of distant machinery vibrating through the walls.

221

"Well, not officially," Isadora said with a sly smile, the glint of mischief in her eyes. "But it was easy work for the plasma cutter."

Chapter 40

After exiting the subway system, Isadora brought them to a safehouse, a modest apartment nestled in an unremarkable building near downtown. The small living room was sparsely furnished with a worn-out sofa, a simple coffee table, and a few mismatched chairs. The fridge in the kitchen made a humming noise and contained water and a few other basic essentials.

"It isn't much," Isadora said, "but it'll have to do until we figure out our next steps. I need to step out briefly, but I'll be back later."

"Thank you," Shepard said, taking her hand.

Sam smiled at her.

Isadora looked back at him as though she was weighing something important. "I hope you're worth it," she said, before leaving.

With the place to themselves, Shepard grabbed two bottles of water and some light snacks and returned to the couch. Sam dug into a bag of potato chips as though he hadn't eaten in a month.

"Slow down or you're gonna be sick."

Sam set the bag aside and downed the bottle of water. "You didn't need to do this," he said, an earnestness in his eyes.

Shepard set her water down on the table. "It's not like me to do something like that. I'm a team player. Always have been. I don't lone-wolf it."

Sam sat up straight. He seemed to be regaining some of the energy he'd lost. "So what changed?"

She studied his face. When the angle was just right, she could see he was a perfect mix of her and Peters. Even now that he was older than both of them, she could still spot those key features—the turn of his nose, the prominent dimples. He even wore his hair like Peters, combed back and off to the side. It was eerie. This wasn't some random stranger she'd risked everything to save. He was her flesh and blood, now her only son. Never mind how hard it was to reconcile the way she felt with the late-middle-aged man sitting before her. In the span of three weeks, Sam had gone from an infant to just shy of a senior citizen.

"Is it painful?" she asked.

Sam looked himself over, uncertain what she meant.

"The growth spurt. I expect being stretched out like that can't be very pleasant."

He shook his head. "No, I don't feel any physical pain."

"You feel another kind of pain?"

"Fear is maybe a better way of putting it," he told her. "Fear of dying. I suppose in a way, I'm having a human experience at breakneck speed. Only a few days ago, the thought of death never entered my mind. But then I woke up this morning and saw that the skin on my arms had become looser and that my knees were hurting when I slid out of bed."

"I know the feeling," she said, torn between wanting to laugh and wanting to cry.

224

"And since my life will be infinitely shorter than most, it means I'll miss out on what everyone else experiences. The joys, the sorrows."

Shepard let out a sick little laugh. "I have enough sorrow for the two of us. Trust me when I say you aren't missing anything there."

He grew still for a moment, watching her. "I noticed a change in your expression back at the lab after Dr. Singh revealed where the forge was located."

Clearing her throat, Shepard waved her hand dismissively. "You mean after I found out Mercer, someone I considered a friend, had been replaced by a Drax agent?"

Sam nodded. "Since you put it that way. But that wasn't what I was talking about. I saw a deep flash of pain in your eyes when Singh spoke. It almost looked like you'd seen a ghost."

She hesitated, torn between revealing a deeply held secret and maintaining the stoic façade she had so carefully constructed over all these years. But something in Sam's eyes—a depth of understanding that spoke to shared loss—compelled her to lower her defenses.

"No, you're right," she finally admitted, her voice trembling. "Something did happen a long time ago. Something I thought I'd dealt with."

As she began to speak, the memories of that fateful expedition came flooding back. The excitement of discovery, the sense of anticipation as she and her colleague, Dr. Joel Torres, navigated the labyrinthine passages of what promised to be a groundbreaking discovery for the fields of archaeology and linguistics.

"We were on an expedition to uncover a lost Mayan city," she began, her voice soft but steady. "Joel and I had been working together for years, exploring ancient ruins and unearthing artifacts that shed light on civilizations long gone. This particular expedition was our most ambitious yet, and the stakes were high."

She paused, her eyes distant as she recalled the excitement that had accompanied their discovery. "We stumbled upon an undiscovered chamber deep within the ruins. It was a groundbreaking find, and I couldn't help but feel that we were on the verge of something truly extraordinary."

Shepard's voice wavered as she continued, the memory of her colleague's reluctance weighing heavily on her conscience. "Joel was hesitant to venture further into the chamber. He had a family, you see—a wife and three children—and the risks inherent in our profession had always weighed heavily on him. But I was headstrong, blinded by the promise of discovery. I urged him to push on, insisting that the rewards far outweighed the dangers."

A pained expression crossed her face. "As we explored, the floor beneath us gave way without warning. We were both sent tumbling into the darkness, but I managed to grab onto a ledge. Unfortunately, Joel wasn't so lucky. I watched in horror as he plummeted into the abyss, his life extinguished in an instant."

She took a deep, shuddering breath, her eyes glistening with unshed tears. "I've never been able to shake the feeling that I'm responsible for his death. If I had only listened to his concerns, if I had been more cautious… maybe he'd still be alive today."

Shepard's voice broke, and she fell silent, the weight of her guilt a palpable presence between them. Sam regarded her with a mixture of sympathy and respect.

"I've carried that guilt with me for years," she whispered, her voice raw with emotion. "The knowledge that my actions led to the death of a dear friend and colleague, and the devastation that wrought on his family… it's a burden I don't know if I can ever truly lay to rest."

As she finished recounting her story, Shepard looked to Sam, her eyes searching his face for judgment or condemnation. But all she found was understanding— the quiet recognition of someone who knew words alone were powerless to undo such a torrent of emotion.

As they sat amidst the quiet of the safehouse, a fragile connection was forged between them. It was a bond born of shared suffering and the understanding that came from confronting one's own demons. And while it offered no easy answers, it provided them with a measure of solace in the knowledge that they were not alone.

Chapter 41

Joint Base Andrews

Peters stood at attention in Bradshaw's office, the atmosphere charged with anxiety. The commander's face was a storm cloud of anger. "What do you mean she isn't here?" Bradshaw demanded, his voice barely restrained.

Peters took a deep breath, knowing the gravity of the situation. "Sir, we've looked everywhere. After fleeing from the lab, Shepard and Sam made their way outside. We lost their trail by the track."

Bradshaw's face turned a deep shade of red. "You do realize the magnitude of what we may have lost? It was the whole reason we were relocating him in the first place!"

Peters weighed his options, deciding he couldn't keep quiet any longer. "While I strongly disagree with Shepard's actions, I understand why she did it."

Bradshaw's eyes widened in disbelief. "What? I've got a call with the Joint Chiefs in ten minutes. The next words out of your mouth better be good."

Peters took a steadying breath. "Shepard's sources informed her that the convoy is set to be ambushed."

"Ambushed? By who?" Bradshaw asked, his voice dripping with skepticism.

"Not clear, sir."

"And her source?"

Peters swallowed hard. "I believe it was Special Agent Douglas, from the FBI."

Bradshaw's expression shifted from anger to incredulity. "You mean this isn't even coming from military intelligence?"

"No, sir."

"So we're just supposed to take Shepard's word, is that it?" Bradshaw's frustration boiled over as he smacked a pen holder off his desk, sending writing utensils scattering across the floor. "No, thank you!"

"There's one other thing, sir," Peters added, not entirely sure how this bit of news would go over.

"What is it, Colonel?"

"Shepard seems to think that Dr. Mercer has been compromised."

Bradshaw's left eyebrow rose. "Compromised?"

"Replaced with a Drax imposter."

The commander put his head in his hands. "Jesus." His eyes searched the room. "Well, we don't have much choice then. Take her into custody and we'll sort it out later."

Peters braced himself, maintaining his composure. "Yes, sir. Should we postpone the convoy until Shepard is located?"

Bradshaw paused, his gaze shifting to the window. The silence stretched out, filled only by the ticking of the clock on the wall. Finally, he turned back to Peters. "No, it goes ahead. But add another detachment of airmen to guard it. Just in case."

Peters hesitated, a knot of worry tightening in his stomach.

"Is that clear, Colonel?" Bradshaw barked.

"Crystal, sir," Peters said, snapping a salute before leaving the room.

Peters made his way to the base armory, a cavernous space filled with the low hum of activity. The walls were lined with weapons and gear, each meticulously organized, while the center held a collection of heavy-duty vehicles ready for deployment. Alvarez, Jake, and Nash were gathered around a table strewn with maps and tactical gear, their faces set in varying degrees of concentration.

"Hey, boss," Jake called out, looking up from his rifle. "What's the latest on Shepard? Has she lost her mind or what?"

Peters shook his head as he approached. "No, she hasn't lost her mind. But she did take Sam off base. The authorities are searching for them as we speak. In the meantime, we have a mission to focus on."

Alvarez frowned. "Why would she do that? What's her angle?"

"She's trying to protect him," Peters replied. "But that's not our concern right now. We have orders to follow."

Nash, who had been silent up until now, glanced up from his gear. "So, what's the plan, Colonel?"

Peters bent forward to activate the holographic table. A whirring sound filled the air as the map of their route sprang to life, the three-dimensional terrain glowing in a faint yellow light. Manipulating the hologram with swift gestures, Peters zoomed in on their destination. "Raven Rock Mountain Complex, near Blue Ridge Summit, Pennsylvania."

Jake, always quick with a question, asked, "Why there?"

Peters pointed to the map. "It's one of the most secure locations we have, and it's close enough for us to reach by convoy."

"What's the makeup?" Alvarez asked, clearly not satisfied with just the destination.

"We're rolling out with five armored SUVs, one MRAP APC, and thirty airmen," Peters explained. "The convoy will be heavily armed and prepared for any eventuality."

Jake leaned back in his chair, crossing his arms. "Why can't we just fly? We're at an Air Force base, after all."

Peters had anticipated the question and had the answer ready. "The terrain around Raven Rock is too rugged. There's no infrastructure to support aircraft or helicopters. Plus, the location is close to a designated no-fly zone. Air transport is not an option."

The men exchanged glances, their dissatisfaction clear. Nash muttered under his breath, "Just our luck, right, Colonel?"

"I don't make the rules," Peters said. "One more thing. The intel we have right now is fuzzy at best, but there are grumblings someone might try and snatch the crystal and the headpiece en route."

Alvarez pulled the charging handle on his pulse rifle. "Not on our watch, they won't."

"Good answer," Peters told them. "See you in the hangar in ten."

The three operators nodded, turning their attention back to their preparations. Peters could see the tension in their movements, the unspoken questions and doubts lingering in the air.

He walked away unable to shake the feeling they were embarking on a suicide mission.

Chapter 42

Washington, D.C.

Douglas pulled up to Capital Ribs and checked the address again, grinning. *Am I really that predictable?*

The smell of smoked meats greeted him as he walked through the door, making his stomach rumble in anticipation. The ambiance was warm and rustic, just the way he liked it. Even the decor spoke to him. The walls were adorned with vintage political campaign posters and historical photographs of Washington landmarks. A large, vintage map of the city covered one wall, dotted with notable BBQ spots across America, highlighting Capital Ribs as the ultimate destination. Plush leather booths provided comfortable seating, while bulbs hanging from the ceiling cast a warm, inviting glow.

Douglas scanned the room, spotting Desiree in a corner booth near the back. Ever cautious, she had chosen a spot that afforded a good view of the entrance. As he approached, he noted the platters of ribs being delivered to nearby tables, the succulent meat falling off the bone, and his anticipation grew.

Desiree looked up from her menu, a knowing smile on her face. "Thought you'd appreciate the choice," she said as he slid into the booth across from her.

He chuckled, nodding appreciatively. "You always know how to pick 'em, Desiree. This place smells like heaven." But jovialities aside, the strain on Douglas' face was obvious.

She set the menu down, her expression shifting to a more serious tone. "I got your message."

Douglas folded his arms, taking in the inviting atmosphere one last time before focusing on her. "About the ambush?" he asked.

Desiree glanced around the room, ensuring their conversation would remain private amidst the din of the bustling restaurant. "I hope you don't think I have any power to find out when and where it's going to happen."

He shrugged. "I don't see why you wouldn't know. Perhaps it's that you don't wanna tell me."

"I resent that," she said, looking hurt. "What more do I need to do to prove I'm on your side?"

Douglas's eyes narrowed, his focus sharpening. "Ronald Reagan liked to say, 'Trust, but verify.' And I must say I've always been rather fond of the fellow."

"I've heard Ravencroft complaining lately about Safe Harbor," she said, clearing her throat. "Says their Drahk'noth is the best he's ever seen, but that their methodology is barbaric, even for him."

"That means a lot coming from a scoundrel like Ravencroft."

"I've also heard him say the quantity of shipments has gone down and he doesn't understand why."

Douglas produced the inhaler. "Probably because of this thing. That top-notch Drahk'noth Ravencroft is so eager to get his hands on? Well, for some reason they got the bright idea to start ingesting it themselves."

Desiree's eyes grew three times bigger. "Oh, wow, pumping your body full of ultra-refined dark matter.

What could possibly go wrong? Explain to me again how humans have managed to survive this long?"

"News flash: we do stupid shit," Douglas said, only dimly aware that the human race wasn't a group he technically belonged to anymore. "Problem is, rather than killing them, which would have been a blessing, it's actually made them extraordinarily potent. Remember our friend Simon?"

"Ah, I see. I was certain the guy in the basement was Drax, but now it makes sense." Her eyes fell to the menu before finding Douglas again. "Isn't it obvious then? These human yahoos have gone rogue. They might talk a good game about worshiping the Drax and treating us like gods, but at the end of the day, what human doesn't wish to be a god as well?"

"I've already passed along as much intel to my contacts in the military as I can. If you hear anything else, let me know."

Desiree crossed her arms. "Of course. So what now? You just gonna let the Air Force handle what's coming?"

"I've got a pair of junior agents staking out Safe Harbor's main warehouse. Traffic to that particular location has dropped by eighty percent, which tells me they may be in the final stages of planning the heist."

"And did your contacts in the military believe you?"

"Sounded like they did," Douglas said. "Although whether the top brass will listen is another story altogether."

Desiree took a deep breath. "There's something else you ought to know." She locked eyes with Douglas, her gaze intense, humorless. "On more than one occasion, Ravencroft brought the director of Safe Harbor…"

"Elijah Morant."

"Is that his name?"

Douglas nodded. "Where'd they take him?"

"Ravencroft was so impressed with the quality of the Drahk'noth they were producing, he took Elijah to meet the Master."

Douglas felt a chill run down his spine, but his face remained impassive. "Is that right?"

"And apparently it made quite an impression on the budding preacher. That's where his reverence for the Drax became a full-on cult."

Bewildered, Douglas sat back and shook his head. "The guy sounds like a total nutcase. But why's the Master so eager to get his hands on Sam?"

Her expression changed. So too did the tone of her voice. "Is that the Endarian child who can manipulate the fifth force?"

"He's only half-Endarian," Douglas corrected her. "And there's little left of the child. He's a grown-ass man now. Probably older than I am."

She looked at him, confused.

"You're just gonna have to take my word for it."

Laughing, she said, "That sure sounds familiar. As for the Master's plan, if he inhabits Sam's body and possesses his powers, he'll be nearly unstoppable."

"Isn't that just what we need," Douglas said, the sarcasm dripping.

"Look, I think you missed the point I was trying to make earlier," she told him, guiding the conversation back. "Bringing this Elijah character to see the Master violated every rule in the book. No one sees the Master except Ravencroft and those who held his position in ages past. It's a really big deal."

"The end zone's in sight and it sounds like they're starting to get sloppy," Douglas said.

Desiree's eyes were shining now. "You get your hands on this Elijah character and press him hard enough, he might just spill the beans on the location of the Master's lair."

Chapter 43

Joint Base Andrews

The convoy gathered at the hangar, the early morning light casting long shadows over the armored SUVs and the MRAP APC. Peters stood by the lead vehicle, surveying the scene with a critical eye. He mentally detailed the layout of the convoy: The MRAP leading the way, followed by the two middle SUVs carrying the precious relics—the crystal and the headpiece. The convoy was rounded out by two more SUVs acting as a rear guard. Peters, Alvarez, Nash, and Jake were tasked with protecting the headpiece while a separate group would secure the crystal, each object housed in a specially designed container.

The trip to Raven Rock Mountain Complex was 80 miles and expected to take just under two hours. Peters knew that the journey itself was fraught with potential hazards, but he was most nervous about the stretch through the mountains. The winding roads and rocky outcroppings provided ample opportunity for an ambush.

As they moved out, the Apache gunships circled overhead, their powerful rotors cutting through the air with a reassuring thrum. Jake, sitting in the back seat of the second SUV, whooped in appreciation of the machines and the protection they provided.

And yet, despite his eagerness to get this mission over with, Peters couldn't shake the nagging feeling of unease as the convoy progressed. The flat, open terrain offered a sense of security, but he knew it wouldn't last. He kept a close eye on the road ahead and the surrounding landscape, his mind racing with contingency plans. The air inside the SUV was tense, with everyone focused on their respective tasks. Nash, positioned in the rear, manned a Gatling gun while Jake sat one row ahead, monitoring the convoy's radio communications.

As they climbed into the mountains, Peters felt his stress level begin to rise. The road twisted and turned, each bend revealing another potential hiding spot for an ambush. He could feel the heavy weight of the mission, knowing that the safety of the convoy—and the relics—rested on his shoulders. Overhead, the Apaches' rotors sliced through the thin mountain air, continuing their ever-vigilant protective duties.

The convoy slowed as they navigated the sharp turns and steep inclines, the vehicles' engines laboring under the strain.

Peters glanced at the passenger seat where Alvarez sat scanning the rock wall to their right. "Stay sharp," Peters said. "We're in the danger zone now."

As they continued their ascent, the acute feeling of vulnerability grew. The rocky outcroppings loomed overhead, and Peters couldn't shake the sensation that they were being watched.

Had Douglas' intel been reliable? Or was it simply messing with his head, acting as nothing more than a distraction?

They were approaching the no-fly zone when the lead Apache pilot radioed in. "Bravo Lima Echo. This is where we leave you."

"Appreciate the overwatch," Jake replied. "Sad to see you go."

"Godspeed," the pilot said, before the choppers peeled away, back to Andrews.

With less than ten miles to go before they reached their destination, Peters' nerves were beginning to settle.

A message came in from the lead vehicle. "Colonel, please be advised I have a minivan about a mile out heading our way."

"Roger that, Sanders," Peters said, his pulse quickening. "Can you get eyes on?"

"Road's windy, sir. But as soon as it straightens, we'll have a look with binoculars. Over."

Peters, Jake and Alvarez shared nervous glances.

Nash called out from the back gunner position. "We good?"

"Not sure," Peters said, gripping the wheel just a little tighter than normal. "We're currently assessing. Hold tight."

Agonizing seconds passed without any word.

"Is it a threat?" Peters asked, unable to wait any longer.

"Sir, we see what looks like a family inside the vehicle. So that's a negative."

Now the road straightened and Peters nudged the SUV into the oncoming lane to have a look for himself. On their right was the sloping side of a mountain. To their left was a cliff. No matter how you sliced it, this sure wasn't an ideal spot for a firefight.

"Haven't they already cleared the vehicle as a family of civilians?" Alvarez asked, when he saw what Peters was up to.

Peters handed him the binoculars. "Then it won't hurt if we have a look for ourselves. Besides, since when is having more eyes on a potential target a bad thing?"

"That FBI guy's gotten in your head," Alvarez snarked as he peered through the magnified lenses, trying to adjust for the movement of the road. "Yup, like he said, just a... wait a second."

The van was closer now, less than a hundred yards away.

"Those aren't people," Alvarez shouted. "They're mannequins."

Peters radioed the entire convoy at once. "The van is hostile. I repeat the van is..."

Peters barely finished his sentence when the minivan accelerated, barreling straight toward the lead MRAP. The explosion that followed was deafening, a massive fireball engulfing the vehicle and sending a shockwave that rattled the entire convoy. Shrapnel and debris rained down as the MRAP was lifted off the ground, the force of the blast tearing it apart. The front of the convoy was obliterated in an instant, creating a chaotic scene of twisted metal and smoke.

"Brace for impact!" Peters shouted, gripping the wheel as he slammed the brakes to avoid the smoldering remains of the MRAP now blocking the roadway.

The radio crackled with frantic voices. "We're hit! Front vehicle down! Front vehicle down!"

Before anyone could fully comprehend the devastation at the front, a metallic ball rolled into the middle of the convoy from the rear, its blinking red light a harbinger of doom. The gravity grenade detonated with a sudden, eerie silence, creating a localized distortion that pulled the rear vehicle inward, crushing it with an invisible force. The soldiers inside had no time to react as the vehicle was compressed into a twisted hunk of metal, their screams cut short.

"We need to move, now!" Nash yelled from the back.

"Everyone out!" Peters commanded, throwing open his door and leaping to the ground. The team scrambled to exit the vehicles, each member moving with the urgency and precision drilled into them by countless hours of training. The sound of gunfire was immediate, bullets pinging off the armored SUVs as they scrambled for cover.

From the cliffs above, attackers began to rappel down on ropes, their descent swift and coordinated. "We've got hostiles coming in from above!" Jake shouted, firing up at the descending figures.

Nash was manning the rear-facing Gatling gun mounted on the SUV, the powerful weapon roaring to life as he unleashed a torrent of hot lead towards the attackers. "Come get some!" he bellowed, his voice barely audible over the deafening barrage of gunfire. He swept the barrel left and right, mowing down several of the attackers before they could reach the ground.

Peters scanned the chaotic scene, noting the relentless efficiency of the assault. These were not ordinary combatants; they moved with an unnatural speed and strength, seemingly impervious to pain. "Alvarez, cover the headpiece!" Peters ordered, motioning towards the vehicle's precious cargo, still in the back seat.

Alvarez nodded, ducking behind the SUV as he reached in to grab it. "These guys don't give up, do they?" he yelled, his voice tinged with frustration.

The attackers on the ground pressed forward, driving into the heart of the convoy. The air was thick with the acrid smell of gunpowder and the sharp tang of blood. Nash continued to unleash a storm of rounds from the Gatling gun, but even that wasn't enough to stem the tide. A fresh explosion rocked the rear of the convoy, the shockwave knocking them to the ground.

A panicked voice screamed over the radio. "We're getting overrun!"

Nash's Gatling gun finally went silent as the last of its ammo was spent. He threw open the door and jumped to the ground, his pulse rifle already in his hands. "They're rappelling down from the cliffs! We need to take them out before they get close!"

Peters crouched behind the SUV, his mind racing. "Jake, watch our left flank! Nash, stay with Alvarez and protect the headpiece!" He peeked around the edge of the vehicle, firing off several pulse rounds at the approaching attackers. His heart pounded as he watched the figures clad in black camo closing in, their faces twisted with a mix of fury and fanaticism.

Jake picked off several attackers as they descended from the cliffs, his weapon cracking with deadly precision. "Keep moving, keep moving!" he called out to the others, his voice an anchor in the chaos.

Peters spotted an attacker closing in on Alvarez, who was trying to shield the alien relic. Without hesitation, Peters sprinted towards them, tackling the assailant to the ground. The two men rolled across the asphalt, trading blows with brutal intensity. Peters landed a solid punch, dazing the attacker long enough for Peters to draw his sidearm and fire a point-blank shot. The body went limp, and Peters pushed it aside, breathing heavily.

The airmen and Delta operators fought valiantly, but the sheer number of attackers was overwhelming. The enemy, some of whom were armed with advanced Drax weaponry, pushed forward, their eyes gleaming with a mad fervor. They appeared to be driven by a cause that made them nearly unstoppable.

Hand-to-hand combat broke out as the distance closed, soldiers and attackers locked in a deadly dance. Peters saw Nash struggling with an attacker, the two men rolling on the ground in a desperate fight for control. He rushed to Nash's aid, delivering a powerful kick to the attacker's side and pulling Nash to his feet. "You okay?"

Nash nodded, wiping blood from his face. "Yeah, thanks. But they're closing in on the crystal!"

Just then a bullet ricocheted off the pavement and tore through Alvarez's side. He went down with a grunt, clutching his wound. Peters rushed over, firing at an attacker who was closing in. "Stay with me, Alvarez!" he shouted, trying desperately to stop the bleeding.

Chapter 44

With the convoy in disarray, the attackers pushed their assault. Peters knew they couldn't hold out much longer. The enemy was everywhere, their ferocity and numbers overwhelming the defensive line. His mind raced, searching for a way to turn the tide.

But in the chaos, there was no clear answer. They were surrounded, outnumbered, and outgunned. The fate of the mission hung in the balance, the precious relics they were sworn to protect now perilously close to falling into enemy hands.

As the attackers pressed their advantage, the remaining airmen and Delta operators were forced to retreat.

"Fall back! Regroup at the secondary position!" Peters shouted, his voice cutting through the chaos. He hefted Alvarez, who was groaning in pain from his wound, over his shoulder. With a grimace, Peters led the retreat, spotting Jake and the headpiece just up ahead.

The convoy's vehicles were now makeshift barricades, offering limited cover as they fell back to a more defensible position. Nash and Jake provided covering fire, their pulse rifles raining death on the advancing enemy.

"Don't let up!" Jake shouted, scanning for any sign of a breach. He fired a burst, taking down an attacker who had managed to get too close. "We can't let them through!"

Peters found a relatively sheltered spot behind an overturned SUV and set Alvarez down. "Stay with me, buddy," he urged, ripping a piece of cloth from his uniform to staunch the bleeding. "We're going to get you out of here."

Alvarez gritted his teeth, nodding weakly. "Just… if I don't make it, tell my son…"

Peters' eyes hardened with resolve. "Save it, soldier, you'll tell him yourself," he promised, though he knew the odds were against them.

Despite their best efforts, the attackers managed to breach the defensive line protecting the crystal. Peters could see the collaborators swarming out of an armored Brinks truck towards the SUV where the crystal was housed. The soldiers there were being overwhelmed, their defensive position crumbling under the relentless assault.

"Jake, Nash! They're breaking through!" Peters barked.

Jake turned, his face grim. "We've got to hold them off!"

The two Delta operators sprinted towards the breached line, firing as they ran. The attackers, sensing victory, redoubled their efforts, their savage strength and disregard for pain giving them a fearsome advantage. Peters watched in horror as the defenders were overrun, the crystal's protective case wrenched from their grasp.

"No!" Peters shouted, feeling a surge of despair. He grabbed his pulse rifle and fired at the attackers, trying to create an opening, but it was too late. The enemy had the crystal, their leader holding it aloft triumphantly.

Nash, his face twisted with rage, tackled the leader, grappling for control of the crystal. They rolled on the ground, each trying to gain the upper hand. But the enemy was stronger, fueled by some inhuman force. He slammed Nash's head into the ground, stunning him, and wrenched the crystal free.

Peters and Jake pushed forward, taking out the enemy fighters around Nash. But by the time they arrived, the crystal was gone.

Chapter 45

Shepard was in the middle of trying to shake off a terrible feeling when the apartment door opened. In walked Isadora, followed by the last person she expected to see.

"Elder Gorian?" Shepard said, rising up off the couch. Sam did the same.

"I thought you might need a friend," Isadora said, walking past them and into the kitchen.

"Is that what we are?" Shepard asked. "Friends?"

Gorian's expression shifted to one of curiosity. "I thought we put that whole episode on Mars behind us. You came to my aid and I gladly returned the favor."

"I suppose that makes us even then," Shepard said, her arms crossed.

Gorian's gaze moved off her and over to Sam, who stood with his hands in his pockets.

"He looks much older than the last time we met," Gorian observed. "And just as unassuming." He smiled, as though contemplating whether or not to say the next bit. He did anyway. "Perhaps the most powerful person in the universe, and he's taken the form of a… what do you call them? A regular…"

"Schmo," Shepard said, completing Gorian's rather cutting observation. "Except Sam is no Schmo."

"I don't doubt that," Gorian countered. "But do you remember your true identity?" he asked him. "Your non-human side?"

Sam shook his head. "I was born in a box barely a month ago."

"Yeah, cut him some slack," Shepard said.

Isadora joined them, popping a bottle of water. "I spoke to Douglas earlier. He said Andrews went on full lockdown after you fled and now the local police are involved. Both your pictures are all over the news."

Shepard nodded, dimly aware that knot in her belly was getting tighter.

"It's only a question of time before they find you, I'm afraid," Isadora informed them.

Gorian adjusted the sleeves of his robe. "Tell me, what precisely did you hope to achieve from this action?"

"I was trying to keep Sam safe." Shepard told him about Douglas' warning.

"Yes, I am familiar." Gorian motioned to the apartment. "They may call this a safehouse, but it won't be long before the Drax manage to track you here. Then what will you have accomplished? Sam will still be gone and you'll either be dead or languishing in a prison cell."

"Both risks I was willing to take," she said, her features set in a look of defiance.

"If the Council truly were the bad guys you've made us out to be," Gorian said, "we could easily have taken Sam without you even knowing."

Sam's jaw clenched and sparks of blue energy began building at his fingertips. "Go ahead and try it."

Gorian raised a hand. "But that isn't how we like to operate." His eyes found Isadora and he made a funny face. "At least not with those we consider friends and

248

allies. By this stage, surely you understand that Sam holds tremendous power. Under the right circumstances, such a power could be used by our side to heal the sun and save humanity. However, if wielded by the Drax, surely they would use it to annihilate all life in this solar system. The decision the two of you make right now could determine which path we take. Thus, it shouldn't surprise you to learn that I've come with an offer."

Shepard's body tensed. She knew perfectly well neither she nor Sam had much to bargain with. Gorian was right. If the fate of the solar system was at stake, the notions of "human rights" and "playing fair" would go right out the window. Which was certainly an argument in his favor. The Council had the ability to simply beam in and snatch Sam while the two of them were sound asleep. And yet they hadn't. Instead, Gorian had come to negotiate, and negotiate was precisely what Shepard intended to do.

"On your end of the bargain, you have Sam," Gorian began. "On our end, we have a guarantee of protection and humane treatment for the both of you."

"And what of my life on Earth?" Shepard asked.

Gorian shrugged. "Well, it seems you've made quite a mess of that. Sadly, undoing such a thing would be beyond our ability. As a result, you would live out the rest of your life with us. Certainly, we could find you a place to live at the facility being built on Suwanose Jima."

"If I were you, I'd take that offer," Isadora said, now peeling an apple.

It certainly was tempting. "But what if I had more to offer than just Sam?"

One of Gorian's eyebrows went up. "I'm listening."

"A possible resting place for the galactic forge's missing half."

Gorian's face was calm, but the subtle twitch of his lip betrayed his hidden interest. "Go on."

"We'll take the first part of your offer," Shepard said. "But we also want to accompany any expedition to retrieve the forge."

Gorian's expression showed doubt. "I'm afraid that would not be possible. There are tests on Sam that must first be carried out."

"Oh, not more tests," Sam said, frowning.

"I assure you," Gorian countered, "unlike your human hosts, the Council's requirements will not be unpleasant in the least."

"It's all or nothing," Shepard said. "Take it or leave it."

"You know how negotiations work, don't you?"

A sly grin formed on Shepard's lips. "You know what a full house looks like, don't you?"

Gorian looked at Isadora for help.

"She's got you there," the Thalasian said, smiling as she took a bite of her apple.

Chapter 46

Douglas sat in the spy van, the glow from multiple screens reflecting off his weary face. Beside him, Jason, the FBI IT specialist, was hunched over a laptop, fingers flying across the keyboard as he tried to hack into Safe Harbor's warehouse surveillance system. A half-eaten donut lay forgotten next to his mouse pad.

"Anything yet?" Douglas grunted, his voice tinged with impatience.

"Almost there," Jason muttered, eyes glued to the screen. "Just need to bypass one more firewall. With any luck, we may even get sound too."

Douglas nodded and turned back to his own task. He was reviewing the footage captured by the van's camera array over the last twenty-four hours. The system responded to his voice commands as he scanned through hours of uneventful recordings. "Next segment," he ordered, fighting off boredom as the screen showed more empty scenes.

Suddenly, something caught his eye. "Halt. Go back." He leaned closer to the screen. The footage was high-definition, but the rain and fog from last night created clouds of vapor that kept obscuring the image. He squinted as a series of flashes appeared on the screen.

"Roll it back again. Enhance," he instructed, his heart rate quickening.

The image cleared slightly, revealing what looked like a convoy of large black SUVs pulling out of the warehouse at four a.m. Leading the convoy was a heavily armored Brinks truck. Douglas' eyes narrowed as he watched the vehicles move like ghosts through the rain-soaked streets.

"Jason, check this out," he said, glancing over at the IT specialist. Jason paused his hacking efforts and peered at the screen.

"That's some serious hardware for an NGO," Jason remarked.

Douglas felt a wave of unease wash over him. He glanced down at his phone and saw two missed calls from Colonel Peters. His heart sank as he realized he had probably just witnessed the team leaving late last night on its way to stealing the alien relics. He dialed Peters' number, his mind racing.

Peters answered on the first ring. "Douglas, this is not a good time."

"I tried to warn you," Douglas said, his voice tense.

"Yeah, but the higher-ups were too skeptical to think straight," Peters fired back, his tone heavy with frustration and anger. "Chain of command and all. Anyway, several airmen are dead. One of my close friends... he's gravely wounded."

Douglas closed his eyes, the weight of the news hitting him hard. "I'm sorry to hear that, Colonel. We just found something that might be related. A convoy of black SUVs and a Brinks truck left Safe Harbor's warehouse early this morning."

"Goddamn it," Peters swore. "That has to be them. They took the crystal. I'll bet they're in the process of handing it over to the Drax as we speak."

"I wouldn't be so sure of that," Douglas said. "This group is so wild even the Drax don't know what to do with them. I heard they've got plans for the relic that would make your hair turn white."

There was a pause. "Any word from Shepard?"

Douglas grew quiet. "Not yet. I heard she left the base."

"You make it sound almost trivial," Peters murmured. He was hurting on many levels and Douglas couldn't help but sympathize with the man. "If you speak to her, give her my best, would you?"

"I will."

Douglas was about to hang up when Peters spoke again.

"I get this is in your jurisdiction now." There was a seething hatred in the military man's voice. "But what I wouldn't give for a little payback…"

"You and me both," Douglas said, commiserating. "I'll keep you apprised."

No sooner had he hung up than a group of four vehicles rolled up to the warehouse, this time only three SUVs with the same Brinks truck from last night.

"That must be them," Douglas said, happy the enemy seemed to have taken at least one loss. Now they needed to find out if they still had the spoils of war.

Douglas got on the phone and immediately called FBI headquarters followed by the local police. Within the next few hours, they would be descending on the Safe Harbor warehouse, warrants in one hand and weapons in the other.

Act 3

The Master's Lair

Chapter 47

"Got it," Jason muttered, finally succeeding in tapping into the video and audio feed. The screens inside the spy van flickered before stabilizing, revealing the interior of the massive warehouse.

Douglas rolled his chair forward, his eyes narrowing as he watched the scene unfold. Inside, Elijah Morant stood before a gathered crowd of followers, his presence commanding and charismatic. Although wiry, he wore a beanie, his left arm covered with a sleeve tattoo. But even over the video feed, the dazzling quality of his eyes was unmistakable. The warehouse had been transformed into a makeshift temple, with rows of people sitting reverently before a stage. The air hummed with anticipation.

On the platform next to Elijah was a tall cylindrical object covered by a large velvet sheet. Elijah raised his hands, silencing the murmurs of the crowd.

"Brothers and sisters," Elijah began, his voice resonating with fervor, "today is a momentous day. A day of victory, of divine providence. The Celestial Architects have seen fit to bless us with their power, guiding us toward perfection."

The crowd erupted in cheers and applause. Elijah waited for the noise to subside before continuing.

"For too long, humanity has wallowed in ignorance and mediocrity. But we, the Ascendants, have been chosen to transcend. To become more than human. The Architects have revealed to us the path to enlightenment, and today, we take another step on that journey."

Douglas watched, his heart pounding, as Elijah's hands moved to the velvet sheet. With a dramatic flourish, he pulled it away, revealing the tall cylindrical object underneath. Inside the suspension tube was a nearly naked young woman, her body contorted and struggling. A black helmet enclosed her head, hiding her features but not her fear.

Elijah approached the control panel connected to the tube, holding up the crystal. "Behold the instrument of our celestial ascent," he proclaimed. "With this crystal, we shall harness the power of the fifth force. Through sacrifice, we shall be purified."

He inserted the crystal into the control panel. Instantly, the woman's body began to convulse, her limbs thrashing against the confines of the tube. A low hum filled the air, growing in intensity as the power surged through her. The crowd began to chant, their voices rising in unison, hands lifted toward the heavens.

"Purify us, O Architects! Elevate us beyond our mortal coil!"

Douglas felt a sickening churn in his stomach as he watched the woman suffer. Her convulsions grew more violent, her body writhing in agony. Elijah stood before the control panel, his face a mask of glee.

"This is the path to enlightenment," Elijah continued, his voice rising above the cacophony. "Through the crucible of suffering, we shall emerge as beings of light and power. The Celestial Architects demand our devotion, our sacrifice. And in return, they grant us their divine essence."

Finally, he pressed a button labeled "purge." The woman's body tensed one last time before going still, her struggles ceasing abruptly. From a hose connected to the tube, a violet liquid began to pour, filling a tiny cup placed beneath it.

Elijah raised the cup, holding it up to the light. The look on his face was one of elation and triumph, as if he were holding the very essence of divinity itself.

"Behold the Master's blessing," he declared. "Through this, we become one with the Architects."

He brought the cup to his lips and drank. The effect was immediate and powerful. Elijah's body shuddered, and he nearly stumbled, but caught himself. When he looked up again, his eyes shone like two brilliant sapphires, glowing with an unearthly light. This wasn't your run-of-the-mill Drahk'noth. The crystal's power had altered it, corrupted it and made it infinitely more powerful.

The crowd erupted into a fervent frenzy, their chanting reaching a fever pitch. Douglas felt a cold dread settle over him. His mind raced as he watched Elijah bask in the adoration of his followers. This was beyond anything he had anticipated. The level of devotion, the willingness to sacrifice, and the sheer power Elijah now wielded were terrifying beyond measure.

"How many cops and agents are taking part in the raid?" Jason asked, his worried gaze never leaving the screen.

Douglas swallowed hard. "I'm not sure, but something tells me not nearly enough."

As they continued to watch, they witnessed the transformation in Elijah's demeanor. The man's movements had become more fluid, his presence more commanding. It was as if he was truly becoming something more than human.

Chapter 48

Ixchara, Guatemala

The large teardrop-shaped craft skimmed over the thick Guatemalan jungle, hunting for signs of fifth force radiation.

Shepard, Sam and Gorian were on the bridge eyeing the viewscreen. Around them, Council ensigns manned various flight control stations as they navigated the ship. They wore light blue uniforms with a two-headed snake over their right breast. Apart from the odd permutation here or there, they appeared almost entirely human.

"Sir," one of them called out. "I've just detected a reading three miles south of us."

"Let's have a look," Gorian said, motioning forward.

The ship made a ninety-degree turn and was over the target in a flash. And yet, for those inside its inertial bubble, it felt as though they were stationary.

Below them, sticking out from a thick canopy of tropical foliage, was the crest of a weathered pyramid. It was nearly indistinguishable in the vast sea of greenery.

"Ixchara," Shepard whispered. "Until now, it's been nothing but the stuff of legends. A Mayan pyramid lost to time and reclaimed by the jungle now for many hundreds of years. You wouldn't believe how many archeological teams have set out searching for this place, only to come up empty."

"The burial place of the legendary ruler, Itzamna," Gorian said with a smile. "You're not the only one who knows your Mayan history."

She nodded. "His name means 'wise one.' And yet, according to the legends, he was buried with all of the men and women who built his final resting place because they'd been cursed."

This caught Gorian's attention. "Seems a little ironic that the wise one's final resting place should have such a horrible legacy, don't you think?"

"Human history is filled with contradictions, I'm afraid."

The craft set down in a clearing not far away. Gorian brought them to a room on board where they could get equipped. "Qu'el here will provide whatever you need."

Qu'el smiled. He was muscular with light hair and sharp eyes. "You'll need a weapon and some protection from any fifth force radiation," he told her.

"I'm guessing you don't have any extra MAGsuits lying around."

He grinned, a little puzzled by her comment. "No, but we can give you what we use." He handed her a belt with a flat, square-shaped device.

"What's this?" she asked, securing it around her waist.

He tapped it once and Shepard's body was suddenly surrounded by a shimmering field of energy. Qu'el took a glowing bladed weapon off the wall and swung it at her. She lunged back, but the blade struck the force field just above the knee, shooting off sparks.

Sam's eyes went wide.

So too did Shepard's. "Wow, that's quite impressive."

"The system can differentiate hostile from friendly action and will block or allow accordingly. Go ahead, try and turn it off."

Shepard reached down to the device on her belt and went to press it, expecting resistance. And yet she felt none. The field turned off.

Qu'el handed a field generator to Sam. He then gave both of them earpieces and glasses. "The earbuds we'll use to communicate while inside the temple."

"And the glasses?" she asked.

"We've retrofitted them to sync with any man-made AI systems you may be using."

Shepard put both on. She then tapped her other ear, bringing RUTH back online.

"Hello, Dr. Shepard, great to be with you again. I've detected eyewear units. Would you like me to add them to your devices?"

"Yes, please." Shepard glanced around the room. "Tell me if you can see okay?"

RUTH locked onto Sam's aging face. "Oh," the AI said, startled. "Who's the old fogey?"

"Excuse me?" Shepard said, horrified, before the realization struck her. "She's practicing her slang."

"Yes, apologies if you were offended, Samuel."

Sam waved. His hands were wrinkled now and he had the general appearance of someone in their seventies. "None taken."

RUTH turned her attention back to Shepard. "I'm sensing heightened vitals. Are we heading on another expedition?"

"Yes, RUTH," Shepard replied. "And the last time I was in Guatemala at a site very much like this one, let's just say things didn't go very well."

"I'm sorry to hear that," RUTH said, commiserating. "But back then you were missing a very important ingredient."

"Patience?" Shepard asked, not liking where this was heading.

"Me," RUTH said and in her mind's eye Shepard could almost see the AI smiling.

"Proud of yourself, aren't you?" Shepard asked.

"I try."

Qu'el disappeared around the corner for a moment and returned with what looked like a sleek rifle. "It's no showstopper, but it'll take down just about anything that comes at you."

For Sam, Qu'el provided an energy pistol and holster. "You've used one of these before, haven't you?" the armorer asked.

Sam nodded. "Of course."

Qu'el then suited up before excusing himself.

Shepard turned to Sam. "I'm proud of you," she told him.

Sam looked at her quizzically. "You are? For what?"

"You've never shot a weapon in your life, have you?"

He shook his head.

"You lied," she added.

Sam glanced around, feeling guilty. "I suppose I did. But I don't get it. You're proud that I lied?"

"No," she said. "I'm proud you're finally getting in touch with your human side."

•••

The trek through the jungle was arduous, the dense foliage making every step a struggle. Shepard led the way with Sam close behind, followed by Qu'el, Gorian, and at least twenty Council soldiers. The ruins of the ancient Mayan temple emerged from the undergrowth like a sleeping giant. The once-majestic structure was now discolored and worn, vines and tree roots growing up its sides, intertwining with the stone like a constricting serpent.

Qu'el held out a scanner, its display flickering with readings. "I'm picking up what might be an entrance," he said, moving closer to a thick stone slab that sealed off a section of the temple. The stone was ancient, with faint carvings that had long since faded into obscurity.

Council soldiers advanced to place charges around the edges of the slab. Shepard watched as the substance began to sizzle and smoke, eating away at the stone. Within moments, the slab dissolved, revealing a dark, narrow passageway beyond.

The group proceeded cautiously inside. The air was cool and damp, carrying the scent of earth and decay. The sound of dripping water could be heard in the distance. The walls were rough and cold to the touch, covered in a layer of moisture that made them slick.

Qu'el continued to scan the surroundings, his eyes fixed on the device. "I'm picking up lifeforms," he reported, his voice tinged with concern. "The signal is weak, but they're definitely here."

Gorian scoffed, dismissing the warning with a wave of his hand. "Probably some wildlife that's gotten in. Nothing we can't handle."

Shepard glanced at the armorer, her brow furrowed. "What's the concentration of fifth force radiation you're picking up?"

Gorian checked his own scanner, the readings flashing across the screen. "Enough that you wouldn't want to be in here without an energy field protecting you."

The group moved deeper into the temple, their senses heightened. The passageway twisted and turned, leading them further into the heart of the ancient structure. The flickering light from their energy weapons cast eerie shadows on the walls, creating the illusion of movement.

As they rounded a corner, the passage opened into a larger chamber. The walls here were covered in more intricate carvings, depicting scenes of sacrifice and reverence. The chamber was lit by a faint, unnatural glow, emanating from the stone itself.

Qu'el scanned the room, his device beeping softly. "The lifeforms are closer now," he said, his voice barely above a whisper. "But the signal is still weak."

Shepard felt a chill run down her spine. "Stay alert," she warned, scanning the room for any signs of danger. The group spread out, their movements cautious and deliberate. The silence was deafening, each step echoing through the chamber like a drumbeat.

From here, the tomb descended into a wider, labyrinthian area, with small rooms lining the winding never-ending corridors. More carvings appeared, but these ones weren't of words, but of people. One of them Shepard was certain depicted Thalor and his brother Aloine.

"It's Endarian," Gorian said, glancing around with an air of reverence.

Shepard activated her comms. "RUTH, please start compiling."

RUTH's voice came through clearly. "Yes, Dr. Shepard. From what I can see, the walls in this section are recounting the rise and fall of the Endarian civilization."

"Any clues yet on where the rest of the forge might be?" Shepard asked.

"Not yet, I'm afraid," RUTH replied. "I'm still compiling data and will let you know if I find anything useful."

It wasn't long before the group came to a narrow walkway that spanned an empty chasm. The void below was so deep that their lights were swallowed whole, leaving the depths shrouded in impenetrable darkness. The walkway, made of ancient stone, looked precarious, its edges crumbling slightly under their weight.

Shepard turned to Sam, her expression serious. "Look straight ahead, Sam. Don't look down, no matter what."

Sam nodded, his face pale but determined. They began to cross, their footsteps echoing ominously in the cavernous space. The air was thick with tension, each step feeling like it could be their last.

It was nerve-wracking, the vast emptiness below seeming to pull at them, trying to drag them into the abyss. The walkway seemed to narrow with every step, the darkness below yawning hungrily.

Halfway across, a Council soldier lost his footing, his boot slipping on the worn stone. He teetered on the edge, arms flailing for balance. Panic flashed in his eyes as he began to fall, a cry escaping his lips.

Shepard froze, unable to stop seeing the face of her colleague Joel disappearing into the darkness all those years ago.

Qu'el, quick as lightning, lunged forward and grabbed hold of the soldier's arm. "Hold on! I've got you!" he shouted, pulling the soldier back to safety.

The soldier, pale and shaken, nodded gratefully, clutching Qu'el's arm for support. The group continued, their resolve strengthened by the close call. Each step was taken with the utmost caution, their breaths held until they reached the other side.

As they stepped off the walkway, they found themselves in an open plaza. The floor beneath them was an intricate and beautiful mosaic, depicting scenes of a long-lost civilization. The vibrant colors and detailed designs were a stark contrast to the dark, foreboding chasm they had just crossed.

On three sides of the plaza were rooms and apartment complexes carved into the stone. It was clear now that this was no mere temple; it was an underground city. The walls of the structures were adorned with carvings and symbols, telling the story of the people who had once lived here.

Regaining her composure, Shepard looked around in awe, her fear from earlier melting away as she took in the incredible sight. "This place... it's unbelievable," she whispered, her voice filled with wonder.

For a moment, the group allowed themselves to marvel at the beauty and mystery of the underground city.

"How much more is there?" Sam asked, gripping one of his tired knees.

"Hold up for a second," Shepard called out to the others, tending to him.

"Maybe I just need to sit for a second," he said, motioning to a slab of stone sticking out from a nearby wall.

Shepard brought him over there.

"Yes, that's more like it."

Glancing behind her, she noticed half of the Council soldiers were gone. Concerned, she turned to Gorian. "Where are the others?"

Gorian's expression remained calm. "I sent them off to hunt for the source of the energy reading. It's the only way we'll find what we're looking for."

Shepard nodded but couldn't shake the uneasy feeling gnawing at her. As they moved forward, she caught a glimpse of something white in the distance, flitting past a doorway. She stopped and aimed her light, trying to make sense of what she had seen.

"Did anyone else catch that?" she asked, her voice a little shaky.

Qu'el checked his sensors. "Sensors are much cleaner now. The beam must have been bouncing off the walls up there, giving a false reading."

Shepard shook her head, trying to dismiss her anxiety. Was she just freaking herself out? The further they went, the more the tension in the air grew. The carved walls seemed to watch them, recounting the ancient tales of the Endarians.

With Sam rested, the group pressed on, their footsteps echoing in the vast emptiness. The wide-open spaces swallowed the light from their torches, creating an almost tangible darkness. Every sound, every movement seemed amplified, making the hairs on the back of Shepard's neck stand on end.

For that reason, she kept close to Sam. He was looking a lot more pale than usual, his eyes darting around nervously. "I think someone's down here with us," he said, fear in his throat, his hand resting on the grip of his pistol.

"Someone or something," Shepard wondered, more to herself.

That was when the communicator came to life. The message was garbled and filled with static. But even through the interference, Shepard could make out the voices on the other end and they were filled with terror.

Chapter 49

A strange noise pierced the stillness, a screeching and clicking that seemed to come from all directions at once. Shepard paused, her heart pounding in her chest. Soon, the others heard it too. The sound grew louder, more insistent, echoing off the stone walls of the underground city. Qu'el's eyes widened as he checked his sensor, which was currently going haywire.

"There are strong signals coming from all around us," he called out, his posture rigid.

Before they could react, Council soldiers came running toward them from beyond the narrow walkway they had just crossed, their faces contorted with fear.

"They're coming! They're coming!" the soldiers screamed.

A second later, Shepard and the others saw what was chasing them—the creatures from the depths, fast and nimble, their bodies a nightmarish blend of sinew and bone. They made that same strange clicking and screeching sound as they closed the distance with terrifying speed.

One soldier spun around on the walkway, raising his energy weapon to fire. But before he could pull the trigger, a creature lunged at him, its clawed hand slashing through the air. The blow knocked him aside, sending

271

him tumbling into the darkness below, his scream echoing as he fell.

Moments later, more of the white creatures emerged from the recessed structures around the plaza. They charged in, their bodies stark against the dim light. Their skin was milky white and almost translucent, with thin but powerful limbs ending in long, razor-sharp claws. Their faces were eyeless, blank slates that added to their eerie appearance. They moved with a terrifying grace, their bodies contorting in unnatural ways as they closed in on the group.

Within seconds, the plaza erupted into chaos. Everyone was firing their energy weapons, trying to fend off the onslaught. Beams of light cut through the darkness.

Shepard fired her weapon, hitting one of the creatures square in the chest. It stumbled back, a hole burned through its torso, but then it started to get up, the wound healing rapidly. She glanced at Sam, who was doing his best to keep up, his pale face filling with fear. "Are you seeing this?" Shepard cried out, trying to stem the panic bubbling up inside of her.

"Keep firing!" Gorian shouted, his voice cutting through the din. "Don't let them surround us!"

Qu'el's field generator buzzed as a creature slammed into him, knocking him to the ground. He rolled away, his shield absorbing the impact, and fired a shot that took off the creature's arm. It screeched and writhed, a dark liquid spurting from the stump.

"They won't stay down!" Qu'el yelled, scrambling back to his feet.

The creatures were everywhere, swarming from all sides. Shepard saw one leap from a nearby building, landing on a Council soldier with a sickening thud. The soldier's shield held, but the force of the impact sent him sprawling. Another creature pounced, its claws raking against the shield, trying to get through. Eventually, it gave way and the soldier shrieked in agony as he was torn apart.

Sam was surrounded by three of the creatures, their eyeless faces turned toward him as they clicked and screeched. He raised his hand, and a burst of blue energy shot out, knocking them back. But they were relentless, getting up almost immediately, their bodies twisting unnaturally as they resumed their attack.

One of the monstrosities lunged at Shepard, its claws outstretched. She sidestepped, feeling the rush of air as it missed her by inches. She fired point blank, sending it crashing to the ground. But even as it lay there, its body began to knit itself back together.

They reached the far side of the plaza, finding temporary refuge behind a large stone structure. The creatures hesitated, clicking and screeching as if sensing their prey was momentarily out of reach.

"We can't keep this up," Qu'el said, breathing heavily. "There are too many of them."

Shepard nodded, her mind racing. "We need to find a way to stop them. There's got to be something we're missing."

The creatures gathered at the edge of the plaza, their eyeless faces turned toward the group, waiting for their next move. The eerie silence that followed was almost worse than the noise, the anticipation of the next wave hanging heavy in the air.

"Whatever it is," Gorian said, gripping his weapon tightly, "I suggest we figure it out fast."

Screeches echoed off the stone walls. Shepard tensed, scanning for any sign of an opening.

As if on cue, a burst of gunfire erupted from behind the creatures. Peters, Nash, Jake, Dr. Singh, Mateo, and a few dozen airmen stormed into the plaza, weapons blazing. The airmen wore MAGsuits, their sleek, armored exoskeletons glistening in the dim light. Energy blasts and bullets tore through the air, cutting through the creatures with relentless precision.

Peters led the charge, his pulse rifle spitting brilliant bolts that dismembered one of the creatures. It fell to the ground, thrashing as it tried to regenerate. Nash followed behind, his pulse rifle mowing down another creature that leaped at him from the shadows. Jake and Mateo flanked them, their weapons adding to the barrage.

Dr. Singh stayed near the rear, a plasma pistol in one hand while he used his other to adjust a portable scanner. "Aim for the head!" he called out.

The creatures, though formidable, were not invincible. Limbs were severed and bodies were torn apart. Some of the creatures fell, their regenerative abilities overwhelmed by the sustained fire. Others, seeing their numbers dwindling, began to retreat back into the recesses of the underground city.

Gorian and his Council soldiers pressed the advantage, their weapons flaring as they drove the creatures back. Shepard and Sam fought side by side, their resolve unwavering as they cut down the enemies that dared to come close.

A creature lunged at Peters, its claws extended. He sidestepped and swung his weapon like a club, smashing it across the face. The creature staggered, and he fired a point-blank shot, sending it sprawling.

"Nash, swing left!" Peters shouted. "Don't give them a chance to regroup!"

The heavy weapons operator did just that, switching to his portable Gatling gun and opening up. A single deadly volley tore a creature's legs out from under it, leaving it squirming on the ground where Nash finished it off.

The combined might of the Council soldiers and the airmen turned the tide. The creatures, now outnumbered and outgunned, retreated fully into the darkness, their screeches fading into the distance.

Silence fell over the plaza, broken only by the heavy breathing of the soldiers and the hum of their equipment.

Shepard wiped the sweat from her brow, scanning the area for any remaining threats. "Is everyone all right?" she called out.

"Bruised and battered," Nash replied, helping a fellow airman to his feet. "But most of us made it."

The plaza resembled a medieval battlefield, a grisly tableau of death and destruction. Dozens of the pale, sinewy fiends lay in twisted heaps, their blood pooling on the intricate mosaic floor. Among them were the bodies of a handful of Council soldiers, their energy weapons still clutched in lifeless hands. The air was thick with the metallic scent of blood and the acrid tang of spent energy charges. The once-serene and ancient underground city was now marred by the remnants of a fierce battle, a stark reminder of the cost of their mission.

The medics in the group quickly dispersed to care for the wounded. Peters found Shepard at once and touched her shoulder. The reverberation from her energy field knocked his hand away. The sight made her laugh. "I guess you'll need to wait till later to arrest me."

He joined her in laughter, despite the hint of sadness dancing in his eyes.

"What's wrong?" she asked.

"You were right," he told her. "About the ambush." He grew quiet for a moment.

She looked around, noticing someone was missing. "Hey, where's Alvarez?"

Peters shook his head. "Probably in surgery right now. He got shot during the ambush. The doc said an inch in either direction and he might have been a goner."

She shook her head in disgust. "Dammit! Why didn't you stop the operation?"

"I tried," Peters insisted. "Believe me. But Bradshaw wasn't willing to take the chance."

She thought she understood perfectly. "The intel wasn't trustworthy enough, I take it?"

"It wasn't that I didn't believe you. It's just—"

She cut him off. "Your duty to the flag and the chain of command. I get it."

They locked eyes. "It's a strength, you know. Not a handicap."

"Tell that to Alvarez's family." She realized at once how harsh that had sounded. "Listen, I'm sorry. And thank you." She motioned to the chaotic surroundings. "Without you guys, I'm not sure we would have made it."

The light had returned to Peters' eyes. "First thing I saw when we arrived was Sam blasting away."

Shepard turned to Sam, who looked exhausted but unyielding. "He's right. You did well, Sam."

He nodded, managing a faint smile. "Thanks. I suppose I can still surprise myself sometimes."

Dr. Singh approached, his scanner beeping. "We need to move fast. There could be more of them."

276

"Agreed," Gorian said, his tone somber. "Gather your things and move out."

Peters gave a similar order to his men.

Between two of the recessed dwellings was an archway that led to another part of the temple. Clutching her weapon, Shepard and the others pushed on, distinctly aware they were being watched.

Chapter 50

Outside the Safe Harbor warehouse, the FBI and police tactical teams prepared to breach the building, their movements synchronized and purposeful.

Douglas, standing near the building's main entrance, gave the order, his voice steady despite the tension that gripped him. "All teams move in."

In one coordinated move, they all surged forward, breaching several entrances at the same time. Inside, chaos erupted. Elijah's followers, dressed in dark, nondescript clothing, appeared almost immediately, their eyes wild with rage, their movements unnaturally swift and precise. They met the intruders with a ferocity that took the tactical teams by surprise.

The battle was immediate and intense. Cult members, their bodies augmented no doubt by Drahk'noth, fought with a brutal efficiency that made them nearly impervious to pain. Bullets seemed to slow them but not stop them, and their strength was far beyond that of a normal human. One officer fired point blank into a cult member's chest, only to watch in horror as the man continued to advance, his face twisted in a snarl.

Douglas tried to ignore the knot tightening in his stomach. These weren't just fanatics; they were something more. He scanned the dozens of individual battles going on all around him, looking for anything that might give his team an edge. A cult member flinched and covered his ears as a high-pitched feedback squeal emanated from a nearby radio.

"That's it," Douglas muttered to himself, eyes widening with realization. He grabbed his radio and issued a quick command. "Use flashbangs and sirens. High-frequency sounds seem to affect them. Repeat, high-frequency sounds."

The tactical teams adapted quickly, deploying flashbang grenades and turning on high-pitched sirens. The effect was immediate. Cult members recoiled, their hands flying to their ears, their faces contorting in pain. This gave the FBI and police a crucial opening. They pressed their advantage, pushing the cultists back inch by inch.

Just when it seemed the tide might turn in their favor, a new wave of cult members surged forward, driving the tactical teams back. The warehouse was a battlefield, littered with debris and echoing with the sounds of gunfire and screams.

In the midst of the chaos, a figure moved with lethal grace, taking out cult members with a combination of precise gunfire and brutal hand-to-hand combat. It was Desiree. She had followed her own leads to the Safe Harbor warehouse, and now she was fighting alongside them.

He couldn't help but admire her skill as she made her way towards him, cutting through the chaos. "Nice of you to join us," Douglas said as she reached him, a grim smile on his face.

"Couldn't let you have all the fun," Desiree replied, scanning the battlefield. "What's the plan?"

"Keep them off balance with the high-frequency sounds," Douglas said, gesturing to the tactical teams. "It's their weakness."

Desiree nodded, her expression hardening.

Together, they moved back into the fray, coordinating their efforts. Flashbangs and sirens continued to disorient the cult members, allowing the police and FBI to keep them off balance.

As the chaos raged on, Douglas couldn't shake the feeling that this wasn't going to end well. The cult's strength was formidable, but so was their resolve. They would fight to the bitter end, driven by Elijah's twisted vision.

But with Desiree by his side and a newfound understanding of their enemy's weakness, Douglas felt a renewed sense of purpose. They would take down Elijah and his followers, no matter the cost.

"Where's Elijah?" she asked, scanning the room with sharp eyes.

Douglas caught sight of him in the distance, ducking into one of the side rooms.

With a few team members in tow, Douglas and Desiree maneuvered through the melee, edging closer to their target. The path was fraught with peril, cultists lunging and firing at them from all directions. Douglas stopped and took cover behind a stack of wooden crates, firing his weapon to cover Desiree as she moved forward.

They reached a reinforced door near the back of the warehouse. One of the FBI agents planted a breaching charge. Moments later, the detonation went off with a deafening roar, blowing the door inward and revealing a room filled with dozens of isolation tubes. Inside of each was a human figure. More tubes filled a raised platform in the rear of the chamber. That was where Elijah stood, desperately working the buttons on a console.

"Elijah, it's over!" Douglas shouted, stepping forward. "Stand down, and no one else has to get hurt."

Elijah's smile widened. "You underestimate the power I now possess," he said, holding the control panel aloft. In the center, the Endarian crystal glowed ominously.

With a flourish, Elijah pressed the purge button. Inside the tube, the woman's body convulsed violently, the energy coursing through her with terrifying intensity. A second later, he pressed a cup beneath a spigot.

Douglas and Desiree exchanged a tense glance.

"We have to stop him," she said, realizing what might happen if he drank that liquid.

Douglas raised his weapon and fired, missing.

Elijah brought the cup to his lips, the violet liquid running down the sides of his face. "Behold the future!" Elijah bellowed, his eyes like two black holes, sucking in all the light in the room. The cult leader raised his hands and a wave of force emanated from him, sending Douglas and his team sprawling.

Regaining their footing, the police and FBI agents opened fire. But their bullets stopped inches from his body, as though stuck in a gravity well. There they spun harmlessly before tumbling to the ground.

Desiree lunged forward, and Elijah swatted her aside with a casual flick of his wrist. She crashed into the wall, groaning in pain. "Douglas, we need a plan," she gasped.

Douglas nodded, his mind racing. Elijah's powers were formidable, but they had to find a way to exploit a weakness. "Keep him distracted," he said, moving to flank their adversary.

Elijah laughed, a chilling sound that echoed through the room. "You think you understand power? I am the force that bends reality itself!"

While Elijah's attention was focused on Douglas and the police, Desiree took advantage of the distraction. She moved with fluid grace, slipping behind the cult leader. Her eyes locked onto the glowing crystal in the console. With dexterity and speed, she yanked the crystal from the console, her fingers wrapping around it tightly.

Elijah whirled, his eyes wide with fury. "You dare to take what's mine?" he bellowed, raising his hand to strike her with a fresh blast of energy.

Desiree inserted the crystal into the energy baton, but Elijah's attack hit her squarely in the chest, dropping her to her knees. The intensity was overwhelming. He was killing her.

The FBI agent sprinted toward them right as Desiree flung the baton in Douglas' direction. A split second later, she collapsed.

Douglas caught it, his grip tightening around the handle as the crystal glowed.

Elijah's face twisted with rage as he saw the weapon in Douglas's hands. "You want some too?" Elijah roared, reaching out to unleash a torrent of dark energy towards Douglas.

But Douglas was faster, striking him with the baton's now vastly improved power. The force of the contact sent a concussive blast through the room. Elijah was thrown back with immense force, his body crashing through an empty isolation tank, shattering glass and spilling liquid everywhere. He continued his trajectory, smashing through a cinderblock wall with a deafening crunch.

The room fell silent, the aftermath of the battle leaving the air thick with tension and dust. Douglas stood panting, the baton still humming with residual energy. He looked over at Desiree, who lay lifeless at his feet. He knelt beside her. "Stay with me," he pleaded, but her eyes were already closing.

She managed a weak smile. "We did it," she whispered, her voice barely audible.

Douglas held her hand as she slipped away. A tear fell from his eye and onto her cheek, where it hung for a moment before sliding out of sight.

"He's not dead," one of the officers shouted.

Douglas glanced up and caught a flicker of movement over where Elijah lay. He and other officers hurried over. The cop was right. Elijah was still alive, his chest rising and falling in shallow breaths. The energy baton at the ready, Douglas quickly realized the cult leader was no longer a threat. Elijah's eyes, once filled with malevolent energy, were now clouded with delusion and pain.

His thin lips twitched into a weak, deranged smile. "I'm coming to join you, Master," Elijah whispered, his voice barely audible. "On Enceladus, we will be together again for eternity."

Elijah's eyes closed, his body finally going still.

Griscole arrived carrying a containment unit that had housed the crystal. Carefully, they detached it from the baton and placed it inside. Douglas watched as shimmering blue light danced tantalizingly through the viewport. "Do me a favor, call Commander Bradshaw at Joint Base Andrews and tell them we have their stolen artifact."

Griscole turned. "Where are you going?"

Douglas was heading back to collect Desiree's body. "It's time I paid my respects to a fallen…" He paused, searching for the right words. Then finally he found them. "Family member."

Chapter 51

Ixchara, Guatemala

As they navigated over the rubble of a collapsed pillar, RUTH's voice chimed in through Shepard's earpiece. "I should let you know, the markings in this new area mention Aloine seventy-six percent more often than in earlier sections of the temple. Therefore, I am confident we are heading in the right direction."

Peters glanced around, taking in the ancient architecture. "Whoever built this place sure was ahead of their time."

Nash nodded, inspecting the intricate carvings. "Endarian technology probably helped."

She paused, her voice lowering. "Of course, there's also a darker side to its history. Legends speak of a grisly past following the temple's completion, something that probably led to the rumors of it being cursed and its eventual abandonment."

Jake chimed in. "I'm not surprised they deserted the place. It's filled with bloodthirsty monsters that won't die."

From the back, Mateo had a realization of his own. "There's little doubt fifth force radiation exposure was the cause of the creatures' mutations and their superb healing abilities. Remember the young airman we rescued from the anomaly in Atacama? Radiation exposure completely healed his wounds."

Singh nodded. "Yes, you're right. What's strange is I studied one of the creatures' severed limbs, one of its hands, and it appeared to be human."

Suddenly, Shepard was struck with something. "The temple builders were sealed in after construction because they'd been cursed. But what if they had already started showing signs of radiation poisoning? Strange mutations that frightened the local population, leading to them being locked inside the temple?"

Jake's eyes widened. "Are you saying these things we've been fighting were once human beings?"

The thought was almost too horrible to contemplate, but Shepard nodded. "Hundreds of years of exposure must have turned them into monsters."

They continued walking, the revelation hanging heavy in the air. Soon they reached a large stone wall. In front of it was a glass-covered pod containing a seat. Beside the pod stood a stand with an octagonal readout.

Nash frowned, a sense of foreboding washing over him. "I have a bad feeling about this."

The group gathered around the peculiar setup, the air thick with tension, the low hum of the field generators creating an almost otherworldly atmosphere. The intricate carvings on the stone wall seemed to pulsate with an ancient energy, reflecting the light from their equipment.

Shepard examined both the pod and the pad. "This must be the entrance to Aloine's tomb."

Gorian stepped forward, scanning the area with a device. "The radiation levels are high, but with our fields, we should be protected."

Eyeing the pad, Qu'el frowned. "It looks like a control panel, but there's no obvious way to activate it."

On a whim, Peters approached and slid his gloved hand into the depression. He left it there for several seconds, but nothing happened.

"Maybe it requires an Endarian touch," Shepard said, looking at Sam. "Wanna give it a shot?"

He nodded. "Why not?"

With slow, labored steps, Sam approached the pad, his hand hovering over the surface. A second before he did so, he shut off his shield generator.

"Sam, stop!" Shepard shouted. "You'll be irradiated."

"It's okay," he said as he placed his hand on the pad. No sooner had his skin made contact than a soft glow began emanating from the stand. It spread rapidly across the floor, illuminating the stone wall with a cascade of ancient symbols. Once dormant, the pod now also hummed to life.

Suddenly, large letters in the Endarian script were projected onto the stone wall. It took less than a second for RUTH to translate what was before them. "'The greatest act of strength is to offer oneself, expecting nothing in return.' It appears to be a quote of some kind," the AI said.

"Cute," Jake scoffed. "It might not get us inside, but it'll sure brighten your day."

Just then, the pod's glass door opened with a whoosh. They stepped back, alarmed.

"The heck is going on here?" Nash demanded.

"'Offer oneself for nothing in return,'" Shepard quoted. "If I didn't know any better, I'd say they were asking for a sacrifice."

Mateo's expression became grave. "Given the Mayans' history, that wouldn't be completely unheard of."

"Whoever among you is expendable, please step forward," Gorian said, his tone almost amused.

"Perhaps we should decide by age," Peters suggested, glancing at the wary faces around him. "Who's the oldest one here?"

Most of the guards on both sides were young.

"They don't call you Elder Gorian for nothing," Jake said, shrugging. "I'm just saying."

"This is ridiculous," Gorian shot back. "Why would my life be worth less than any of yours?"

Sam stepped forward. "I'll go."

"Not a chance," Shepard said, cutting him off. She pushed past Peters and jumped into the pod, deactivating her force field.

Jake, Peters and Nash all sprang to stop her, but the glass door was already closing before they had a chance. She pressed her fingers against the glass and Peters did the same. "Don't do this," he begged her. "There's got to be another way."

Green mist began filling the pod. Purely on instinct, Shepard drew in a deep lungful of air. But Peters wasn't playing any longer. He brought his fist down on the glass, trying to shatter it. The pod continued to fill with smoke until Shepard was no longer visible. He leveled his rifle and squeezed the trigger. At the last second, Jake knocked it away, the pulse beam going wide.

"The hell are you doing?" Peters shouted, desperation in his voice.

"Are you mad?" Jake shot back. "You would have cut her in two."

A moment later, the green mist retreated, revealing Shepard. She lay in the pod, unmoving.

New words were projected on the door. RUTH translated. "'A sacrifice has been made.'"

And with that, the stone slab began to disappear into a recessed part of the wall.

At the same time, the pod door began to rise. Peters reached in and scooped Shepard out at once. He tried to check her vitals and begin chest compressions if necessary, but something was blocking him.

"Her shield generator's still on," he said in surprise. "She must have put it back on after entering the pod." Sam bent down next to him. But the others were busy staring into Aloine's tomb. "You people make me sick," he snarled.

A hand touched the side of his helmet. He followed it all the way down to Shepard. Her eyes were open, staring at him.

"You're alive?" he chanted joyfully.

She sat up. "It was a test," she said, shaking the cobwebs loose in her head. "Not of bravery, but of faith and conviction."

"And stubbornness too," Peters said, helping Shepard to her feet.

Together they stood with the others, staring inside the immense rounded crypt chamber. In the center was what looked like a cryounit standing upright. Inside was the figure of a man with an elongated skull. Was he dead or merely asleep? It was impossible to tell. Yet he was far from bone and ash. He was fully formed and bore a striking resemblance to Thalor.

"This must be Aloine," Gorian exclaimed.

Surrounding him were piles of offerings and items he was meant to enjoy in the afterlife. One of those stood out, its shape much larger than the others, its edges smooth and rounded. But it was obvious this particular object wasn't an offering.

It was the other half of the forge they'd been searching for.

Chapter 52

Jake and Nash cautiously approached the cryochamber, their flashlights casting eerie glows on the ancient walls. The figure inside lay motionless, his features serene and reminiscent of Thalor, but with an ethereal quality that suggested an otherworldly presence.

"This is incredible," Jake muttered, sweat running down his forehead. "Can't tell if this guy's alive or not."

Nash nodded, peering closer. "It's like he's in some kind of suspended animation."

Meanwhile, Shepard, Peters, and Mateo made their way to the other side of the tomb, where the forge's other half stood. Its smooth, rounded edges were a stark contrast to the ancient relics around it. A faint light glowed from its internal mechanism, indicating it was still operational. They shared a look of relief.

"This is it," Shepard said, eyeing the device's sleek lines. "It's a beautiful sight."

Across the room, Jake called out, "Shepard, any idea if this guy's ever gonna wake up? We've pressed every button and nothing's happening."

Shepard turned to face him, her mind racing. "Aloine might be waiting for some pinnacle event before he reawakens. Didn't Lena mention something about Ascension?"

"Sounds like something out of the Bible," Nash added flippantly.

A light flashed in Peters' eyes. "What are the chances some of the religious figures we've read about throughout history have really been Aloine or others just like him?"

Shepard shook her head. "Intriguing thought. Perhaps he accounts for more than we realize."

Their conversation was abruptly cut short by the sound of shouting from outside the chamber. The crackle of gunfire followed, echoing through the ancient hallways.

With the massive stone door wide open, leaving a gap thirty feet wide, Peters quickly became aware they were in a terrible defensive position. "We need to fortify our defenses, now!" he yelled, rallying the Council troopers and airmen.

As they rushed toward the entrance, they were met with a chaotic scene. The battle outside had intensified, and the once-cohesive line of defense was faltering against a new breed of Drax soldiers. These next-generation Praetorian Guards were unlike anything they had faced before—sleek, powerful androids that cut through their forces with brutal efficiency.

"Take cover!" Peters shouted, diving behind a fallen pillar as a barrage of energy blasts whizzed past. The air was thick with smoke and the acrid smell of burning metal.

Gorian, wielding his energy weapon, stood shoulder to shoulder with Shepard. "We can't let them take the forge or we're done," he growled, his voice filled with frustration.

Qu'el, the Council armorer, was already setting up a defensive position with the remaining troopers. "Hold the line!" he bellowed, his voice cutting through the chaos.

Jake and Nash, having left the cryochamber, joined the fray. "They're getting closer," Jake said, watching as the enemy advanced mercilessly.

The battle raged on, the Council soldiers and airmen fighting desperately to hold their ground. The Drax Praetorian Guards moved with terrifying precision, their attacks relentless.

Suddenly, more Drax soldiers appeared, their sleek forms glinting in the dim light. Shepard's heart sank. These must be the next-generation battle androids Douglas had mentioned. They were more powerful, more lethal than anything Shepard's team had faced before.

"This isn't looking good," Peters muttered, scanning the battlefield.

One of the Praetorian Guards lunged at Shepard, its movements almost too fast to track. She barely managed to deflect the blow with her field generator, the force of the impact sending her sprawling.

"Stay down!" Peters shouted, firing at the advancing android. His shots found their mark, dropping the Drax soldier.

"We can't hold them off much longer!" Gorian yelled, his weapon overheating from continuous fire.

Shepard struggled to her feet, her mind racing for a solution. They needed to find a way to turn the tide of this battle before it was too late.

As the battle intensified, the human and Council troops were forced to retreat deeper into the chamber. The ancient walls reverberated with the sounds of energy blasts and kinetic rounds, the air thick with the acrid smell of gunpowder and ozone. Sam and Shepard dived for cover behind a pile of offerings, doing their best to return fire against the onslaught of Praetorian Guards.

Energy rounds flew across the room, striking the ancient stone and scattering fragments everywhere. A shot ricocheted off Aloine's cryopod, creating a spiderweb crack in the glass. Shepard's heart skipped a beat at the sight, but there was no time to worry about it now.

"Keep firing!" Peters shouted, his voice barely audible over the din of battle. He and the remaining Council soldiers and airmen held their ground, their field generators shimmering as they absorbed the impact of incoming rounds.

The Praetorian Guards, with their sleek, powerful forms, pressed their advantage, forcing their way inside the chamber. Their movements were precise and deadly, each one a calculated strike aimed to incapacitate or kill.

Shepard spotted Ravencroft among the androids, his sinister presence unmistakable. She tried to line up a shot, but the chaos of the battle made it impossible to get a clean aim. Frustration gnawed at her as she ducked back behind cover.

Suddenly, from the shadows at the edges of the chamber came a new threat. The white crypt creatures, with their milky, translucent skin and sharp claws, attacked the Praetorian Guards from the rear. The creatures moved with terrifying speed and agility, their screeching and clicking sounds filling the air.

With ferocity, they hacked and slashed at the robots, tearing off plate armor and cutting hydraulic fluid hoses. The Praetorian Guards, caught off guard by this unexpected assault, faltered under the intensity of the attack.

Seeing the tide turning, Ravencroft pulled two smoke grenades from his belt and tossed them into the chamber. The grenades exploded with a hiss, filling the room with thick, choking smoke. Visibility dropped to zero as rounds continued to fly in all directions.

Shepard struggled to see through the smoke. The sounds of battle became muffled, and for a moment, everything seemed to blur into a disorienting haze.

Moments later, the smoke began to clear. The room, once filled with the cacophony of battle, fell eerily silent. Shepard looked around, trying to make sense of the scene. The Drax Praetorian Guards were gone, their retreat marked by the trail of destruction they left behind. The white crypt creatures had also vanished, their presence now a haunting memory.

Shepard scanned the chamber, relief flooding through her as she saw the forge still standing, its faint light glowing nearby. Aloine's cryopod, though cracked, remained intact. But then she looked down by her side, where Sam had been crouched during the fight. Her heart sank as she realized he was gone.

"Sam!" she called out, her voice echoing in the cavernous chamber. Panic set in as she frantically searched the area, hoping to catch sight of him. "Sam, where are you?"

Peters and the others regrouped, their expressions grim. "We need to find him," Peters said, his voice brimming with anger. "We can't let him fall into their hands."

Shepard nodded, panic quickly giving way to resolve. "Spread out," she ordered. "He can't have gone far."

The team fanned out, their eyes peeled for any sign of Sam. The chamber, now silent and filled with the aftermath of the battle, felt like a tomb more than ever.

After close to an hour of searching, the team had to face the stark realization that Sam was gone. The Drax had taken him.

Chapter 53

Washington, D.C.

Douglas was on his fifth beer when Monique pushed her way into the apartment. The umbrella stand had fallen blocking the door and she had to stoop down and move it out of the way before she could enter. As she did so, her eyes grew wide with shock. "Mr. Dwight Douglas, what on earth is going on here?"

The sink was piled with dishes. On the kitchen table was a half-eaten pizza, the box left open. The coffee table was an even sorrier sight. Two-day-old cereal bowls sat side by side with empty cans of Milwaukee's Best. He hadn't even lifted a finger once to tidy the place since Keller's body had been found.

"There's pizza if you're hungry," he told her. The television was on the sports channel. The Forty-Niners were playing the Seahawks. He thought someone was winning fourteen-zero, but Douglas wasn't really paying attention.

Monique glanced at the pizza again and scoffed. "I don't do pizza, Daddy. And it's stale as all get-out." She cleared a stack of old newspapers off the couch and grabbed a seat.

"You look nice," he said, grinning. "Whatshisface taking you out?"

Her face twisted into a disapproving grimace. "I'm assuming you mean Jamal. And he already took me out to Jordi's. Was lovely. He's waiting in the car downstairs. I told him I'd just be a minute. He insisted we stop by and look in on you."

"He sounds like a keeper," Douglas said, sitting up straight.

"I heard how you caught the guy who killed Keller," Monique said, treading like someone moving carefully through a very dense minefield.

"It all happened so fast, I never had a chance to process it," Douglas said. "I'd been pushing so hard to set things right. To avenge her, I never stopped to... what's that word?"

"Grieve, Daddy." She pushed closer and took one of his hands.

"And your sister," he began.

A complicated array of emotions crossed Monique's face. She shook her head, struggling to maintain her composure. "The funeral was nice."

"That stuff I told you, how she wasn't herself. You remember?"

"How could I forget? You sat me down and told me Desiree was some kind of robot."

"Never mind all that," he said, maybe a little too forcefully. The mist of alcohol floating around him might help loosen the emotions, but it restricted his ability to communicate. "I don't know why I said it."

"It wasn't true, was it?" Monique asked, worried about what he might say.

Douglas shook his head. "Desiree was your sister and she was an amazing person. A principled person. Right up to the end. I just wanted you to know that."

Tears were running down Monique's cheeks now and Douglas reached over to wipe them away. "Your old man can be a real shit sometimes, I know that. I've dropped the ball more than once and you've always been there." He squeezed her hand. "I just hope you can forgive me."

She laughed. "Of course, don't be silly."

"We were four once, our little family. Now we're only two. Time is one of those things you can never get back. What do you say we stop wasting it?"

Monique smiled and kissed him on the cheek. She stood and made her way to the door. "Sleep tight, Daddy. I'll see if I can't swing by tomorrow and help you clean up."

He blew her a kiss as she closed the door.

Slowly, his mind shifted back to the bigger picture. To the ongoing fight over the fate of the human race. And to Elijah's final words, something about rejoining the Master on Enceladus. Along with the crystal, Douglas had also passed along that added bit of intel. Desiree had told him during one of their meetings that the cult leader might just be able to lead them to the Master's secret lair. God willing, she had been right and the collective nightmare they'd all been living would soon be over.

Douglas' gaze fell back to the television once again. He raised his beer. "This one's for you, Agent Keller. And for you, Desiree. Class acts through and through." He took a long swig and then rubbed two fingers together before the screen went black.

Chapter 54

Council Base Command

Shepard, Peters, and the rest of the human delegation disembarked from the Council transport ship into an enormous hangar, this one even larger than the Overwatch base on the moon. The vast docking bay was lined with rows of sleek, silver, egg-shaped craft being serviced by a multitude of humanoid technicians. The hangar was illuminated by a cool, ambient light that cast long shadows across the bustling floor.

Shepard's eyes tracked one of the smaller craft as it lifted off silently and glided effortlessly toward a massive hangar bay door, its metallic surface reflecting the ambient light.

At the same time, another shuttle opened nearby and Isadora disembarked, surrounded by half a dozen Thalasian commanders, all dressed in black. They moved with a coordinated precision, their expressions stern and focused.

Commander Bradshaw appeared next to Shepard. "About Sam," he began.

"I was only trying to protect hi—" she started to explain before he cut her off.

"Peters begged me not to court-martial you. Did you know that?"

"No," she said, eyeing the way his jaw was tensing. "But I'm not surprised. For what it's worth, I appreciate you not throwing me in jail."

"Don't thank me too soon," Bradshaw said coolly. "I haven't made up my mind yet. Either way, we'll discuss all of this later. For now, our focus should be on the mission at hand."

Awaiting them were the Council elders. Lysandros stood at the forefront, his smooth skin and large, wise eyes giving him an air of authority and ancient wisdom. Xiulan, with fish gills on the sides of her neck, exuded a calm and serene presence. Sylas, hairless with a slit mouth and no nose or ears, observed the scene with a detached curiosity. And finally, Naima, with shar-pei-like skin, looked both formidable and thoughtful.

"Where are we?" Shepard asked, looking around in wonder at the bustling activity and the sheer scale of the hangar. They'd been summoned directly from Ixchara by Bradshaw and ordered to accompany Gorian to the rendezvous point.

"You're inside a rather cleverly camouflaged space station," Lysandros explained, his voice resonating with calm authority. "We are currently orbiting Mars. Some of you may know it as the moon Phobos, but there is nothing natural about this celestial body." He then lifted his arms in a friendly gesture. "Welcome, delegations from Earth."

The human delegation exchanged glances, absorbing the enormity of their location. Commander Bradshaw, Dr. Singh, Dr. Mateo, Peters, and the Delta operators, including a patched-up Alvarez, looked around in awe.

Lysandros continued, his voice carrying a grave tone. "What we are about to undertake is of the utmost importance. The Drax have been planning a cataclysmic event, one that would result in the death of your solar system. If they succeed, billions will die, and the Drax will repeat their sick endeavor all over again. It is for these reasons we must act swiftly and decisively."

Isadora, standing with her Thalasian commanders, nodded in agreement. Shepard exchanged a glance with Peters. The gravity of their situation was undeniable, and the stakes had never been higher.

Glancing around, she noticed an important figure was missing. "Where's Elder Gorian?" she wondered aloud.

"He left to attend to some important matters," Lysandros replied.

Commander Bradshaw stepped forward, his face somber. "I've reviewed the plans you submitted. Perhaps now is a good time to go over them."

Lysandros nodded, gesturing for Bradshaw to take the floor. The commander moved to the center of the gathered group, his presence drawing their immediate attention.

"Intelligence gathered by our allies on Earth has revealed the location of the Drax stronghold, perhaps their most closely guarded secret," Bradshaw began, his voice firm and resolute. A holographic display appeared, showing a map of the solar system with a halo around Saturn's icy moon Enceladus.

Murmurs spread through the crowd.

"And it has also become clear over the last few months that the Drax have entered the final stages of their plans for our planet and the solar system it inhabits.

302

As a consequence, they've become overconfident and sloppy, and we plan to take full advantage of that."

A few scattered cheers swept through those gathered, led mainly by Jake. The newfound sense of unity and purpose was undeniable.

"As you know, the element of surprise here is paramount," Bradshaw continued, his gaze sweeping over the assembled soldiers and Council members. "A reality that comes with its own risks. For that reason, we have decided not to conduct any reconnaissance on the oceans beneath Enceladus's frozen outer crust for fear of alerting the Drax. What does that mean? Mainly that we will be going in without any knowledge of the defenses we're likely to encounter, nor the size of the force that will be arrayed against us. Nevertheless, this may be our only chance of defeating the Drax once and for all.

"As we speak," he continued, "Council transports will have landed at key bases around the globe, gathering as many soldiers as we could outfit. With any luck, by this time tomorrow, the Drax will be no more, and humanity will once again be free."

Roaring cheers and applause erupted from the crowd as Bradshaw stepped down, the collective enthusiasm of the assembled forces echoing through the vast hangar.

Shepard exchanged a glance with Peters, who gave her a reassuring nod. The path ahead was fraught with danger, but they were ready. They had to be.

As the applause died down, Lysandros stepped forward once again. "We have one more matter to discuss before we proceed. Although we know little of the Drax's stronghold beneath the oceans of Enceladus, we expect their defenses are likely to be formidable. But we have a plan to counteract them. Isadora and her Thalasian commanders will lead the initial assault, drawing the Drax forces out and weakening their defenses. Once the outer perimeter is breached, our combined forces will move in to secure a landing zone."

Isadora nodded. "We will not fail," she said coolly.

The meeting continued with final preparations and strategic discussions, each member of the delegation sharing their thoughts. As they dispersed to make ready for the impending assault, human and Council forces moved to complete last-minute preparations. Soldiers checked their gear, technicians made final adjustments to their ships, and commanders gave additional instructions to frontline units. The atmosphere was charged with a whole range of emotions.

Shepard took a deep breath. There was much to do before the fleet set off for Saturn's moon and little time to do it.

Chapter 55

Enceladus

Ravencroft entered the throne room, particularly anxious for the conversation that awaited him. The gothic chamber, bathed in a ghostly glow, seemed to pulse with the Master's consciousness. At the center, suspended above a pedestal, was the dark sphere housing the Master's pure consciousness, surrounded by a web of conduits and hoses. Ravencroft advanced slowly, flanked by two Drax Praetorian Guards who carried Sam between them.

Sam, once a child but now appearing as an eighty-year-old man, was frail and weak, his once-bright eyes now clouded with age. His body, stooped and thin, trembled as he was brought before the Master. Ravencroft's heart pounded as he approached the sphere, bowing deeply, his gaze fixed on the ground.

The Master's voice reverberated through the chamber, deep and commanding. "Who is this old man before me?" he demanded, confusion and displeasure evident in his tone.

Ravencroft straightened, trying to maintain his composure. "My liege, this is the one you sought. He was a child not long ago, but he has been aging at an accelerated rate."

The Master's presence seemed to grow, the very air around them thrumming with his scrutiny. "How can I merge with something so old? I asked for a child."

Ravencroft lowered himself even further, desperation creeping into his voice. "I beg your forgiveness, my liege. We did not anticipate this accelerated aging. He was a child when we first encountered him, but it seems the fifth force has affected him in unforeseen ways."

The Master's displeasure was almost palpable, a wave of dark energy that sent a shiver down Ravencroft's spine. "I do not tolerate excuses, Ravencroft. You have failed me once again."

Ravencroft's voice trembled as he spoke. "My liege, there is more. Our spies tell us the humans, along with the Council, have discovered your location and that they are likely on their way here. We must evacuate."

The Master's consciousness seemed to swell with anger. "Evacuate? No, Ravencroft. This unfortunate turn of events may prove useful. This may be an opportunity to destroy the resistance once and for all."

Ravencroft dared to look up, his eyes meeting the glowing sphere. "But my liege, the risk—"

"There is no risk," the Master interrupted, his voice echoing through the chamber with finality. "They will come, and when they do, they will face their end. Prepare the defenses and ensure that the child—this old man—is ready. He may prove useful after all."

Ravencroft bowed deeply, his heart heavy with the weight of his failure. "Yes, my liege. I will see to it immediately."

As Ravencroft and the guards led Sam out of the chamber, the Master's presence remained a suffocating weight in the air. The plan was set, and the trap was ready to be sprung. The resistance would come, and they would meet their end in the very lair they sought to destroy.

Chapter 56

Shepard found Peters in a quieter part of the docking bay inspecting his upgraded MAGsuit. Caldwell had been ecstatic to reveal this latest version, outfitted with thrusters specifically for their mission in the oceans of Enceladus.

"Guess it makes this the Mark 3," she said.

Peters half-turned. "Huh?"

"MAGsuit Mark 3."

"Oh, yeah," he replied, distracted.

She crossed her arms. "Look, I can see you're busy. I'll just come back ano—"

Peters turned fully around. "No, it's fine. What's on your mind?"

Shepard sat on a crate next to him, rubbing her hands. "It's just, I know tomorrow's probably the biggest day of our lives."

"Not to mention the most dangerous," he added.

"Exactly, which is why I wanted to make sure nothing was left unsaid between us. You know, just in case."

"We'll be fine," Peters said, taking her hand. "Have faith."

"I wish I shared your confidence," she said, although scanning his eyes, she could see even he was struggling to believe his own reassurances. She stood awkwardly. "They put me up in my own room. It's got a holographic display where I can watch any movie ever made. So that's pretty cool."

Peters laughed. "The Council pirating Earth movies. I think I've seen everything now." He hooked a thumb over his shoulder, indicating the setup behind him. "They gave me a thick blanket. Figured I could push some of these crates together and form something resembling a bed."

"Oh," she said, her brow furrowing. "That's no way to sleep, especially with what's coming." She swallowed. "You know, there's more than enough room in my bed if you…"

Their eyes met and Shepard struggled not to look away. She felt her skin grow warm.

Peters stood. He cupped the nape of her neck with his hands and brought her into a kiss. Time slowed to a crawl. He pulled away, peering deeply into her eyes. "Yes, I'd like that very much."

Chapter 57

Enceladus

The following day, the vast expanse of Enceladus loomed before the allied armada, a formidable collection of ships cobbled together by the Council for this very purpose. The icy moon hung like a shimmering sphere suspended in the inky blackness of space. The ships glided silently toward it, their sleek forms reflecting the distant light of the sun. On the bridge of the command ship, the atmosphere was tense with anticipation.

Bradshaw, Shepard, and Peters stood in their MAGsuits, helmets off, alongside Lysandros, the Council leader. The bridge was a buzz of activity, with officers and technicians moving between consoles, monitoring the fleet's progress. A junior Council officer stepped forward, his face illuminated by the soft glow of the holographic display that flickered to life before them.

"Over the last few hours, cloaked probes have arrived on Enceladus, burrowing through the ice and scanning for any unusual sources of energy," the officer reported. His voice was steady, but the gravity of the situation was clear. As he spoke, the holographic display shifted to show a detailed map of the moon's surface, highlighted with various points of interest.

The display zoomed in on one such point, revealing a bright, pulsing source of energy located at the foot of a giant underwater mountain range. The officers gathered around the display, their eyes fixed on the glowing spot.

Lysandros frowned slightly as he studied the image. "Have you located an entry point through the ice sheet?" he asked.

The officer nodded and brought up another image on the holographic display. This one showed a large venting crack in the ice, its jagged edges forming a natural pathway down into the depths below. "The gravitational forces exerted by Saturn have formed wide tears in the ice," he explained. "This venting crack appears to be our best entry point. It's wide enough to allow for the deployment of our assault teams."

Lysandros turned to Shepard and Peters, his expression serious. "Very well. The fleet will descend on that point."

As ordered, the ships began their descent, the icy surface of Enceladus growing larger in the viewport. The holographic display on the ship's command console showed their trajectory, guiding them toward the venting crack that would be their entry point.

As they neared the fissure, the ship's powerful lights illuminated the jagged edges of the ice, casting eerie shadows that danced across the surface. The crack yawned open before them, a gateway to the unknown.

The ship shuddered as it entered the opening, the temperature dropping rapidly as they descended into the icy depths. The walls loomed close on either side, their surfaces glistening with frost and ancient ice formations.

As they descended further, the images outside the viewport changed, revealing a vast underwater cavern filled with strange, luminescent flora and intricate ice structures. The source of the energy signal was close now, its pulsing light growing stronger with each passing moment.

Shepard held her breath, grasping onto a nearby control console. "No turning back now," she said, her body filling with adrenaline.

And with that, they sped toward the Master's lair. Shepard thought of Sam in that instant, hoping against all odds that he was still alive. The battle for the fate of their world was about to begin.

•••

Two Praetorian Guard troopers gripped Sam by his arms, holding his aged body up as it drooped under its own weight. The Master's imposing presence filled the room as he addressed Ravencroft. The chamber hummed with the latent energy of the unfinished forge, its ominous glow casting long shadows.

"I have changed my mind," the Master announced, his voice echoing through the chamber. "Sam is to be put inside the unfinished forge and lashed there if necessary."

Ravencroft's brow furrowed with uncertainty. "My lord, the two halves have not yet been united."

"That's correct," the Master replied. "The device will not be at its full power, but it should suffice."

Ravencroft hesitated, glancing at the frail figure of Sam. "And what about the old man? Won't it kill him?"

The Master laughed, a cold, mirthless sound. "That is a chance I'm willing to take. Now, insert him inside the device along with the remote targeting equipment to destroy the incoming fleet."

"But we were unsuccessful in securing the headpiece or the stone, my lord," Ravencroft continued, desperation creeping into his voice.

"It is for that reason that I made one of my own," the Master said.

A new android entered the room, carrying a crude-looking crown laced with circuitry. It moved forward, intent on placing the makeshift device on Sam's head.

With a sudden burst of life, Sam struggled to free himself, blue orbs of fifth force energy growing in the palms of his hands. His eyes blazed with defiance as he fought to break the androids' grip.

A silent order passed from the Master to one of the androids, which responded with swift brutality. It punched Sam in the gut, the force of the blow causing him to bend over, coughing blood, the blue energy dissipating into the air.

"You see? There's still some life left in him," the Master said to Ravencroft, his voice dripping with contempt. "Now hurry."

Ravencroft nodded, directing the Praetorian Guard to place Sam inside the forge. The aged half-human, half-Endarian was strapped into the device, his frail form looking pitiful against the cold, hard machinery.

The android placed the crude crown on Sam's head, securing it in place. Sam groaned in pain, his eyes fluttering, but the Master merely watched with a satisfied air.

The unfinished forge began to hum with energy, its mechanisms coming to life. The chamber filled with a harsh, pulsating light as the device powered up. The Master turned his attention to Ravencroft, who stood nervously by.

"Ensure the remote targeting equipment is properly integrated," the Master ordered.

Ravencroft moved to comply, his hands shaking as he worked.

Soon the final connections were made, and the forge's glow intensified, casting eerie shadows on the walls. Sam's body convulsed, his face contorted in agony as the device drew upon his latent fifth force energy.

The Master observed the scene with cold satisfaction.

The chamber seemed to hold its breath, the air thick with tension as the Master made ready to initiate the final phase of his plan. All he needed was for the enemy to show their faces.

Chapter 58

As the allied fleet navigated through the murky depths of Enceladus's ocean, the anxiety grew. The dim glow from the fleet's lights pierced the darkness, revealing the rough, alien terrain below. On the command deck of the flagship, a junior navigation officer pointed ahead, his voice tight with tension. "We should be nearing the target location any moment now."

Shepard gazed through the viewport at the colossal underwater structure as it emerged from the depths. Twinkling lights were the first sign of its ominous presence as they approached. Then the rest of it came into sight. Nestled against the base of a mountain, the complex rose from the ocean floor, its towering spires reaching toward the heavens like the twisted fingers of a Gothic cathedral.

Suddenly, a beam of blue energy streaked through the water, striking the transport ship directly beside them. The beam seemed to slice through the ship's shields effortlessly. A moment later, the ship detonated in a brilliant burst of light, sending a shockwave through the water. The explosion was followed by an immediate implosion as the vast pressure of the ocean crushed the remnants into oblivion, metal crumpling like paper.

Lysandros's eyes widened. "What was that?"

Before anyone could respond, another deadly beam cut through the murky waters, hitting another transport. This time, the ship was split in two, debris scattering into the abyss as the immense pressure did its gruesome work. The surrounding water filled with floating wreckage and the eerie, drifting lights of destroyed vessels.

A look of concern cast a shadow over Bradshaw's face. The situation was growing dire, and every second counted.

"They're using the forge," Shepard said.

Peters turned to her. "But how is that possible if we have the other half?"

"I'm not sure," she replied, suddenly afraid. "Perhaps it works, but it's just less potent."

"Looks potent enough for my taste," Bradshaw said, crossing his arms.

"We should turn back and regroup," Lysandros suggested, his voice tinged with urgency.

"No," Bradshaw said firmly. "We've come this far. It's do or die."

Determined, Bradshaw ordered Shepard and Peters to make haste towards their assault craft. They bolted from the command deck, weaving through the chaotic corridors of the ship. Around them, crew members darted about, preparing for the inevitable battle. The ship shuddered with every nearby explosion, lights flickering ominously as the structural integrity was tested to its limits.

They arrived at the hangar, where their assigned assault craft awaited them. Dr. Singh and Mateo stood near the ramp. "Good luck out there," Singh said, his face etched with worry.

Inside, Alvarez, Nash, and Jake were already waiting, their expressions filled with anxiety. Shepard and Peters took their places, buckling their safety harnesses.

The hatch closed with a thud, sealing them inside. The craft lifted off smoothly, coursing through the hangar bay before plunging through the force field that separated the ship from the frigid waters outside. The cold, dark ocean swallowed them whole as they joined the rest of the fleet in the treacherous approach to the Master's lair.

A horde of allied assault transports sped toward the lair like a school of hungry piranha, sleek and deadly. Defensive batteries from the facility erupted into a cacophony of energy fire, illuminating the dark waters with deadly streaks of light. The pilot of Shepard's ship jerked the controls, trying to maneuver them out of the line of fire. Around them, several ships were hit, disintegrating in bursts of fire and debris.

Ahead of the pack, a group of Thalasian ships took point, their pilots expertly targeting the defensive turrets. Precision shots from their weapons systems disabled one turret after another. Jake whooped and hollered, his enthusiasm infectious even in the dire situation. "Take that, you bastards!" he shouted.

Alvarez muttered, "I can't wait to get out of this tin coffin."

The lead ships began their assault on the facility's outer hull. Powerful lasers cut through the thick metal, creating gaping holes in the structure. Following closely were specialized craft equipped with shield generators. They moved in swiftly, deploying energy shields that sealed the openings, keeping the water out but allowing the troops to enter.

In twos and threes, the nimble craft penetrated the membrane and set down in a wide-open chamber within the lair. The atmosphere inside was chaotic, filled with the sounds of battle and the acrid smell of energy discharge bouncing off the dank, forbidding walls.

As the doors to the transport slid open, the team saw the ferocity of the battle unfolding before them. Drax troopers, relentless and heavily armed, swarmed in from every entrance. Allied craft continued to shuttle in more friendly troops, trying to establish a foothold in the enemy stronghold.

Energy rounds and kinetic projectiles filled the air, creating a deadly latticework of destruction. The Drax troopers moved with inhuman speed and precision, their enhanced reflexes and strength making them formidable opponents. Allied soldiers, both human and Council, fought valiantly, using their advanced weaponry and field generators to hold their ground.

A Drax trooper lunged at a Council soldier. The soldier parried with an energy blade, the clash sending sparks flying. Another fired a barrage of energy bolts at an allied soldier, who narrowly dodged, returning fire with a pulse rifle that sent the Drax sprawling.

The battle raged on, the cavernous chamber echoing with the sounds of war. Energy shields flared and shimmered, absorbing impacts before collapsing. Bodies fell on both sides, the floor slick with a mixture of human and alien blood.

In the midst of this chaos, Shepard and her team disembarked, weapons at the ready. They moved swiftly, joining the fray. Jake took point, his weapon spewing a continuous stream of suppressing fire. Alvarez and Nash flanked him, covering their sides. Peters and Shepard brought up the rear, scanning for threats and opportunities alike.

A Drax trooper charged at Shepard, its eyes glowing with malevolent intent. She sidestepped, bringing her weapon up and firing point blank into its chest. The trooper staggered, but its advanced armor absorbed most of the impact. It swiped at her with a mechanical hand, but she ducked and fired into its back, cutting it down.

Peters shouted, "We need to push forward!"

The team pressed on, carving a path through the chaos. Amid the cacophony, a group of allied soldiers managed to break through a line of Drax troopers, securing a small perimeter. They signaled for Shepard's team to join them, providing a brief respite in the relentless assault.

Bradshaw's voice sounded in the team's earpiece from the command ship. "Status report."

"We're inside," Peters shouted over the din. "Facing heavy resistance."

Just then a gravity grenade went off in the landing zone, crushing two craft at once along with all of their occupants.

"If this keeps up," Jake said, sniping the Drax trooper who had tossed the grenade from a balcony above them, "we're not gonna last much longer."

"He's right," Peters shouted to Bradshaw. "Forget holding anyone back in reserve. We need everyone now."

"I'm afraid you'll have to make do, Colonel. That initial volley from the forge took out two of our main transports."

Peters signed off.

"So that's it then?" Nash said, watching a fresh batch of landing craft touch down.

Peters nodded. "We push ahead with what we have."

As if in response, a giant set of doors opened, revealing thousands of Praetorian Guards backed up by mech units. The fire now was withering. Dozens were cut down on either side. It was turning into a slugfest and as of now, they were on the losing side.

Chapter 59

Hunched behind a supply crate, Shepard popped up to fire and noticed an access door to their right. She signaled the others, who gave her the thumbs-up. Together, they skirted the battle at the landing zone, hoping they might be able to circle around and divide the Drax's attention.

"RUTH," Shepard cried, as they charged toward the door. "I hope you're taking careful notes of every nook and cranny."

"I am, Dr. Shepard," the AI said in a jolly voice. "I began mapping the visible parts of the facility the moment we landed."

"Good to hear."

Peters drew even and pushed ahead, punching a button on the wall to open the hatch. Up it swung, revealing a dank, narrow corridor. Small fixtures overhead cast dim pools of light into the distance. For the first time since they landed, the haptic feedback system began registering something other than gunpowder and ozone. The air here was heavy with the smell of metal and coolant, which hinted at the high-tech machinery operating just out of sight. The corridor was silent except for the hum of machinery and the unsettling hiss of decompressing gas.

They pressed on, two dozen airmen following suit, their footsteps echoing through the metallic corridor. The air was thick with the acrid scent of energy discharge and the distant sounds of battle. Peters led the way, scanning the path ahead for any signs of the enemy. Suddenly, he spotted a stray Drax trooper up ahead. With a swift, practiced motion, he raised his weapon and fired, the shot taking the trooper down instantly.

As they moved forward, Jake glanced through the porthole of a passing room and called them back. "Hey, guys, you need to see this," he said, his voice tinged with urgency.

They doubled back and entered the room, only to be floored by what they saw. Row after row of glass capsules lined the walls, each housing a dark substance that seemed part gas, part liquid, swirling ominously within its confines.

"Drahk'noth," Shepard said, her voice barely a whisper, visibly shaken by the sight. "Look how much there is."

"Each one represents a human life that was snuffed out," Alvarez reminded them, his voice filled with sorrow and anger.

Peters removed the bandolier of explosives he was wearing and began priming them. Shepard, noticing his actions, asked, "What are you doing?"

"Putting them to rest." With a determined look, he tossed the bandolier down the long causeway, the explosives sliding and clinking against the metal floor.

They rushed out of the room, turning a corner only to come face to face with a large group of Praetorian Guard units. For a moment, both sides were surprised, the silence hanging thick in the air. Alvarez was the first to raise his weapon, but before anyone could fire, the facility was rocked by a massive explosion. The force of the blast knocked everyone off their feet, the shockwave reverberating through the structure.

The androids struggled to get up, their mechanical limbs twitching and sparking from the impact. The humans recovered first, their training and instincts kicking in. They unloaded their weapons into the Praetorian Guard, a hail of bullets and energy rounds tearing through the metallic bodies. The air was filled with the sound of metal clashing and breaking, the androids reduced to chunks and spare parts scattered across the floor.

As the smoke cleared, it revealed the aftermath of the explosion and the ensuing firefight. The corridor was littered with the remains of the Praetorian Guard, their once-formidable forms now reduced to scrap. The team took a moment to catch their breath.

"Everyone okay?" Shepard called out, her voice echoing in the now-silent corridor.

"All good here," Jake replied, "except I might need some fresh underwear."

A commander of one of the human brigades came over the radio. "There's just too many of them. We're getting pushed back."

There wasn't any time to waste. Peters and the rest of the team charged forward before RUTH's voice chimed in. "By my calculations, if you head left, it should lead to an upper balcony."

They all exchanged a quick glance before agreeing to follow her advice. Racing to the end of another long up-sloping corridor, Peters punched the button next to the latch. It opened, revealing they were indeed on a raised catwalk. From here they could see throngs of Drax troopers below pouring fire on the beleaguered and ever-diminishing allied attack force.

After clearing the catwalk of the enemy, they began lobbing grenades down onto the Drax soldiers, knocking out huge swaths of them with every explosion. Many were killed before the enemy turned their attention to the threat from above. As good a plan as it was, the catwalk's downside was that it provided very little cover. Rounds from the Drax below pinged all around them. One cut through Nash's suit, nicking his thigh. He grimaced as the self-sealing mechanism prevented his suit from decompressing. "Ain't nothing but a flesh wound."

Normally Jake would bust out laughing at a line like that, but the withering fire had sapped his humor. Soon, it became so intense, they were trapped, lying flat for fear of getting picked off.

"A soldier at Gettysburg once said during the second day of battle that balls were flying so thick that you could hold out your hat and catch it full," Peters told them, crouching low.

"Now we know how he felt," Jake said, a twinkle in his eye.

They were beginning to lose hope that anything would keep the Drax from overwhelming them when an unfamiliar voice came over the radio.

"I hope you've left some for us," he said.

Just then several heavily armed transports pushed through the membrane, unloading onto the advancing Drax with heavy energy weapons.

"Who is this?"

"Elder Gorian," came the indignant reply. "Who else would it be?"

324

The craft set down as more allied soldiers joined the fray. Behind that group came even more transports. The tide was beginning to turn.

"I thought we were out of soldiers," Peters radioed back as he and the others on the catwalk rose up to rejoin the battle.

"As you know, millions of Council citizens were lying in cryosleep, waiting for a time when the Drax were no more," Gorian explained. "I thought it was more than fair that at least some of them be awakened to do their part."

Jake whooped as the Drax were now the ones retreating. "You can run, but you can't hide," he called out. "You go and tell your Master we're coming for him."

Chapter 60

Inside the throne room, Sam's frail and barely conscious body was still attached to the forge.

Ravencroft, his heart pounding, stepped forward and bowed deeply. "My lord," he began, trembling, "the allies have been reinforced. They are pushing deeper into the facility."

"How is this possible?" the Master exclaimed, his voice booming through the chamber. The first crack in his confidence was evident.

Ravencroft kept his head bowed low, whispering, "I await your command."

The Master's orb seemed to pulse with renewed intensity. "Then I will do what should have been done from the start," he declared, his tone resolute.

"My lord?" Ravencroft asked.

"I will merge with this flesh," the Master stated, his attention settling on Sam's sagging form.

Ravencroft glanced at the old Endarian, who was barely conscious, his breaths shallow and labored. "But do you think that's a good idea, my lord?" he ventured cautiously.

"My immense power will fill him up, make him grow stronger, younger," the Master replied. "No more questions. Prepare for our union."

Reluctantly, Ravencroft obeyed. He turned to the Praetorian troopers stationed nearby and ordered them to bring in the necessary equipment. The troopers moved swiftly.

Sam was removed from the forge, his body limp and unresponsive. He was brought to a new device, his arms and legs splayed apart, bound by restraints. The Master's orb loomed above him, the conduits and hoses snaking towards the device like the limbs of some great, slumbering beast.

Ravencroft oversaw the preparations, his anxiety growing with each passing moment. The troopers worked quickly, setting up the intricate machinery required for the merger. The device hummed to life, the glow of the Master's orb intensifying.

The room was filled with an ominous silence, the air thick with tension. Ravencroft's mind raced, doubts and fears swirling within him. He glanced at Sam, who lay helpless and vulnerable, and then at the Master's orb, pulsating with malevolent energy.

As the final preparations were completed, Ravencroft took a step back. The troopers finished securing Sam in place, his limbs bound by the restraints, his body exposed to the immense power of the Master's orb.

"Proceed," the Master said gleefully. "It has been eons since I've known what it is to have a physical form."

Ravencroft, his hands trembling slightly, reached out and activated the machine. The room was filled with a low hum as the device powered up, its lights flickering to life. Sam, sensing the impending merger, turned his head away, a look of resigned dread on his face.

A conduit extended from the Master's orb, snaking towards the machine to which Sam was attached. The connection was made, and an intense beam of crimson light shot through the conduit, linking the Master's consciousness with Sam's body.

Sam writhed violently as the energy flowed into him. The room was bathed in a dramatic light show, the red glow pulsating with a rhythm that matched the Master's triumphant anticipation. Sparks flew from the machinery, and the air crackled with energy.

Sam screamed, his muscles twitching and spasming as the merging process continued. His skin glowed with an ethereal light, the power of the fifth force coursing through him. The conduits hummed louder, the energy building to a crescendo.

Then, with a blinding explosion of red and blue light, the machinery around them shorted out and fell silent. The room was plunged into darkness, the only remaining light coming from the flickering remnants of the failed equipment.

"Sire, are you still there?" Ravencroft called out, his voice tinged with panic. The orb was silent, its usual glow dimmed. In the background came the sound of the nearby battle.

Turning to Sam, Ravencroft saw the first signs of transformation. Already, Sam's face was beginning to look younger, the lines and wrinkles fading. His eyes fluttered open, revealing a pair of silver orbs that glowed with an otherworldly light.

Ravencroft took a step back, unsure of what to make of this new entity before him. The merging had been successful, but the result was more terrifying than he had anticipated.

"I am here," Sam said, his voice a mix of his own and the Master's, resonating with an eerie, dual timbre.

The power in his voice sent shivers down Ravencroft's spine.

"My first order of business is a little housekeeping," Sam said, turning to Ravencroft, as he raised his hand, palm out.

"No!" Ravencroft shouted as a jet of violet energy streamed from Sam's outstretched palm, piercing him through the chest. Shuddering, the Drax commander fell to his knees and took a final ragged breath before collapsing dead.

Chapter 61

With the Drax on the run, the humans surged forward, emboldened by the enemy's retreat. The corridors of the lair echoed with the sound of heavy boots and the shouts of the advancing forces. More than once, groups of Drax troopers took cover in an attempt to delay their advance, but they were cut down swiftly, their resistance proving futile against the sheer determination and numbers of the human soldiers.

Next, a fresh detachment of Praetorian Guard entered the fray, their powerful, next-generation android forms presenting a tougher challenge. The human line stumbled, but they managed to overwhelm them with sheer numbers and coordinated tactics. Each step forward pushed them deeper into the complex, closer to their ultimate goal.

Peters, Shepard, and the Delta operatives led the charge, their MAGsuits humming with energy. RUTH's voice crackled through their comms. "I'm detecting an unusually large power source behind the next bulkhead. It suggests we may have found the Master's throne room."

They arrived at a utilitarian-looking blast door adorned with crude markings. "This must be it," Alvarez said, struggling to keep up.

Peters punched the access button, and the door opened with a swoosh, releasing a gust of stale air. The room was filled with white wisps of smoke and an awful smell that made them recoil. "Something died in here," Jake exclaimed, moving to plug his nose before his hand impacted the visor of his helmet. "Damn haptic feedback," he swore.

The chamber was massive, with a high vaulted ceiling that seemed to stretch endlessly upwards. Black metallic archways framed the room on either side, creating a Gothic, cathedral-like ambiance. In the center of the room was a giant black metal sphere, seemingly lifeless and cold.

"Maybe he offed himself," Nash said, his voice tinged with hope.

"Somehow I doubt that," Peters replied as they crept in, scanning every corner for signs of an ambush. A contingent of soldiers followed them, their weapons at the ready.

As they moved deeper into the chamber, the smell grew worse, a mix of decay and something acrid, almost chemical. Smoke swirled around their feet, obscuring the ground and making each step feel like a descent into the unknown.

Peters signaled for the team to spread out, covering all angles. They moved cautiously, their senses heightened, ready for any sudden attack. The sphere loomed in the center, a silent sentinel that seemed to watch their every move.

Shepard's voice broke the silence. "RUTH, any signs of life?"

"None detected," RUTH replied. "But the power readings are off the charts. Whatever is in here, it's pulsating with incredible power."

331

Peters nodded, his jaw tightening. "All right, stay sharp. We don't know what we're dealing with yet."

Shepard was distinctly aware that this throne room was as much a holy shrine as it was a seat of power. The Master truly was their god; without his essence, the Drax would cease to be. The sphere, they had learned, was where his consciousness resided and yet it appeared to be either empty or dormant.

"Over here!" Jake yelled, motioning to the human figure lying next to the sphere.

They gathered around. Shepard's heart sank as she turned him over. She recoiled. This wasn't Sam. The figure had a six-inch hole carved through his chest.

"It's Ravencroft," Isadora told them, shaking her head with derision.

Before anyone could say another word, a boy stepped out from behind the sphere.

Shepard rose to her feet and gasped. It was Sam. But he was no longer the eighty-year-old man she had last seen in Guatemala. He looked more like the child she'd visited growing up back on Earth. Except, instead of the sweet smile, this new Sam's face was twisted in rage, his eyes gleaming with a cold, merciless light, like two neutron stars.

"What happened to you?" Shepard said, disturbed and afraid.

Sam grinned, slamming his hands together. From the impact erupted a shockwave, sending everyone tumbling backward. The force was immense, crackling with unrestrained power.

Then Sam rose in the air, suspended on invisible strings like some demonic marionette, his body alive with licks of violet energy.

He began gliding toward them, his bare feet hovering several inches above the ground. A handful of soldiers raised their pulse rifles and opened fire, but the rounds impacted an invisible barrier.

Annoyed, Sam made a flicking motion with his hand and turned the soldiers into dust. The act was effortless, a mere exertion of his newfound power. An evil laugh escaped his lips as he examined his hand, marveling at the energy coursing through it. "How I've missed this," he said, his voice a chilling echo of the Master's.

Other groups of soldiers opened fire, only to suffer the same fate. Sam's power seemed limitless, his control absolute. At one point, Shepard, still on the ground, watched as Sam suddenly grabbed at one of his hands, his face contorted with inner conflict.

"What's going on?" Alvarez asked, leveling his weapon but holding his fire.

"Sam is still in there," Shepard said, her voice a mix of hope and fear. "Somewhere." She staggered to her feet and moved towards him, her steps unsteady but determined.

"No, Shepard, don't!" Peters cried out, his voice filled with desperation.

Shepard held out her hands, pleading. "Sam, don't do this."

Jake ran out to grab her, his intent clear. But Sam's head snapped toward the oncoming threat. With a flick of his wrist, he flung Jake aside, sending him colliding with the now empty sphere. Jake impacted it with a sickening crunch, his body crumpling to the ground.

Shepard looked on in horror at the sight of her friend's lifeless form. But running to him now would only get them all killed. She turned back and locked onto Sam's glowing eyes. "I know you're still in there."

333

Sam's face contorted in pain, a vicious battle waging within him. The blue energy of the fifth force began to grow as he struggled for control.

"Enough!" The Master's voice echoed with authority as the blue light flickered and went out. "I've had my fun. Now it's time to finish this." He raised one of his hands, where a dense sphere of red energy began to grow, pulsating ominously from his palm. The entire room became electrified as streaks of lightning erupted from the ground, racing up Sam's body. It was clear he was about to create a cataclysmic detonation that would annihilate all of them.

Some of the soldiers began to run away in panic. But the sound of Sam's laughter, distorted and malevolent, chased them, echoing off the walls and down the dank corridors of the complex.

As Sam continued his cackling, his free hand suddenly grabbed hold of his other wrist, pushing the surging ball of energy down his own throat. His laughter turned into a grotesque gargle as he choked on the very power he had summoned.

Shepard stood frozen, horror-struck by the sight, until a pair of rough hands grabbed her and pulled her behind a nearby crate. Her heart pounded as Sam stumbled, his face a mask of confusion and agony. His skin began to glow, cracks of blue light appearing all over his body.

"No!" he cried out, his voice filled with anguish and desperation. The crimson light intensified, and with a final, piercing scream, his body exploded, vaporizing on the spot. The force of the blast sent shockwaves through the room.

In the aftermath, a thin wisp of smoke, loosely in the form of a man, hovered in the air for a moment before dissipating completely. The Master's presence was gone, leaving an eerie silence in the room.

Shepard rose and ran to the place where Sam had stood. She fell to her knees, tears streaming down her face as she sobbed uncontrollably. The weight of the loss was overwhelming.

Nash and Alvarez rushed to check on Jake.

A radio call crackled to life from one of the human commanders in another part of the complex. "I don't know who pulled the plug, but a whole battalion of Drax troopers just dropped dead."

"How is he?" Peters asked.

Alvarez was bent over Jake's lifeless body. Next to him, Nash looked grief-stricken. "His neck must have broken on impact."

Peters clenched his fists, struggling to maintain his composure.

Bradshaw came over the airwaves a moment later. "We just heard the mission was a success. Great job in there."

"Thanks Commander," Peters said, his voice flat.

"Oh, I also wanted to give you a heads-up. You folks are about to have a visitor."

Chapter 62

A glowing yellow orb pushed through the membrane and came to rest outside the throne room. As the energy field dissipated, an oval-shaped craft took its place. A hatch opened and a tall man with an irregularly shaped head emerged.

Shepard stood, still overcome with sadness at the loss of Sam and Jake.

Strange as he appeared, each of them knew precisely who it was. "Aloine," Peters said, his words filled with reverence.

Aloine approached, his gold and blue robe brushing the floor as he neared. The few soldiers who remained parted and reformed in his wake, like water around a river rock.

"Why so sad?" he asked, his voice deep and soothing.

"We lost many lives defeating the Master," Shepard explained, staring down at the mark left on the floor.

"Energy is never lost," Aloine reminded them. "It merely awaits a new form."

"As that which is created by the fifth force," she said.

A gentle smile formed on Aloine's lips. "Precisely. The one who lured the Master, what was it you called him?"

"His name was Sam," Peters said, standing now by Jake's body.

Shepard's brow furrowed. "What did you mean, 'lured?'"

"A man of Endarian blood sent to absolve the human race of its sins," Aloine explained.

She shook her head. "I'm not following you. What sins?"

"Ignorance," he replied. "Aren't you familiar with the prophecy?"

"Arrival, Awakening and Ascension," she recounted. "But we weren't certain what it meant. Who was ascending? And to what?"

"Why, the human race, of course," Aloine told them. "Sam, as you call him, was the final piece of a much bigger picture. Without witnessing the power Sam possessed, the Master would never have left his sanctuary to merge. You see, it was Sam's role to tempt such a foolish move. And your job to see that the two of them met."

Shepard's head was swimming.

"The human race is now free," Aloine told them, his features radiating joy. "But liberty comes with its own challenges. I hope your race will do better than mine." He glanced around until his eyes found the forge. "I believe you have some things that belong to me."

"Things?" Shepard asked. "Oh, yes, of course. The headpiece, the forge and the crystal."

He smiled. "How else will we heal your dying sun?"

Chapter 63

Washington, D.C.

It was after midnight by the time Douglas stepped out of the FBI's D.C. field office. He was too tired to even pay attention to the grumble in his belly.

A voice called out to him from the bottom of the stairs. "Burning the midnight oil, I see." Isadora winked as she waited for him to descend.

The corners of his mouth rose into a smile as they embraced. "I'm glad you made it back in one piece," he whispered. He pulled back and held her at arm's length. There was a bandage over her right eye and another covering her left ear. "Well, almost in one piece."

They walked together to his cruiser. "The Drax are gone," she announced. "Humanity has finally lifted the Drax's vile boot from its neck."

He grunted.

"Geez, you're hard to please. You'd think news that good would make a man's day, maybe even his lifetime."

Douglas folded his arms on top of the cruiser as Isadora swung around to the passenger side. "I'm thrilled, don't get it twisted. But you were off on another planet when it all happened."

"I don't understand."

"Do you have any clue what went down the minute that compressed ball of pure thought burst?"

"The Master?"

Douglas nodded.

Isadora's eyes searched around for the answer. The sound of a firetruck siren wailed in the background. And behind that, an ambulance. Realization began dawning in her eyes.

"I can see you don't watch the news." He laughed as both of them slid into the car. "Over the last twenty-four hours, hundreds of thousands, maybe even millions of seemingly normal people just dropped dead."

"Drax agents," she said, her jaw hanging open.

"And what happens to those robotic fools after they die?"

"Poof," she said, splaying out her hands. She sat straight, smiling. "So I take it you've been up to your eyeballs."

"And then some," Douglas barked, turning on the car and pulling out.

"Things will only get better from here," Isadora said, raising three fingers. "I promise."

He glanced over, grinning. "I heard the Council's already been hard at work thawing out the rest of their population and settling them on Suwanose Jima. Wonder how that's gonna go."

She nodded. "So do I. A rather grumpy Gorian told me the island's not even finished yet and already a few hundred thousand Council residents have arrived. The Japanese government's been tight-lipped about the whole thing. I'm assuming they're waiting for things to stabilize before they make a big announcement."

Douglas chuckled. "That should be interesting." He turned to Isadora. "And what about you? I suppose you and the other Thalasians are out of a job now."

"To be honest, I hadn't thought about that."

"Ever considered applying to the bureau?"

That made her laugh out loud. "And become an FBI agent?"

He nodded. "You were quite good at it. Maybe one day you could even have my job."

"Why? Are you quitting?"

"Nah, an old dog like me? Free time and I don't mix well. Turns out, when the Master went bye-bye, so too did Director Matthews."

"He was one of them?"

"I had a feeling all along," Douglas admitted. "I just couldn't prove it."

"And now they're putting you up for his job?"

"I've heard rumors."

"You should take it."

"We'll see. But if I stay, I'll be in the market for a new partner."

Isadora wasn't sure. "Replace Agent Keller? Those are some big shoes to fill."

"And you've got some pretty big feet."

She pointed at him, grinning. "Easy, buster."

"I call 'em like I see 'em," Douglas said, stopping at a red light. "Give it some thought, at least."

Smiling, she asked, "What are you doing now?"

"Dropping you off and heading home to sleep."

"No, you're not. I can hear your stomach grumbling from here," she said, putting a hand over her mouth, trying not to giggle. "I know a great rib place not ten minutes away. They're open late."

"Ribs, eh?" he said, mulling the idea over.

"I knew you'd change your mind. They say the way to a man's heart is through his stomach."

"You know me all too well," Douglas replied, his features filling with a sense of peace he hadn't known for a very long time.

Chapter 64

One Year Later

The Swan 42 cut through the light waves of the Mediterranean Sea. Shepard came up from below decks carrying two mackerel dangling from a stringer.

"Might as well cook up the two we caught yesterday," she said, laying a kiss on Peters before setting them on the cutting board.

"We as in you," he said, laughing. Next to him, a trail of smoke wafted up from the barbecue.

Shepard joined him. "I tried to give you some credit, at least."

"It was my fishing rod, how's that?"

"Deal."

He looked out at the horizon. In the distance was the Italian coast and beyond that the setting sun. She stopped and followed his gaze. The sight was breathtaking as golden rays danced on the water, creating a shimmering path that stretched to the horizon.

"It's still hard to get used to," she said.

"The sun?"

"Yeah, looking so normal. It's nice, but I still need to pinch myself every so often."

His eyes traced down to something else she was holding. A strip of white plastic.

"That what I think it is?" he asked, surprised.

Shepard grinned, holding up a pregnancy test showing two red lines.

Peters' eyes went wide. Leaping from his seat, he scooped Shepard into the air, twirling her around.

She laughed and squealed, begging him to set her down.

As he did so, a tear rolled down her cheek.

He wiped it away. "Those are tears of joy, I hope."

She nodded, although she was thinking of Ryan and of Sam and how much she would have loved for them to be here.

Peters could see now what was troubling her. He cupped her face and kissed her.

She ran a hand over the stubble on his cheek. "I know how much you've always wanted a family."

"A family with you," Peters amended as a devilish glint began forming in his eyes. "You know, I just had the craziest idea."

Shepard waved her arms in a warding motion. "Your last crazy idea nearly put me in traction."

"Hey, it's not my fault you can't hike."

"Mount Kilimanjaro? I still don't know why I said yes."

"Because you love me."

She looked at him, beaming. "So what's this latest expedition you want to send us on?"

"Somehow, I managed to convince Nash, Mateo and Alvarez to chip in on a forty-footer of their own. Thought maybe we could sail around the world and meet them near Hawaii."

"Are you mad?"

"I might be," he said, his arms outstretched. "But what are you afraid of? Without the Drax constantly stirring up trouble, the world's a much safer and happier place. In fact, last year was the only one on record without a war. Hard to believe, isn't it? The human race finally getting along."

Once Aloine had used the forge to heal the sun's damage, he'd loaded every scrap of Endarian tech onto his ship and left. To where? He wouldn't say. All for the better as far as Shepard was concerned. Such an awesome power, they had learned, had no place in mortal hands.

"One last adventure before our twosome becomes a threesome."

Shepard took a seat and filled their glasses. Given the news, hers was now Perrier. They clinked goblets, turning back to enjoy the setting sun. "Okay, I'll think about it."

"Come on, don't make me pull rank."

"Cool it, Colonel," she chided him. "A 'maybe's' as good as you're gonna get right now."

He put the fish on the grill and slid in next to her, enjoying the moment. It felt like heaven and both of them hoped it would never end.

A Note to Readers

Thank you for joining me all the way to the end of a story I've been eager to share for a long time. What started as a simple thought experiment evolved into this narrative.

With the galaxy's vast resources, what possible reason would aliens have to invade Earth? The common trope is they'll come for our water. Yet, in our solar system alone, water is abundant. Metals and minerals, too, are plentiful throughout space. It's likely that within a century, humans will be mining asteroids instead of Earth's depths.

This led me to wonder if there was something else aliens might seek—some precious resource we don't even know exists. From there, the concept of Drahk'noth and the Drax's efforts to gather and refine it emerged. It served as a metaphor for our ignorance and, paradoxically, our arrogance as a species.

The ongoing debate over the existence of UFOs (or UAPs) exemplifies this. For those open to the idea of superior beings visiting us, evidence abounds. Yet such a reality is also chilling. Perhaps my tendency to explore the darker aspects of human nature made this a story worth telling.

Having read this series, some of you may have learned something new. Others, perhaps not. Regardless, my goal was never to convince you of alien existence or that the human mind could refine exotic substances. My aim was to entertain you. And maybe, just maybe, to get

346

you to see the universe—and our place in it—in a slightly different light.

Thank you for journeying with me.
James D. Prescott

Glossary:

Drax:
An alien race that uses humans in order to harvest refined dark matter from their minds.

The four fundamental forces:
These are the four natural forces that govern the interactions of matter. They are made up of gravity, electromagnetism, the weak nuclear force, and the strong nuclear force.

The fifth force:
A previously unknown fundamental force responsible for propagating the emergence of matter into the physical universe.

Fifth force radiation:
A form of exotic energy emission created by the manipulation of the fifth force, much the same way gamma rays are a byproduct of nuclear interactions.

The Council:
A loose confederation of humans previously seeded across the galaxy by the Drax.

Thalasians:
A sect of humans dedicated to helping the Council overthrow the Drax.

Real life versus fiction

While The Fifth Kind is a work of fiction, several of the elements that went into building the story were drawn directly from newspaper headlines and scientific magazine articles as well as from medical and academic journals. Here are just a few.

Aurora UFO Crash:
In April 1897, a mysterious airship reportedly crashed in the small town of Aurora, Texas. According to contemporary newspaper accounts, the wreckage contained the body of a "Martian" pilot, which was subsequently buried in the local cemetery. The incident has been the subject of much debate and investigation over the years. While I took a few liberties with this particular legend, given that it's one of the earliest accounts of a crashed UFO, I thought it might serve as an intriguing entry point for the final installment in the series.

Black Knight Satellite:
An object of unknown origin that has been observed in Earth's orbit for several decades. Conspiracy theories suggest it is an ancient extraterrestrial satellite, possibly monitoring Earth. The origins of these claims are based on various observations, including unexplained radio signals and images from space missions. Despite numerous theories, the object has not been conclusively identified, and mainstream science generally attributes the sightings to space debris or natural satellites.

AI Mind-Reading:

AI mind-reading refers to the emerging technology that uses artificial intelligence to interpret brain activity and translate it into readable data, such as thoughts or intentions. This field, while still in its infancy, has shown promise through various experiments where neural signals are decoded to control devices or communicate thoughts. Advances in neuroimaging and machine learning have accelerated progress, raising ethical and privacy concerns alongside its potential medical and technological applications.

Celestial Phenomenon over Nuremberg:

On April 14, 1561, residents of Nuremberg, Germany, witnessed a remarkable celestial phenomenon. According to a broadsheet published at the time, the sky was filled with what appeared to be an aerial battle between various shapes, including spheres, crosses, and cylinders. This event has been interpreted in modern times as a possible mass sighting of unidentified flying objects (UFOs). While the true nature of the phenomenon remains a mystery, it inspired numerous theories, ranging from natural atmospheric events to extraterrestrial encounters.

Perseverance Rover Mission Helicopter:

The *Perseverance* rover, part of NASA's Mars 2020 mission, carried a small helicopter named *Ingenuity*. *Ingenuity* was the first aircraft to attempt powered flight on another planet. Its primary mission was to demonstrate the feasibility of aerial exploration on Mars, providing reconnaissance for the rover and capturing high-resolution images of the Martian terrain. Since its first flight on April 19, 2021, *Ingenuity* has successfully completed multiple flights, surpassing expectations and paving the way for future aerial exploration of Mars and other celestial bodies.

Ezekiel's Wheel:

Ezekiel's Wheel refers to a vision described by the prophet Ezekiel in the Hebrew Bible. In the vision, Ezekiel saw a whirlwind and a cloud with flashing fire, from which emerged four living creatures, each with four faces and four wings. Beside each creature was a wheel, intersecting another wheel, allowing movement in any direction without turning. These "wheels within wheels" have been interpreted in various ways, from symbolic representations of divine presence and mobility to early descriptions of UFOs. To this day, the enigmatic nature of Ezekiel's vision continues to inspire and confound.

Additional References

By no means definitive, here are only some of the more interesting and compelling UFO cases from the past few decades:

The Westall UFO Mass Sighting
In 1966, over 200 students and teachers at Westall High School in Melbourne, Australia, witnessed a UFO landing in a nearby field. The silver, saucer-shaped craft was observed hovering and then descending before taking off again at high speed. Despite the significant number of witnesses, the event was downplayed by authorities, leaving many questions unanswered.

The Kecksburg UFO Incident
On December 9, 1965, a fireball was seen streaking across the sky over several US states and parts of Canada, eventually landing in Kecksburg, Pennsylvania. Witnesses reported seeing a metallic, acorn-shaped object. The area was quickly secured by the military, and despite official claims that nothing was found, many believe the object was extraterrestrial.

Michigan UFO Event
In March 1994, hundreds of people, including law enforcement officers, reported seeing strange lights in the sky over south-western Michigan. The lights moved in erratic patterns and were tracked by radar. The event gained significant media attention, but no official explanation was provided.

The Falcon Lake Incident
In 1967, Stefan Michalak claimed to have encountered a UFO while prospecting near Falcon Lake, Manitoba, Canada. He reported seeing a craft land and, after approaching it, was burned by a grid-like exhaust vent. Michalak suffered from physical symptoms, and the incident remains one of Canada's most well-documented UFO cases.

The Pascagoula Abduction
On October 11, 1973, Charles Hickson and Calvin Parker claimed they were abducted by aliens while fishing on the Pascagoula River in Mississippi. They described being taken aboard a craft by strange beings and subjected to physical examinations. Their detailed accounts and emotional distress drew widespread attention and it remains a significant abduction case.

The Allagash Abductions
In 1976, four men on a camping trip in Allagash, Maine, reported being abducted by a UFO. They claimed to have seen a bright light and later, under hypnosis, recalled being taken aboard a craft and subjected to medical examinations. The consistency of their stories and the corroborative hypnosis sessions have made this a notable case in UFO abduction lore.

Thank you for reading The Fifth Kind: Ascension—the conclusion to the Dark Nova Series!

I really hope you enjoyed the ride!
As many of you already know, reviews on Amazon are one of the best ways
to get the word out and allow me to keep producing the kinds of books you enjoy reading.

Please consider leaving a rating or review!

Made in the USA
Las Vegas, NV
05 August 2024

93414239R00215